THE UNIVERSITY OF MICHIGAN
CENTER FOR JAPANESE STUDIES

MICHIGAN PAPERS IN JAPANESE STUDIES
NO. 12

MICHIGAN PAPERS IN JAPANESE STUDIES

"THE STING OF DEATH" AND OTHER STORIES
BY SHIMAO TOSHIO

Shimao, Toshio

translated, with introduction and interpretive comments
by Kathryn Sparling

Ann Arbor

Center for Japanese Studies
The University of Michigan

1985

ISBN 0-939512-18-1

Center for Japanese Studies
The University of Michigan
108 Lane Hall
Ann Arbor, MI 48109

Cover design from a painting by Eric Ernst

Library of Congress Cataloging in Publication Data

Shimao, Toshio, 1917-
  "The sting of death" and other stories.

  (Michigan papers in Japanese studies; no. 12)
  Translation of six stories.
  1. Shimao, Toshio, 1917- —Translations, English.
I. Sparling, Kathryn, 1946- . II. Title.
III. Series.
PL838.H57A27 1985   895.6'35   83-26313
ISBN 0-939512-18-1

Printed in the United States of America

For Susanna Finley Rapp

CONTENTS

Preface

The stories of Shimao Toshio were first called to my attention in 1972 by a Japanese friend and classmate who was herself a writer of short fiction. Finding them compelling, horrifying, and ultimately wonderful, I thought of putting them into English some day.

I actually began this project in 1976, with *Shi no toge* [The sting of death], included in this volume, and have worked on them intermittently ever since. Sometimes the contagious hysteria—of the "sick wife" stories in particular—has overwhelmed me, and I have had to stop. I have always come back to them, mostly because they made intimate sense no matter what turn my own life was taking, and because they seem to represent a commitment, rare in modern Japanese literature, to life and to the responsibilities it brings. So the characters in these stories have been with me for nearly ten years, continuing to fascinate me. I introduce them here in the hope that even in pale translation they may seem as real and as valuable to other readers.

These stories are more dense and difficult in Japanese than in this English version, which inevitably conveys, in other respects as well, a slightly different impression. My aim was to be rather more literal than otherwise in my translation; I hoped to avoid smoothing over the unusualness of Shimao's prose by preserving (even at some cost) subtle echoes of the recurrent images embedded there, resisting the temptation to explain, rationalize, or otherwise unmix metaphors. Often I have not succeeded.

For one thing, I have generally not been able to retain ambiguity—a striking characteristic of Shimao's prose—but have had to make exclusive choices. Through several stages of editing, I have done away with unclear antecedents and other obstacles to immediate comprehension of the literal meaning of the text. Long sentences and in some cases paragraphs have been broken up where I was finally convinced that the length exceeded what normal English prose would tolerate.

* * *

Kakeromajima, where the first two stories are set, is one of the larger islands of the Amami Archepelago of the Ryukyus, which stretches from about 200 miles south of Kyushu to Okinawa. Since Meiji the Amami Islands have been part of Kagoshima Prefecture, except for the Occupation years, 1946 to 1953, when they were under American military rule along with Okinawa. From ancient times until they were taken over by the Shimazu of Satsuma in 1609, they were part of the Ryukyu Kingdom ruled by Okinawa. The culture and the language combine elements from both the Ryukyus to the south and mainland Japan to the north. The climate is subtropical. Even today the industry is mostly fishing and agriculture; sugarcane (the brown sugar candy Toë serves the lieutenant in "This Time That Summer"), bananas, and pineapples are the major products. The largest island in the archepelago, Amami Ōshima ("Great Island"), where Shimao and his family lived until 1975, produces the famous Ōshima *tsumugi*, a kind of pongee. During the Second World War the Amami Islands were the site of many secret military bases, where special attack-force units (suicide squadrons) like Shimao's were stationed. Like Shimao's wife, many of the people are Christian, as a result of Catholic missionary activities in the nineteenth century, but in general, traditional ways, including religious and folk beliefs, prevailed until well after the war, though they are now quickly disappearing under the influence of national education and, inevitably, television.

*   *   *

Many people have helped me with this manuscript, more people than I can thank individually here. Wayne Lammers, now teaching at the University of Wisconsin, did a directed reading course with me several years ago, for which he prepared a good translation of about the first third of *Shi no toge*. Undoubtedly, some of his phrases have found their way into my version. I am grateful for his help and generosity. I am greatly indebted to Shun'ichi Katō and Yōko Katō, Susumu Nagara, and Mutsuko Endō Simon, all of the University of Michigan, for their invaluable and most gracious assistance in reading the Japanese texts. Advice from native speakers is especially reassuring when venturing to declare a sentence ambiguous. James I. Crump kindly helped me with English word choice, particularly military terms.

Most of all, I am grateful for the help and moral support of John Campbell, Director, Elsie Orb, Administrative Associate, and the editor of this series, Bruce E. Willoughby, at the University of Michigan Center for Japanese Studies, and to Cindi Larson, who typed and retyped my almost illegible manuscript, on my capricious schedule, more times than I care to admit.

INTRODUCTION

Until a recent "boom," Shimao Toshio, writer of short fiction, critic, and essayist, was not widely known, even in Japan. He has never won the Akutagawa or the Naoki Prize, and to my knowledge, none of his works has appeared in English translation. He is less well known than other writers (Yasuoka Shōtarō, Kojima Nobuo, and Shōno Junzō) with whom he has associated and whose works have been liberally translated into English.[1] Yet, there are those who consider him to be one of the best contemporary writers in Japan.

Essentially, he has been a writer's writer, admired by other writers, critics, scholars, and especially aspiring writers. His fiction, mostly short stories until "The Sting of Death" was completed in 1977, has been considered avant-garde, difficult of access, and excruciating, a reputation that is based on his early surrealistic works, such as "Everyday Life in a Dream," many of which appeared in reasonably obscure, specialized journals. But his influence on contemporary writers would seem to be considerable because of both the revival of interest in surrealism immediately following the Second World War and the creation of a subgenre of more or less autobiographical fiction—dubbed *katei no jijō shōsetsu* ("domestic exigency novels"). This terminology derives from the five-year-old Shin'ichi's refrain in Shimao's "The Sting of Death." Whenever his parents begin to fight, Shin'ichi shouts, "Here we go with domestic *exigencies*" (*katei no jijō ga hajimatta*), "Stop your domestic *exigencies!*" (*katei no jijō wa yamero*).[2] Kojima Nobuo (*Hōyō kazoku* [Family embrace], 1965) and Miura Shumon (*Hako niwa* [Miniature garden], 1967) have achieved greater popular recognition for this sort of work.

Perhaps one reason for Shimao's comparative obscurity has been his personal reticence, his preference for removing himself from the public eye. That Shimao has spent so comparatively little of his life in Tokyo, the center of the Japanese literary establishment, certainly is a factor. Scholars and journalists who wanted to interview him sometimes have had to travel to the Amami Islands to do so. Thus, those who have written about him have usually been personal acquaintances from his early days as a struggling novelist.[3] Shimao's obscurity is also the result of his identification with subgroups outside the mainstream of Japanese literature—Catholic writers, for example, or writers of "local color fiction" (*chihō bungaku*).

1

But those who happen upon Shimao Toshio's fiction are spellbound. Mishima Yukio has described him, with grudging admiration, as "formidable, appalling" (*osoroshii sakka*).[4] He has also been called a relentless "demon for observation" (*Kansatsu no ma*).[5] With few exceptions, his works are not pleasant reading, but they are not unapproachable. They deal with supremely personal, yet always recognizable, experiences, emotions, compulsions, and fantasies of elemental human existence—for example, the man turned inside out like a sock in "Everyday Life in a Dream," the molted cicada in "The Sting of Death." Although mesmerized by the horrible accuracy of these stories, the reader is warmed by the earnest, committed, almost passionate voice of the narrator.

Shimao Toshio, the son of a successful silk importer, was born on 18 April 1917 in Yokohama. Both his parents were originally from Odaka-machi, Sōma-gun, in Fukushima, and Shimao spent many of his summer vacations there. Although he writes of himself as a traveler, a perpetual wanderer who does not quite belong anywhere, he seems to consider Odaka-machi his place of origin. When he was eight, his family moved to another port town, Kobe, because of his father's business.

As a child Shimao was sickly, and he himself comments that, from childhood, physical weakness set him apart and turned him to writing about his own mode of existence as an alternative to that of normally healthy people. In 1923 he suffered a critical illness, but just what the disease was is unclear. (Yoshimoto Takaaki has suggested that Shimao's self-image is that of one perpetually suffering from a nameless critical illness.[6]) When to the doctor's amazement he began to recover, he was sent to his grandmother's home in Sōma-gun for total rest, and eventually his entire family came to take him home again. The day after his father left Yokohama for Fukushima, their home was destroyed in the Great Kantō earthquake. These events had a lasting effect on Shimao: the tiny thread that separates life and death and the seeming capriciousness of fate that brings a sudden reprieve from almost certain death are common themes in his later fiction.

From childhood Shimao seems to have been introspective, a self-conscious loner who was a voracious reader, fascinated by the printed word. When he was in the second year of elementary school, his father bought him a small mimeograph machine with which he produced, in the next ten years, some fifty-five booklets that gradually contained his own poems and short stories. At thirteen he was enrolled in Kobe First Commercial School since it was assumed that he would be a businessman and inherit his father's business. But he spent much of his time writing short stories, already strongly autobiographical, and putting out a literary magazine that he wrote, composed, and mimeographed himself. When he was seventeen, his mother Toshi, the first literary and intellectual influence on Shimao, died, and his father assumed complete responsibility for his upbringing. In 1936 Shimao was sent to Nagasaki, yet another port town, to attend Nagasaki

Higher Commercial School, where he was on the staff of the little magazine *LUNA*.[7] The following year he began another private publication, *Jūyon seiki*. [The fourteenth century], but abandoned the project when the first issue was banned as a danger to public morality.[8]

In 1939 he went on to the international trade division of the same school and joined a student tour group to Taiwan and the Philippines, still theoretically with the goal of pursuing a career like his father's. During this time he also became friendly with Agawa Hiroyuki and contributed to the literary magazine *Kooro*.[9] The next year, at the age of twenty-three, he transferred to Kyushu University in Fukuoka, where he became friends with Shōno Junzō. At first he was in the economics department, but he retook the entrance exams and changed the following year to a more compatible major, East Asian history. During this period he made several trips to China and Korea, of which he later published accounts. In the summer of 1943, carrying a watermelon and a collection of his own poetry, he went with Shōno Junzō to Sakai to pay a formal call on the romantic poet Itō Shizuo, whose support and encouragement of his literary endeavors Shimao enjoyed for years thereafter. Because of the war, he graduated six months early, in September 1943 (his graduation thesis was on the Uighur Turks in Yuan Dynasty China). The same month he privately published *Yōnenki* [An account of my childhood], a collection of early poems, stories, and parts of his diary from his days in Nagasaki. The collection was intended, one suspects, as a literary farewell to the world.

He immediately applied to the Naval Officers Candidate School, which he entered in October, and the next month he began torpedo-boat training. He received his commission as Lieutenant Junior Grade, and in November 1944, at twenty-seven years of age, he was assigned as the commanding officer of a special attack torpedo-boat unit of 183 men and was stationed at Nominoura on Kakeroma Island. During his ten months there he met his future wife, Ōhira Miho, who was an elementary school teacher in a neighboring village and had been educated in Tokyo. He writes that the intensity of their romance was predicated on the exoticism and extraordinary circumstances of his imminent self-immolation. She had pledged not to survive him.

On 13 August his squadron was placed on standby alert, but before they actually received sailing orders, the war ended. In September the squadron was demobilized, and he returned to his father's house in Kobe. The following March he married Miho, who had managed to obtain transportation to Kobe on a boat operated by the black market. For several years they lived in Kobe, and the marriage produced two children, Shinzō, born in 1948, and Maya, in 1950.

Shimao reluctantly taught world history, historiography, and Chinese cultural history at several colleges, including Kobe Foreign Language Institute. He also resumed his literary career in earnest. Two of the stories in this volume,

"The Farthest Edge of the Islands" and "Everyday Life in a Dream," were published
in 1948 and helped establish his reputation as a young writer of promise. In 1950
he was awarded the first Postwar Literature Prize for his story *Shutsu Kotō-ki*
[Exodus from the island]. During this period he participated actively in literary
circles and was invited to become a member of the prominent *Kindai Bungaku*.[10]

He resigned his teaching position in 1952 and moved his family to Tokyo,
the center of the Japanese literary world. He began teaching high school world
history and social studies to make ends meet while he increased his connections
with young writers, most notably those who came to be known as the "Third Generation of New Faces" (*Dai-san no shinjin*), in particular, three groups: *Genzai no
Kai, Ichini no Kai,* and *Shin Nihon Bungakkai*.[11] One assumes these are the groups
referred to with ambivalence in "The Sting of Death." During these years he
suffered from a mild form of tuberculosis (as did the husband in "The Sting of
Death"). As a writer he was extremely prolific and produced twenty-one stories in
approximately a year and a half.

Toward the end of the summer in 1954, Miho began to show signs of severe
mental distress, and the immediate cause seems to have been the discovery that
her husband had been unfaithful to her (as in "The Sting of Death"). She was
hospitalized in October, then released to his care. The next May, he was hospitalized along with her, for a period of about five months, to attend to her personal
needs. His writing career was interrupted, but experiences during this period
inspired his "sick wife" series (*byōsaimono*), of which three are included here. In
October 1955 they returned to the southern islands, to Naze on Amami Ōshima, so
that Miho could regain her emotional stability in the comfort of familiar surroundings, and again he found part-time teaching jobs to support him while he
wrote. In December of the following year, he was baptized into the Catholic
Church, the church of his wife. It was during this period that he produced most of
his "sick wife" series, a group of short stories originally published between 1955
and 1961, beginning with *Ware fukaki fuchi yori* [Out of the depths], which described the transition from home life to hospitalization, and *Nogareyuku Kokoro*
[The heart that slips away]. The stories, based on their life together in the mental
hospital, continued one after another.

A few years later, he shifted his gaze backward to the months of his wife's
psychological disintegration while the family was still attempting to care for her
at home and to maintain some semblance of family life. This series begins with
Ridatsu [Pulling away], dealing with the initial crisis that resulted in his withdrawing from his relationship with the other woman and choosing to devote all his
energies to his wife's welfare, and includes "The Sting of Death." These stories
were published in 1960 as a collection of short stories, which won Shimao considerable recognition. Much later, in 1977, they were re-edited and published as a
novel.[12] Shimao states that he wrote all these stories both as a kind of "prayer to

his wife," in propitiation for his sins, and as an attempt to help them deal with the psychological crisis. He considered it, he said, almost a sacred "mission" to write.[13] His wife participated in the process, reading his drafts, correcting his prose, and insisting on revisions of conversations and the like when what he wrote did not correspond with her view of "the truth." This practice is suggested in "The Sting of Death," when the husband, Toshio, comments that he is unable to write because he always chooses material from his own life, and at every word he would risk inciting his wife's symptoms.

Shimao also began writing reviews and essays on contemporary literature and becoming increasingly involved in the study of Ryukyuan culture. In 1957 he became the curator of the Kagoshima Prefecture Amami Museum of Japanese-American Culture and, at that time, began a society for the study of the Amami Islands and edited its publication, of which he in fact wrote a substantial portion. In 1958, the Amami branch of the Kagoshima Prefecture Library was established, and Shimao became its head.

In 1962 he turned again to his experiences during the war, in particular the days surrounding the surrender. Now that almost twenty years have passed, he treats his material much more realistically than in "At the Farthest Edge of the Islands" and some surrealistic dream sequences published immediately after his return from the war. In September 1962, he published *Shuppatsu wa tsui ni otozurezu* [When we never left port], undoubtedly the most famous of his many stories about his war experiences.

In April 1963 Shimao was invited by the United States government to make a tour of this country, including Puerto Rico and the Hawaiian Islands. In 1965 he visited Poland on his way to Moscow to participate in a conference on Russian and Japanese literature, returning for an extended tour of Eastern Europe in 1967, then back to the Soviet Union in 1970 and on to India for a conference on Asian and African literature. Much of Shimao's writing in recent years has been essays, many recording his observations on his travels through the Ryukyu Islands and abroad.

He has generally spent part of each year in literary circles in Tokyo, though withdrawn from the public eye, and part on Amami Ōshima, where his home has been. One sadness in his life, perhaps as a result of the sort of marital discord and perpetual unrest depicted in "The Sting of Death," is that his daughter Maya was physically weak and experienced learning disabilities. She is the subject of some of his later writing, both fiction and nonfiction.[14] His wife in recent years has embarked on her own writing career, developing a considerable following and winning acclaim from the critics.[15] In 1975, after twenty years, Shimao resigned his job as curator of the Amami Museum and moved to Ibusuki on southern Kyushu. After frequent moves, following a pattern established early in his life, he moved back to Chigasaki, near his birthplace, Yokohama. Perhaps his recent rise in popularity is not unrelated to this move closer to the center of the literary scene.[16]

The six stories represented here in English translation are intended to give an overview of Shimao Toshio's fictional oeuvre. These stories, written over a period of about fifteen years, are chosen for variety, balance, and length. They are arranged not in the order in which they were written but according to the time in which the stories are set. Thus, the earliest story is first in the volume, but the second story is the most recently published. They combine to form a longer story, told in different voices, about characters who occupy recognizably continuous roles but whose contours and particulars change from segment to segment. The pure, almost mythical Toë of "The Farthest Edge of the Islands," for example, is not Miho of "The Sting of Death," though there are references in the latter to scenes that appear in the former. Nor has the struggling young writer of "Everyday Life in a Dream" simply matured into Toshio of "The Sting of Death."

The last three stories here have been taken out of the context that Shimao eventually assigned to them—"The Sting of Death," for instance, ultimately became chapter two of the novel of the same name, which, I hope, will someday be translated in its entirety. There is, of course, a long tradition in Japanese literature, from classical poetry through the modern anthology, of rearranging and providing new contexts for works written by oneself or by another; Shimao has engaged over the years in this pastime, recombining his own stories in various ways.

This volume by no means exhausts the scope of Shimao's fiction. There are no stories here, for instance, about childhood or student life, and none of his many travel stories. Some of his most famous stories—"When We Never Left Port," for example—have not been included. But the stories presented here do offer a considerable variety of style, from the pristine storybook language of "The Farthest Edge of the Islands," to the young intellectual's jargon of "Everyday Life in a Dream," to the visionary, hysterical, occasionally ritualistic prose of the "sick wife" stories, to the sober, difficult, almost ponderous narration of "This Time That Summer." Shimao's approach to his material varies as well. "Everyday Life in a Dream" is the only representative here of a large number of stories usually called surrealistic by the critics, stories whose plots progress by the logic of dreams. The individual experiences of real life are lived through a combination of conscious and unconscious perception. These stories are the least approachable and the least charming to the casual reader, but they serve, among other things, to highlight patterns in the more realistic fiction. "The Farthest Edge of the Islands" is a symbolic heightening of reality in another way, a romantic fairy tale beginning at the extremity of experience, at the farthest edge of the world. The other stories are presented as precise, close chronicles of reality by a participant in that reality whose attention never wavers and who never allows himself to avert his eyes from a world that he sees as his responsibility and in a sense his fault. All but the first story, "The Farthest Edge of the Islands," which is in third-person narration, are told in the first person by the character who plays Shimao's role in the life that inspired the fiction.

The stories collected here, however, show even more continuities than differences. Some specific images—for example, the Ryukyuan mythological amphibious goblin, the *Kenmun* who tests its victims by engaging them either in *sumō* wrestling or in verbal argumentation, or the methane gas that bubbles to the surface of murky water—appear from story to story, gradually shedding light on the role they play in individual contexts. Except for the first story, the prose is uniformly difficult: there are logical gaps; the grammatical subject is often unclear; the sentences are long and full of sudden turns and surprises; and words have double meanings, or hidden meanings, exploited later like implications reinterpreted and only gradually understood. One is often forced to reread a paragraph in consideration of what succeeds it. Reading the text becomes an experience analogous to the process it depicts. The relationship between life and art is specifically the subject of "Everyday Life in a Dream," but implicitly part of all the stories here. Fiction for Shimao is the transformation of personal experience; life and art are the two essential elements of his being, each of which exists partly for the sake of the other.

There is no escapism in Shimao's fiction. Even the dream and the fantasy are intensified experiences of individual reality. These stories are painful to read; there is a masochism about them. Among the critics they have tended to inspire emotional literary pirouettes rather than sober analysis. The same preoccupations recur in all six stories: the plasticity and ultimate meaninglessness of time from the point of view of the individual; confrontation with death and disintegration, both physical and psychological; the face of humanity with its mask removed, the mind reduced to an elemental state; and the possibility of redemption or resurrection, of expiation through self-examination and the act of writing. The stories are as sharp as Ensign Hayahito's metaphorical "awl concealed in a bag," as relentless as Miho's tireless cross-examination of her husband. And these stories have a special beauty, the flights of fantasy and desperation giving to all of them a luminous intensity that belies the turgidity of his prose.

8   "The Sting of Death" and Other Stories

Notes to the Introduction

[1]All these writers have won the Akutagawa Prize for works since translated into English: Yasuoka for *Kaihen no kōkei* ([A view by the sea], trans. Kären Wigen, [New York: Columbia Press, 1984], pp. 105-96); Kojima for *Amerikan sukūru* ([The American school], trans. William F. Sibley, in *Contemporary Japanese Literature*, ed. Howard Hibbett [New York: Knopf, 1977], pp. 119-44); Shōno for *Pūrusaido shōkei*, of which there are two English translations; Yoshiyuki for *Shūu* ([Sudden shower], trans. Geoffrey Bownas, in *New Writing in Japan*, ed. Mishima Yukio [Hammondsworth, Middlesex: Penguin, 1972], pp. 99-122).

[2]See Okuno Takeo in *Shimao Toshio sakuhin-shū* 4 (Tokyo: Shōbunsha, 1962), p. 295. *Katei no jijō*, literally "conditions in the family," spoken by the child Shin'ichi, is always rendered in *katakana*, indicating perhaps a childish pronunciation and certainly that he does not understand the meaning of the words he is using.

[3]Yoshimoto Takaaki and Okuno Takeo edited *Gendai hyōron* [Contemporary criticism], of which Shimao became a contributing member in 1953. Both were among those who gathered at Yokohama to see Shimao and his wife off when they left for Naze on Amami Ōshima in October 1955. Matsuoka Shunkichi knew him very slightly as a torpedo-boat pilot during the war. Surprisingly enough, even Mishima Yukio, author of a brief but famous essay on Shimao (n. 4), was a fellow member of the short-lived, five-member group Kōyō [Glittering], organized by Shōno Junzō immediately after the war.

[4]"Mateki na mono no chikara" [The power of the demonic], in *Mishima Yukio hyōron zenshū* (Tokyo: Shinchōsha, 1971), p. 331. This famous article is reprinted in Aeba Takao, ed., *Shimao Toshio kenkyū*, (Tokyo: Tōjusha, 1976), pp. 30-31.

[5]Satō Yasumasa, "Shimao Toshio to Katorishizumu" [Shimao Toshio and catholicism], *Kokubungaku: Kaishaku to kyōzai no kenkyū* (October 1973): 113; also reprinted in Aeba, ed., *Shimao Toshio kenkyū*, pp. 294-301.

[6]Yoshimoto Takaaki, "Shimao bungaku no genryū" [The fountainhead of Shimao's literary works], *Kokubungaku* (October 1973): 60-61.

[7]*LUNA* was a poetry journal—originally mimeographed but eventually printed—published in Kobe in 1936 and 1937. It was edited by the young poet Nakagiri Masao (1919-), later known for poetry inspired by his war experiences. Contributors were aspiring poets from all over the country. Shimao's poetry was included under the penname Shimao Hyōhei. The journal eventually grew into the better-known *Arechi*.

[8]This apparently innocuous publication, which carried Shimao's much-discussed story "Okii no teiso to Mako" [Okii's chastity and Mako], was banned by the Home Ministry, and most copies were disposed of by the secret police. The editors were reprimanded and made to promise they would not write anything of a similar nature as long as they were students at Nagasaki Higher Commercial School. Shimao was apparently regarded with suspicion by the police for some time thereafter, and they continued to watch his movements and questioned relatives and neighbors as far away as Fukushima. See "Watakushi no bungaku henreki" [My literary wanderings], in *Shimao Toshio hishōsetsu shūsei* 5 (Tokyo: Tōjusha, 1973), pp. 251-52.

[9]*Kooro* was a little magazine published at Fukuoka Middle School mainly by student intellectuals who tolerated the participation of the commercial school students. The name

comes from the first chapter of the *Kojiki* and refers to the sound *kooro kooro* made by the Heavenly Spear of Izanagi no Mikoto as it stirred the original chaos before forming the Japanese Islands. According to Shimao the word was chosen for its association with creation, in a day when the allusion would surely be recognized. There was an autobiographical, romantic—though not nationalistic—tinge to its contents, which reflect above all an effort to retain literary "purity" as writers in a wartime society. The publication was begun in 1939 and was abandoned in 1944, when its young members were drafted one after another. See Kōno Toshirō, "Shimao Toshio ni okeru shishōsetsu no hōhō: *Kooro* to *Kōyō* no jidai o megutte" [Shimao's autobiographical approach: a look at the *Kooro* and *Kōyō* eras], *Kokubungaku* (October 1973): 130-36; also Shimao's "Watakushi no bungaku henreki," pp. 249-66.

Agawa Hiroyuki (1920-), born and raised in Hiroshima, was a member of a subgroup of *Kooro* at Tokyo University. Later, like Shimao, he became a naval officer, and he was stationed in China when the war ended. He wrote autobiographical fiction about the war and the aftermath of the bomb in Hiroshima. His *Kumo no bohyō* [Clouds for gravemarkers] (1955) offers an interesting comparison with Shimao's *Shuppatsu wa tsui ni otozurezu.*

[10]*Kindai bungaku*, published from January 1946 to August 1964, was one of the most important forces in modern Japanese literature and literary criticism. It was founded in 1946 by Ara Masatō, Haniya Yutaka, Hirano Ken, Honda Shūgo, Odagiri Hideo, Sasaki Kiichi, and Yamamuro Shizuka, all prominent figures who had flirted with Marxism and were interested in the proletarian movement and its repression in the 1930s. Somewhat controversially, membership was expanded in 1947, then again greatly in 1948, to include writers of some stature with little or no thought to their political or social ideology, and the journal became known for its active encouragement of new writers and the publication of experimental works. Shimao, admitted with this last group, remained a member until 1958, when the group again shrank to a unified core.

[11]*Daisan no shinjin* is the name given a rather diverse collection of writers who became known after the immediate postwar period. Shimao is one of the older of this group, whose youth generally corresponds to the war years and the disillusion that followed. Most of them write autobiographical fiction and all are superior craftsmen. Agawa Hiroyuki, Endō Shūsaku, Kojima Nobuo, Miura Shumon, Shōno Junzō, Yasuoka Shōtarō, and Yoshiyuki Junnosuke, among others, are generally grouped together.

Genzai no kai [The present generation club] was a literary journal carrying fiction, poetry, critical essays, and documentary articles, with a split emphasis on art for art's sake and social conscience. The most famous members in addition to Shimao were Shōno Junzō and Abe Kōbō. It was published from 1952 to 1956, but in 1954 the editor Date Norio and others withdrew to start the well-known *Yuriika* [Eurika].

Ichinikai [The one two club] was a lesser-known little magazine sponsored by the influential commercial literary journal *Bungakkai*. Several of the "Third Generation of New Faces" were members.

Shin Nihon bungaku [New Japanese literature] was founded in the same year as its rival, *Kindai bungaku*, by members of the Marxist movement who had either defected or been imprisoned in the 1930s and who returned to communism or socialism after the war. It was intended as a new leftist literary movement. Among the nine founders were Nakano Shigeharu and Miyamoto Yuriko, soon joined by Odagiri Hideo, Noma Hiroshi, and others. The group, which generally advocated a "democratic revolution," was criticized by Cominform in 1950 and subsequently divided into moderate and radical groups, who remained separate until 1952. One immediate cause of the split was the controversy over Shimao's story "Chippoke na abanchūru" [A dumb little *aventure*], which appeared in the May 1950 issue of *Shin Nihon bungaku*. It was criticized as being "anti-revolutionary, four-and-a-half-mat-room decadent *petit bourgeois* fiction" (see Shimao Toshio, *Shuppatsu wa tsui ni otozurezu* [Tokyo: Ōbunsha, 1973], p. 338). Despite intermittent ideological disputes within its membership, and with the Japan Communist Party, publication continues today.

[12]The collection of stories, *Shi no toge* (Tokyo: Kōdansha, 1960) includes "Ie no naka," "Ridatsu," "Shi no toge," "Chiryō," "Nemurinaki suimin," "Nemuri naki nemuri," and "Ie no soto de." In volume 4 of *Shimao Toshio sakuhin-shū*, 1962, cited above, "Shi no toge" occupies the same central position in a different selection of stories: "Ie no naka," "Ridatsu," "Shi no toge," "Gake no fuchi," "Tetsuro ni chikaku," and "Hi wa hi ni." The novel *Shi no toge* (Tokyo: Shinchōsha, 1977) includes as chapters "Ridatsu," "Shi no toge," "Gake no fuchi," "Hi wa hi ni," "Ryūki," "Hibi no rei," "Hi no chijimari," "Ko to tomo ni," "Sugikoshi," "Hi o kakete," "Hikkoshi," and "Nyūin made," including new stories published separately after 1963 and together in other anthologies: *Hi no chijimari* [The shortening of the days] (Tokyo: Shinchōsha, 1965), and *Hi o Kakete* [Taking our time] (Tokyo: Chūōkōronsha, 1967).

[13]See "Tsuma e no inori: Hoi" [Postscript to a prayer to my wife], translated in the appendix.

[14]See the short story "Maya to issho ni" [Maya and I], originally published in *Shinchō*, February 1962; reprinted in *Shimao Toshio sakuhin-shū* 5, pp. 32-49. See also in Shimao Toshio, *Garasushōji no shiruetto* (Tokyo: Sōjusha, 1972), "Nyanko" [Kitten], pp. 141-47, and "Maya," pp. 155-61.

[15]Her *Umibe no sei to shi* [Life and death by the sea] (Tokyo: Sōjusha, 1974) won the coveted Tamura Toshiko Prize for women's writing the following year. Illustrations are by Shimao Shinzō. Two short selections from this volume are translated in the appendix.

[16]Since this book went to press, Shimao has moved to the south once again. He now lives in Kajiki, on the northern shore of Kagoshima Bay.

THE FARTHEST EDGE OF THE ISLANDS

This story takes place long ago, when the whole world was at war.

* * *

One could say that Toë lived among the roses. Surrounded by a hedge of rose bushes, in the middle of a garden carpeted with withered rose leaves, she lived in a room separated from the main house. Here in Kagerōjima, the roses bloomed the year round. On three sides of the room was a wooden veranda, connected to the main house in one spot by a removable breezeway. When night came, she would close the sliding paper doors on three sides of the room and light a candle lamp. And she lived here without ever closing the wooden shutter doors and locking up tight.

* * *

All day Toë's sole occupation was to play in her room with all the village children. They came barefoot, gathering in Toë's garden, and she taught them songs.

Beach plovers, beach plovers, why do you cry?

Nobody knew how old Toë was, but she looked extremely young. Her head was round like a little bird's, and she was plump and girlish, although she weighed remarkably little. As for her face, it was not so different from the other girls of the island, except that there was something striking about her mouth. When she smiled, it stretched horizontally, thin and firm. Among the people of the village, both children and adults, there were many who thought that Toë was fundamentally different from themselves. This was simply because for a long time Toë's family had been thought of in such a way; there was no other reason. Still, nobody found it strange that thanks to the entire village, Toë was able to spend her days playing with the children. Two or three of the village old people knew that Toë had not been born in the village.

* * *

In those days there were troops stationed in the neighboring village of Shohaate. For that reason, there was something unsettled in the air in Toë's village, and people trembled with the presentiment that the world war would soon cast its shadow in the vicinity of Kagerōjima. How many soldiers would come, and what would they do? Would something not occur to cause trouble for the village? What sort of person would the commanding officer be? Such were the various worries of the people in the village.

But eventually they learned many things. There were a hundred eighty-one soldiers in Shohaate, and the young lieutenant junior grade who commanded them was just as useless as a lamp in broad daylight. It was rather the second in command, an ensign named Hayahito, still in the prime of early manhood but experienced and decisive in all matters, who had the dignity and authority of a true military man in his dealings with others. The one hundred eighty subordinates — excluding Ensign Hayahito, the one hundred seventy-nine subordinates—did, in fact, sympathize with their young chief officer, but they had apparently surrendered themselves completely to the strict discipline of the second in command. This was the state of affairs. And so, as for the daily occupation of the commanding officer, it was generally considered that if he made the rounds of Chitan, Sagashibama, Tagamma, Sungibara, plus Ujirehama on the opposite shore, and if he checked on the twelve caves and the crude wooden barracks, well, that would suffice.

Lieutenant Saku—so this chief officer was called—was rumored in the village to be tall and thin. In direct contrast, they said, Ensign Hayahito was short and stocky, with a broad, ruddy face.

In his heart the second in command was not fond of Lieutenant Saku, though on the surface the two seemed to get along well enough. At times, such as when he drank, Ensign Hayahito bored into Lieutenant Saku with cutting words, like a drill concealed in a bag. Upon occasion he would affect extreme intoxication and make a point of behaving roughly to Lieutenant Saku, pushing him and shoving him, but Lieutenant Saku did not protest. Ensign Hayahito often wondered what his commanding officer was thinking. To tell the truth, what Lieutenant Saku was thinking, nobody knew.

* * *

The clouds of war spread as enemy planes gradually began to appear in the skies over Kagerōjima. One day they received bad news: there was to be a major air raid on Kagerōjima. The war had taken an abrupt change, and the enemy was apparently plotting a new strategy. Following the major air raid, the enemy was expected to land on the island itself.

The news swiftly had an effect on Lieutenant Saku's men. In preparation for the air raid, they were ordered to build a revetment in front of the caves to protect their contents from bombing.

Lieutenant Saku received that order after the evening meal, when on the twilight beach people here and there, having nothing more to do today than sleep, gave the longest and most leisurely sigh of the day and lamented the passing of time. A young boy played the harmonica. How could one even imagine a sudden change in such a serene setting?

In the small wooden building, slightly higher than the rest, that housed the main headquarters, the commanding officer, after having lost himself in the pleasures of such an evening, summoned Ensign Hayahito and said, "Ensign Hayahito, this operation must be completed even if it means working all night. Let us begin now." Ensign Hayahito felt the fighting spirit rise slowly within him. Soon, as a result of Ensign Hayahito's strict assignment of duties, in front of the twelve caves one could see the flickering light of lanterns and hear the resounding echo of bumping logs. Actually, these caves held no ordinary supplies. What they contained was only to be used just before the enemy landed on Kagerōjima; no one knew the particulars except the commanding officer and fifty-one men chosen from among the hundred seventy-nine.

* * *

There was turmoil in Lieutenant Saku's breast. The fated day had crept up on him so quickly he felt cheated. At the same time, however, the anticipation of facing this unknown adventure that lay ahead grew stronger. Only one thing still weighed on his heart. That evening, after it was completely dark, he had promised to visit Mr. Toku Tokki's house in the village of Shohaate. You see, the young commanding officer's heart was drawn to Tokki's daughter, Yochi. Once, the lieutenant had given her a piggyback ride. Her soft legs, the cute little palms holding his shoulders, and her breath as it brushed his cheek were unforgettable. Yochi was so small she did not even come up to his chest. Yesterday, when he had passed through the village of Shohaate, Yochi, looking plump with her baby brother Toku asleep on her back, had called excitedly to him, "Lieutenant, Lieutenant. Shohaate's Lieutenant."

He stopped and gazed at Yochi's red lips. Her eyelashes were so long they cast shadows on her cheeks. Her head was big and round and dark, like a toasted rice ball. Moving her shoulders all the while to soothe the baby on her back, she finally mustered her courage and said, "The *Kenmun* comes out under the banyan tree and I'm afraid."

The shawl that tied the baby to her back was too short, and the legs and bare feet that hung below it looked somehow pitiful. She continued, "Come play with me so I won't be afraid, OK?"

As he walked away the lieutenant answered in the dialect of the island, "See you tomorrow."

After he had gone a few steps past her, he turned around and added, "When it's completely dark." In the meantime, he would have some stick candy made for Yochi.

This was the promise he had suddenly remembered. It was quite possible that from tomorrow onward Kagerōjima would become a violent battleground. Kagerōjima itself would not be entirely wiped off the face of the earth, and the people of the island by some quirk of fate might well, like the plants and trees, live on. Ah, even a few of the soldiers stationed on the island would probably survive, left to cry like crickets after a typhoon. But Lieutenant Saku and the fifty-one men had their orders: the possibility of survival was painful to contemplate and not to be hoped for. In his heart, the lieutenant wept. He had to keep his promise to Yochi. That was all he could think of.

*　*　*

Ensign Hayahito and the one hundred seventy-nine men were all busy at their respective duties. There was a sudden turbulence in the night sky, and the effect of the gathering clouds could be felt on the ground as well. A wind seemed to have risen.

The lieutenant went into his office in the wooden headquarters building and immediately summoned his orderly: "Ogusuku. Bring some stick candy and come with me." Ogusuku hurriedly tied some stick candy in a bundle and went down to the beach to ready a rowboat. The lieutenant stepped gloomily into the boat, and quickly Ogusuku began rowing. The slap of the oars reached the ears of Ensign Hayahito, who was supervising operations on the beach. Looking through the darkness out over the water, the ensign saw a rowboat, its bow aimed toward the village of Shohaate, and in it the silhouettes of two men whom he recognized as the commanding officer and his orderly. The bow spun around in the wind, but before long the little boat reached the shore. The lieutenant alighted on the rocks and, accepting from Ogusuku the bundle of stick candy, disappeared into the darkness in the direction of the village. Ogusuku fastened the boat to a stake, then sat down chin in hand and gazed absently over at the opposite shore, where the others were working. He watched the lanterns at the water's edge, their flames growing and shrinking. The sight recalled another from long ago, the lights of the town that grew and shrank like crosses he had watched in painful ecstasy as a child. Apparently, dark clouds had filled the sky.

The house the lieutenant had come to visit was an extremely humble structure, hardly more than a dugout, consisting of just two rooms, a living area, and a kitchen. Even so, there were lots of children in the house. The head of the household, Tokki, had gone about a month ago to Kunya on the other island and had not yet returned.

Tokki's wife Uino said, "Just look at all these children, Lieutenant. In the old days poor Chiisakobe no Sugaru must have looked just like this."[1]

The lieutenant laughed. There really were a lot of them: Tokuguma, Yochi, Tokujirō, Rie, Tokuzō, and finally Tokiyon—little Yochi acted as big sister to all of them. Her younger brothers Tokujirō and Tokuzō and her younger sister Rie, who had already gone to bed, got up again all smiles. With the stern face of an elder sister, she told them to mind their manners. Even with so many children around and the smell of milk in the air, Lieutenant Saku felt there was something unbearably forlorn about the house. It was a sadness that gripped his chest. When that day came, what would happen to these tender children? The thought was unbearable.

"If the enemy invades the island, what shall we do with the children? *Are* they going to invade the island, Lieutenant?" Uino asked him.

"Why would they bother to invade a tiny island like this?" the lieutenant responded, managing an ambiguous reply. Then, unable to bear the role of deceiver, he took his leave. Wasn't it precisely because the enemy seemed about to invade that he had come to say good-bye? Happily eating their stick candy, the children knelt in a line at the entrance way to see him off.

"Good-bye, Lieutenant, Shohaate's Lieutenant."

The lieutenant squeezed the children's hands. Oh, such soft hands. He had not known that there existed anything as soft as those hands.

Yochi added in her precocious way, breathing excitedly, "Lieutenant, Toë said, she said oh she has lots and lots of fish, so she said to tell you to come eat some of it with her."

What lay ahead of Lieutenant Saku was nothing worldly. Soon, the order would come, and the contents of those caves would be set to water; he and his men would climb aboard and dash themselves against the enemy boats—immediately ahead awaited simply the individual, cruel, unnatural destinies of himself and each of the fifty-one men, surely no earthly fate. His knees trembled as he walked back to the rowboat. He dropped into the boat with a thud, and Ogusuku

---

[1]According to legend, Chiisakobe no Sugaru, when asked by the Emperor Yūryaku to gather silkworms (*ko*), misunderstood and collected babies (*ko*) instead.

rowed away from the shore. At that moment, as if a dam had broken, something began to strike the water's surface: it was raining. Pockmarks began to appear over the water. As they got wet, the two men sat in silence. When Saku slipped the peanuts Uino had given him into Ogusuku's pocket, Ogusuku bowed slightly but said nothing. Apparently, the revetments had been completed; in Chitan, Sagashibama, Tamma, Sungibara, and Ujirehama, all was quiet. The rain gently soaked everything.

* * *

The next day, it rained all day.

* * *

And the danger to the island seemed to have passed. The enemy had begun a new campaign against another small island far to the east. The force of the rain gradually mounted until it was a total downpour, forcing them all to take the afternoon off. Tired, the lieutenant lay down in his own room. As he listened to the croaking of little tree frogs under the floorboards, he fell fast asleep.

In his dream, the voices coming from the room next door were loud. What insolence, he thought, then he woke up, surprised at his own irritability. The room was pitch dark. The base once more had been enveloped in the cloak of night, and it was still raining. And there were, in fact, voices next door. He made no conscious effort to listen, but the following fragments of a conversation reached his ears: "Just when we're on the verge of getting who knows what kind of orders . . . and when everyone else is hard at work . . . you see how he is . . . the number four cave . . . this is no time to be sleeping. . . ."

Lieutenant Saku immediately grasped the meaning of those remarks. Remembering Ensign Hayahito's cool, steady snake's eyes, he jumped out of bed with a start. Purposely making his footsteps audible, the lieutenant stomped into the room next door. There, Ensign Hayahito was drinking with a few of the men, and his face, red with drink, gleamed in the light of the three lamps that were burning. Ensign Hayahito greeted the lieutenant, "Well, what do you know. If it isn't our Lieutenant Saku." He was obviously intoxicated and somewhat embarassed.

"We were making so much noise, we must have disturbed your rest." The others looked as though the unfortunate situation had sobered them up a little. Lieutenant Saku stood there and persisted nevertheless.

"Ensign Hayahito, is it true what you said about the fourth cave?"

"True or not, you can check it out for yourself—right, Ishūin?" he said, bringing his red face close to one of the subordinates.

"I see," said the lieutenant, and he quietly returned to his room, took his dark blue raincoat down from its hook, and, still putting it on, walked out into the rain.

Presently, the guard on duty came walking through the rain, passing on the order for all those assigned to the operations at the fourth cave to assemble. Hearing the order, Ensign Hayahito looked startled but smiled wryly. Then, giving his cheek a quick rub with his right hand, as if to hide the smile, he said, "Time for me to repair to my bed, I guess. Ishūin, why don't you guys go to bed now too—unless you're assigned to cave number four, that is?" He was already lying on his bed.

Some fifteen men reluctantly gathered in front of the fourth cave. The sandbag revetment that had cost them so much effort was in a pitiful state of collapse. Apparently the ground there was especially soft, and water flowed immediately below the surface. The water had gushed forth like a small river and completely washed away the revetment. Looking at what was left of the crumbled revetment, the lieutenant saw his own ugly self. The men who had gathered continued to mutter under their breath among themselves. The rain ran under the lieutenant's collar and into his sleeves, and his skin was unpleasantly cold and damp.

"The senior man will count all those present."

When the lieutenant said this, someone said in a low voice, "How does he expect us to get any work done around here?"

When the lieutenant heard this remark, he felt a heaviness in the pit of his stomach. Suddenly, he had been plunged unknowingly into the depths of a great sadness. That sensation gradually changed into a shame that seemed to make his entire body flush crimson. Then, all of a sudden, he felt the anger rise within him.

"Wait!" he shouted, so loud and clear he surprised himself. "You men—you men may all leave now. Go ahead, just go back to bed."

His voice was loud enough to be heard all the way to the village. It happened so suddenly that none of the fifteen or so men moved. They just stood there motionless in the rain, waiting for the lieutenant to speak again. A menacing look flashed across the lieutenant's face, but in the next instant that look had crumbled and he was on the verge of tears. Brandishing his bamboo whip, he bellowed: "What's the matter with you? What are you waiting for? I said you may leave. When I say leave, I mean leave!"

Dismayed and embarrassed by their commanding officer's unprecedented conduct, the fifteen men went back to their respective barracks. Left behind, the lieutenant began to work by himself. First, he dug up the area where the water ran. This was a job of rapidly progressive destruction. The resulting ditch he filled with gravel. Then, one by one he began piling up the sandbags, which were heavy for a man alone. By the time he had finished doing that, it was far into the night, and the rain had stopped. Through gaps in the clouds he could see the moon. It was one night past the full moon. The poor lieutenant's head was filled with a feverish din. As he rubbed his hips and looked up at the clouds, the moon looked very, very grim. He could not help being reminded of his own fate. Tonight he was still alive. When the enemy finally comes to Ushima, Kagerōjima, and the rest, it will almost certainly be on a moonlit night—the thought suddenly struck him like a revelation. He decided to go to bed, and on his way back to the little wooden headquarters, he came to the road that split off and climbed to the mountain pass. ("Toë says, she says oh she has lots and lots of fish. . . .") This pass was not very high, and when you had crossed it, you were supposed to be able to see Toë's village directly below. Suddenly, as though mysteriously beckoned, he found himself choosing that path. Almost immediately after being stationed in Shohaate, he had heard from nobody in particular about Toë of the neighboring village. He already knew it was destiny that Toë was in that village. However, the lieutenant had not yet laid eyes on her. On the way to the pass was a frog, with a voice that sounded human.

At the pass stood a little square shelter where one of the lieutenant's men was on night watch. "Sir. On the pass and as far as I can see from here there seems to be nothing out of the ordinary, and I have heard no strange noises. The rain stopped at 0-0-thirty hours," said the man on night watch, recognizing his commanding officer. The lieutenant nodded and said nothing. Below him the sea sparkled pale in the moonlight. He would not be able to see the village without going a little further around the crest of the mountain. Discerning that the lieutenant meant to descend the path on the other side of the pass, the night watchman asked, "Where are you headed, Sir?"

"In the village under the pale, pale moonlight, beyond the mountain ridge, playing dead on a cutting board there lies a cool fish that has swallowed a pearl. I am determined to see it with my own eyes." Such was the elegant answer the commanding officer gave.

Around the bend a great banyan tree spread its many eerie hands and covered the path. This was the *Kenmun* goblin's tree. The lieutenant could almost hear Yochi's fearful, persistent little voice. When he had passed under the tree, almost at a run, there indeed was Toë's village, nestled as if in the bottom of a bowl, the sleeping little houses side by side. The appearance of this village completely won Lieutenant Saku's heart. It seemed to him that never in his twenty-eight years had he been so impressed by a night view of a village. He was never to see that village in daytime; for him, it simply *was* the village of night. There were remarkably many houses but no one on the streets. Though there were signs of life inside the houses, no light at all emerged from them. It seemed as if the entire village had been created just for Lieutenant Saku to walk around in all by himself. In the moonlight everything was pale, individual forms set apart in outline. And when the lieutenant set foot in the streets of the village, he was enveloped in an indescribably lovely perfume. To what might it be compared? The impression was generally one of sweetness, attenuated pleasingly with the tartness of a mandarin orange. The whole village was damp from the rain a little while earlier, and the air was thick with the scent. Throughout the village were ancient trees, from whose branches hung many roots, like beards. These big trees stood as if shoulder to shoulder, strangely encircling the village. It was said that they bore flowers whose buds opened secretly, quietly, only at night.

For some reason, the lieutenant walked on tiptoe through this seemingly deserted village. Hearing his own footsteps, he felt his heart beat faster, until before long he had wandered into a certain courtyard. What had guided the lieutenant there was the flickering candlelight visible through the paper windows of the little house. Why should there be a light in that one place so late at night? he thought. The lieutenant circled around the hedge of roses and stepped inside the garden; the dead leaves that filled the garden were wet from the rain and gleamed like eyes. There were layers and layers of these leaf-eyes; under the lieutenant's step they squished. He took a look into the room through the paper windows that surrounded it on three sides; on a sumptuous table was a plate of fish, beside which a candle in a silver candlestand flickered dramatically. That was all he could see, no sign of Toë. In order to get a better look, he put his hand on the veranda, and he received a shock: someone was lying on the floor there. He thought he smelled lilies. A young girl in a plain house dress lay there like a stray puppy. Ah yes, it's Toë, thought the lieutenant. Taking out a flashlight small enough to fit in the palm of his hand, the lieutenant shone the light on Toë's face. He was surprised at her large, round face. The faint freckles on her cheek stood out clearly. Blinking at the sudden light, Toë made a gesture as if to hit the lieutenant with her right hand and broke into a big smile, a peculiarly thin, wide smile. Sitting up and putting her hand to the hem of her dress, she said, "I thought you were the moon. I'm sorry. But I wasn't really asleep, you know."

Then she rose and walked with a springy step to open wide the sliding doors and beckon to the lieutenant to come in. When Toë stood in front of the candle light, he could see the outline of her body through her dress. As she replaced the candle, which was about to burn out, Toë glanced at the silver candlestand covered with its shade of figured paper, and her face glowed like a red photo negative. On opposite sides of the candlestand the lieutenant and Toë sat facing slightly sideways and gazed in silence at the now cold plate of fish. The lieutenant was not particularly fond of fish.

"Toë," the lieutenant addressed her suddenly and simply.

"Yes."

Toë raised her eyes to look into the lieutenant's eyes. And he read her fate.

"Who am I?"

"You are Shohaate's Lieutenant."

"And who are you?"

"I'm Toë."

"You go ahead and eat the rest of the fish, Toë."

Toë smiled. She had a special girlish plumpness, and a sturdiness, like a little girl at the mischievous age. The only sign of frailty was in her eyes, which always seemed to focus slightly off to one side. The minute the lieutenant saw those eyes, he knew that he had been taken captive by Toë.

Presently, the Little Dipper began to appear in the eastern sky, and they realized it would not be long before the Morning Star shone over Kyanma Mountain on the island across the water.

*　*　*

At about the time when the second in command, Ensign Hayahito, and the rest of the men had settled into sleep, Lieutenant Saku was walking the road up to the mountain pass. And each time he was startled along the way by that frog whose croaking sounded like human crying. He hated having to meet the guard on night duty at the pass. But by the time Venus shone over Kyanma Mountain on the other island, the commanding officer's room was full of signs of his presence. Yet, thanks to the night watchman, rumors had spread throughout the base about that "daytime lamp," commanding officer Lieutenant Saku, and his nocturnal wanderings.

The enemy attack on the eastern islands was drawing close. At Kagerōjima enemy planes began to fly overhead even in the middle of the night.

*　*　*

One night, the lieutenant was watching the slightly cockeyed Toë, who was singing. So that the light would not be seen from the planes, the wooden doors on the veranda were always shut, and Toë's kimono was draped over the candlestand.

How brief our night together
No sooner evening than midnight,
No sooner has the cock crowed
Than, oh, it's daylight

she sang. A strange, dull persistent hum burrowed into his ears. At first barely audible, it was coming from the south, gradually approaching Kagerōjima.

When Toë had finished her song, she clung tight to the lieutenant.

"The enemy is coming," she said, trembling.

"There is nothing to be afraid of, Toë." The lieutenant smiled, but he was trembling too.

"The enemy, the enemy is coming; I know." Fixing her eyes on the lieutenant's face as if to bore right through him, she said, "Don't go. I know. I know what you're hiding in the caves. I'm scared. Toë is scared. I know about the fifty-one men. I'm scared. Don't go."

*   *   *

Each night when he had soothed Toë and was on his way home, he came to the foot of the banyan tree at the pass. A strange voice from the village below lingered in his ears and stopped him in his tracks. It put him in an unusual frame of mind, as if the entire village were submerged beneath blue waters and the sorrows of the people of the village crystallized into the cry of a curse. Presently, very faintly, like methane gas bubbling up from the depths of the pond, the voice assumed the tones of one young girl gone mad, insistently transfixing the youth who was crossing the pass and leaving the village behind. The voice echoed on and on in a melody like no music he had ever heard. The lieutenant put his fingers in his ears and hurried on, but the melody was still with him. It was Toë, who had run barefoot down onto the beach and was singing, singing "I shall never see my love again. . . ."

Ensign Hayahito, too, began to have circles under his eyes. He had begun to sleep badly at night, for the uncertainty whether or not the commanding officer was really asleep in his room preyed on his mind. Whenever he heard a slight noise from the commanding officer's room, Ensign Hayahito's eyes took on an unnatural gleam.

*   *   *

Eventually, however, he no longer needed to worry. The war had progressed to the point of the inevitable crisis.

Day and night, the commanding officer could not take one step outside the base. Lieutenant Saku would retire to his room in preparation for *that time,* for that fateful day. Then he called together the fifty-one men and gave them instructions for their final hour.

By now the die was cast. It was simply a matter of time.

Since the threat of enemy planes kept them from working during the day, they slept in the caves, rising at night. But even at night, they could not work out in the open: they had to take precautions not to attract attention, for the night brought its own planes, with eyes that could see in the dark.

*   *   *

Can we not imagine how ardently Toë waited? Toë lived for the nights. She completely lost track of what she did during the daytime. She tried laughing aloud for effect, talking all the time, digging potatoes, and planting peanuts. She wore her hair down over her shoulders, put ribbons in it, nibbled sugar in secret, and walked through the village all dressed up, putting on airs. And then, finally, it would be evening.

When evening came, Toë would think to herself, "Tonight he will surely come." And she would sit perfectly still and listen for a sound in the garden. Even the footsteps of the villagers made her jump. Presently, after she had been startled time and time again, she would grow weary of the darkness and go out onto the veranda to gaze at the starry sky. And she would lose herself in contemplation of the past.

She wondered what would become of her, and the tears overflowed and slid down her cheeks.

I saw you this morning, but already by evening
I want to see you again.
For ten or twenty days or more
How could I let you go?

Toë sang this song to herself, and her heart swelled to bursting. Toë did not understand what had happened to her. When she learned of Lieutenant Saku's most mysterious of missions, she had almost lost her mind. Looking then at her own body, how she lamented having been born a human being. She prayed, to the God she believed in. Toë was an adopted child, a secret known only to two or three of the oldest people in the village. Her mother was from a devout religious family, but no sooner had she given birth to Toë than she left this world. This fact Toë came to know, having heard it from no one in particular in the process of growing up. How or when she had come to the house where she now lived, she did not know, but from the time of her earliest memories she had had in her possession a leatherbound book. She was sure this book must have belonged to her mother. When she prayed to her God, she pressed her cheek to the book. The two narrow intersecting strips of cool gold embossed on the cover stole the warmth from her cheek. That she did this, Toe never revealed to a soul. She was certain she would be told that these were the teachings of an evil Western religion, the enemy's religion.

* * *

The lieutenant gradually became irritable, and Toë sensed his anguish. Toë had learned that the lieutenant was called the "daytime lamp" and was shunned by his men. "Poor, poor lieutenant, it's only with me that he acts tough and throws his weight around"—Toë could feel in her own breast the lieutenant's taut, frayed nerves. Suddenly, Toë felt like cursing everything. Why, why, why? Why must he turn his back and leave her? Once, the lieutenant had stayed with her too long. When he saw that the Morning Star already shone over Kyanma Mountain, he turned away and went as fast as he could up over the mountain pass back to the base. Hadn't she then waited, and waited, lingering in the village square, her eyes on the red earth path up the misty mountainside, hoping to catch sight of him.

On Toë's shore the morning mist
On the sleeve of his uniform the crimson stain
Of tears of parting.

And the tears welled up anew and rolled down her cheeks. Even Toë was dimly aware that the enemy was approaching. She knew why the lieutenant could no longer come to visit her, and she knew only too well what the lieutenant would do when the enemy finally came. And yet, night after night, until the Little Dipper hung in the sky and Venus twinkled eerily bright about the crest of Kyanma Mountain, Toë sat out on the veranda. The Morning Star that year was for the two of them the signal to end their tryst, the star of their lovers' parting—but Toë was beyond attaching special significance to such things.

* * *

One day, threading his way through the intervals between enemy planes, Ogusuku, the lieutenant's orderly, came to Toë; hurriedly, he handed her a long, thin, white bundle, and left. Holding her breath, Toë undid the bundle. She felt a sudden pang of alarm; inside was a dagger in a sheath decorated in silver. A letter was attached to it. Slowly making out the awkward characters that looked like twisted nails, she read, "Tonight at midnight, at low tide, on the beach by the salt shack."

In the days before Lieutenant Saku's men were stationed in Shohaate, the people of Toë's village had sometimes gone to Shohaate by waiting for the tide to go out and then going along the beach around the tip of the cape. On the Shohaate side stood a small shack where they burned seaweed to make salt. It was right next to Chitan Beach, which lay in the northeasternmost reaches of the base. This route around the tip of the cape was extremely dangerous, however. For the brief interval that the tide was out, one could make one's way along the beach, but almost immediately the waves came rushing in, crashing against the protruding rock, until the cape resembled the stern image of a standing god, and one could neither advance nor retreat. What was more, in the crevices between the rocks terrible poisonous snakes sometimes lurked, waiting to strike.

As soon as the village had completely settled down for the night, Toë went out onto the beach. But the lieutenant had misread the tide chart. The error wasn't especially noticeable on the beach near her village, but the going would be steep toward the tip of the cape, where a sheer cliff rose from the rising waters. It would be difficult for Toë to work her way around the precipice at the mountain's edge. And the snakes would be particularly dangerous. Along the way were some spots so steep that she could not walk at all. When that was the case, Toë clung to the slippery rocks and made her way through the water. By then, the almost full moon had already set. Under the water were jagged rocks and sharp shells, and she cut her foot. Glowing insects clung to her clothes, and the fishy smell of the tides assailed her nose. Toë wept. It was not that she blamed anybody, she simply wept at her own sad lot in life. When she passed under the place where the banyan trees grew, like Yochi, she was afraid of the Kenmun goblin. Nearly beside herself with terror, occasionally she could hear the sound of oars. Who could be passing by so late at night? Toë was convinced it must be a spirit of the Dead. Sometimes when the wind whistled, she would kneel in the shelter of the rocks, close her eyes, and pray. When the spirit had passed, she would again pick her way between the rocks or through the water, limping from the cuts in her foot.

* * *

Lieutenant Saku awoke. He looked at the luminous dial of the clock at his bedside, and the hands indicated a quarter to twelve. Something vague and misty, like a piece of cotton cloth, had made its way into Lieutenant Saku's head and awakened him. Leaving word with the night watchman that he would be down by the salt shack looking at the night sea—not to hesitate to call if anything should happen, he would just be down by the salt shack and would come running—he left and walked to the shack. Straining his eyes to look through the darkness in the direction from which he knew Toë would come, he discovered that the waves were already lapping against the edge of the mountain. Oh no, thought the lieutenant.

But Toë will come! I know she will come. But what hardship she will have braved to get here. Suddenly his heart swelled, and Toë was more to him than he could bear. He couldn't endure the wait, yet he stood there and waited. Finally, he heard footsteps shyly approaching over the sandy beach. Instinctively he hid behind the rocks. The footsteps came up to where he was and stopped. Emerging from the shadow of the silent rocks, the lieutenant embraced that familiar form and held her fast to him. Toë yielded quietly to his embrace. He could smell her hair, damp with perspiration. The lieutenant lifted Toë's face from his chest and gazed at it. Loose strands of hair stuck whitely to her forehead, glued by perspiration. The lieutenant touched Toë's eyes, and suddenly he felt warm drops on his fingertips. He was also aware of something damp and cold against his trousers. Groping for Toë's body, he found that she was soaking wet from the waist down. Startled, he took a good look and saw that seaweed clung to her waist and hips. He realized now how difficult the route had been that Toë had taken to get there. He felt a crushing pain in his chest. Looking down, he saw that Toë was barefoot, and here and there were traces of blood. He tried to warm Toë with the heat of his own body, but her body refused to be warmed. She had elastic at her wrists and around the ankles of her baggy work trousers. These had become uncomfortably tight. The lieutenant said nothing. Toë, too, listened in silence to the pounding of her own heart. Across the water the peak of Kyanma Mountain was ever so slightly beginning to grow light. This was the first sign that the Morning Star was about to appear.

* * *

"Over there," Toë said. Without turning her head away from the lieutenant, she pointed through the darkness in the direction of the cape. "There was a snake."

So that evening, too, Toë had had an adventure.

The lieutenant marveled at the persistent throbbing in the little breast of this barefoot girl. It seemed to him wonderfully strange that she was by now beyond all thought, while he was nervously monitoring the darkness, so preoccupied with another matter.

Suddenly, once again that peculiar dull hum came from the south and rang insistently in his ear; it was rapidly approaching Kagerōjima. Holding Toë to him —she was small and warm and quivering, like a little captive bird—the lieutenant strained his eyes and ears in the direction of the sound. It was coming closer and was two or three times louder than usual. It came so close that it roared in his ears and made his head ache. Suddenly, before his eyes, there was an explosion of purple, and from the water between Kagerōjima and the other island there arose like a dragon a red pillar of fire. It all happened in an instant. The pillar of fire quickly disappeared, and the strange sound gradually faded off to the north.

The lieutenant had a foreboding of what was to come. He pushed Toë away. Startled, Toë looked into the lieutenant's face.

"Is the enemy coming?"

"It's all right, Toë. I suddenly remembered something I have to do, something very important. Everything's all right. The enemy's not going to come. But tonight's no good. You'd better go home now. Don't worry. I'll send Ogusuku tomorrow with a mesage for you."

"Yes sir," said Toë obediently, uneasily.

"Don't worry, Toë. As soon as it's morning I'll let you know how things are."

"Yes sir."

The lieutenant began to run back toward the base. Toë's almost too docile response bothered him. But the strange explosion he had just seen was no minor occurrence, he was convinced. When he passed by the watchman on duty near the beach, the lieutenant cried out, "Has there been any damage to headquarters?"

"No, sir," the watchman answered brightly.

Presently, the lieutenant could see with his own eyes that the base had been unaffected by the blast. Everyone was sleeping quietly. Even Ensign Hayahito seemed to be asleep. "I suppose I panicked," thought the lieutenant. That Toë was now working her way around the cape, clinging to the rocks, seemed bitter punishment intended for himself.

* * *

The enemy planes that had given them no peace day or night suddenly stopped coming. Two or three days passed in eerie silence. Each day began to seem separate, discrete, as though there were no connection with the day before or the day after. It was unnerving. He ceased to feel, nothing affected him. Then, as though he had suddenly remembered, his blood would seethe. On the days when his blood seethed, rain clouds settled lower and lower in his heart.

* * *

That evening, commanding officer Lieutenant Saku was on Chitan beach watching a bright red cloud at sunset. Like the wings of some monstrous bird, it flew away from west to east, and when presently all was sealed in by the evening mist, the signals clerk on duty came out gasping for breath and informed him that a new dispatch had just been received. For some reason, Lieutenant Saku thought, "This is it. At last." He went to his own room and stared at the dispatch in front of him, rehearsing mentally what was to be done next, when the telephone in the office began to ring loudly. The lieutenant jumped, feeling his body grow light as if he were being lifted from his chair. The signals clerk came running up to his room, shouting, "Lieutenant, lieutenant." When he reached the lieutenant's door he said, "We have just received our orders."

The paper on which the orders had been written was thrust before Lieutenant Saku. On the paper were the words, "In view of enemy activities, stand by to execute mission."

"Assemble all personnel immediately."

Having issued the order through the signals clerk, Lieutenant Saku surveyed his own room in the small wooden building. The perfectly unadorned room looked strangely white, and even the mirror that he had so prized seemed utterly foreign to him now. This mirror was about to reflect things it had never reflected before, he thought. He pictured Toë. The very thought was tragic. All things, however, were to be cut off from him; on the other side of a deep rupture they would recede rapidly like the ebbing tide. With the sense of being in a vacuum, Lieutenant Saku bit his lips, regretting bitterly the fact that he had not made more effort to reach out to the fifty-one men who were now to set out with him and offer them words of kindness. As for Toë, she was by now a part of him, living in every inch of his body.

"Ensign Hayahito. We are leaving, you are in charge now," he called out to the second in command, in the room next door.

Ensign Hayahito gazed fixedly into his young commanding officer's face. They had not been particularly compatible, and he had never in fact learned to like this man, his commanding officer. Even so, the final parting called forth fathomless emotion. At the same time, the ensign was excited at the prospect of taking charge of the unit and finishing operations after the fifty-one men and their commanding officer had gone.

*   *   *

But what happened? Even after the revetment in front of the caves had been completely removed and the boats inside were ready to embark at any moment, much time passed. It was already almost midnight, and the sailing orders had not come. Lieutenant Saku decided, for the time being, to send the fifty-one men to bed—wearing their death uniforms. Nor did he neglect to warn them to be prepared to man the boats at a moment's notice. By now it was almost painful, from one second to the next, to be under normal conditions, all things as usual, nothing out of the ordinary. His heart raced ahead, but the night wore on uneventfully. Lieutenant Saku imagined how he must look, waiting it out in front of the telephone since early evening, showing that he was flustered despite his best efforts. The inside of his head was cold as ice.

Long past midnight, Ogusuku appeared before Lieutenant Saku as if possessed. "Lieutenant. May I have the honor of our settling something outside?"

"What do you want?" the lieutenant said curtly, surprised by the odd phrasing of his request.

"Toë is at the salt shack, sir."

"What?"

With conflicting emotions Lieutenant Saku took a quick look at his orderly's face. "You've been there and told her something, haven't you, Ogusuku?"

Looking frightened, Ogusuku said nothing. Then he handed his commanding officer what seemed to be an envelope.

"Yes, well, don't worry about this any longer. I'll take care of it now. No point in your getting exhausted. Go on to bed like everybody else."

Ogusuku disappeared into the darkness. Lieutenant Saku gazed up at the stars—it was the first time he had felt like looking at the stars since sunset. On a tiny piece of paper inside the envelope it said, in a hurried scrawl, "I am at the salt shack. Please come. Find some way to come to me. I promise not to get upset. Toë."

The lieutenant walked through the base. Soon he found he had come as far as the watchpost on Chitan Beach at the northeastern edge. From there he left the base, and a short walk along the beach brought him to the salt shack. Toë was sitting in the sand as though dazed. Even when the lieutenant stood before her, it took a while for her to notice him. And yet she had seen the lieutenant at the watchpost, and she had been constantly aware of his approach. Toë was wearing a dark kimono of raw silk. Even in the darkness he could see how her white collar lapped neatly at the throat. Toë tried to say something, but her lips trembled so that she couldn't speak. Then she looked at the lieutenant from head to toe, as he stood before her dressed for his final mission. Gently, she reached out and touched his shoe. The lieutenant said, "Toë. This is a drill. I don't know what Ogusuku may have told you by mistake, but it's only a drill."

Toë silently shook her head. The lieutenant, unable to stay any longer, said, "Wait for a letter from me in the morning, Toë. Don't worry." It was all the lieutenant could do to say these words. How could he explain what he did not understand himself?

* * *

Toë put her ear to the sand in order to hear the lieutenant's footsteps as he walked away into the distance. She thought she heard him say something to the watchman on Chitan Beach. His voice was like that of a child. She remembered an evening when the lieutenant had spoken to her in just such a childish voice. Keeping it hidden so that the lieutenant would not notice, Toë had brought with her, wrapped in white cloth, the dagger with the silver carving. This she now held reverently to her breast like a cross. She would wait until daylight. If she were to see something floating in the water, when exactly forty-eight of them had passed through the inlet before her eyes and out toward the open sea, then Toë would fill her kimono sleeves with stones and, clasping the dagger firmly to her breast, walk out into the water. Toë sat perfectly still on the sand. Her body was feverish, and she was aware of nothing around her.

Presently, Toë thought, "Oh look, there is the Little Dipper." In a little while, she thought, "Oh, look how big it is." Then, as though veils were being peeled off one by one, the day grew light, and the green of the land and the blue of the sea showed themselves clearly in the fresh morning air. The little birds began to sing. Was it her imagination, or was there a breeze rustling the leaves on the trees? Soon, in the east around Kyanma Mountain was a line of golden arrows; the stars had all disappeared; and an incredibly big, red sun rose. The tide came softly lapping toward her until Toë very nearly got wet. The waves were like gentle ripples on a lake; sea lice crawled clumsily around in the cracks between the rocks.

Once more Toë clasped the dagger to her. Then she knew that, for the present at least, the danger had passed.

THIS TIME THAT SUMMER

The next morning, I noticed a man from the village, standing in the assembly area directly below headquarters, facing the inlet. I walked by him, but he gave no sign of acknowledgement. His dull complexion, his broad but thin shoulders, his gravity and solidity oozed defiance. He wore a torn undershirt, and his almost equally shabby trousers were a little too short, exposing spindly legs and bare feet. His very appearance seemed to be a demonstration that he could withdraw no further from the spot. Something that would have been unthinkable until yesterday was happening here, I thought, with a mixture of annoyance and fear. Yesterday, the same man dressed that way would have meekly stepped aside to let me pass. Whereas yesterday, except under extraordinary circumstances, people from the village were not permitted on the premises, today it seemed that anyone who showed enough determination would be allowed to enter, for we had lost the power to refuse.

I winced with the officer on duty, who finally had to admit the man though the policy in effect until yesterday had not in fact been abandoned. It had not occurred to me before that both of the wooden flat-bottomed boats in use on the base had been borrowed from people in the village. I had assumed that we had bought them, or that they had been donated. If we had been renting them, then the question of rent ought to have been settled at the very outset; now the news assailed me like ice water poured into my ear first thing in the morning. I had left all such things to the discretion of the appropriate assistant squadron leader, but ultimately the responsibility would be mine. Undeniably there were some matters that I should have kept precise track of, but I had generally paid little notice to such details, thinking that sooner or later our mission would leave it all behind.

"In the space of a single day here they are already demanding we return their boats. They're only thinking of their own self-interest. The instant they realized we had been defeated, they started talking as though they were taking a loss by letting us use the boats for one more hour—it makes you wonder why they lent us the boats in the first place. Earlier they practically forced them on us. I guess their way of thinking is simply different from ours. On the other hand, I can't just stand here and let them walk all over me. I'm going to set things straight right now," said the assistant squadron leader.

After a small typhoon, it was noticed that the two boats in question had drifted away, and they had never been found. I had not been apprised of that fact. It was all very well for the assistant squadron commander to say "I can't just stand here and let them walk all over me," but when it came right down to it, how much of the responsibility would he be willing to accept? When the heat was on, my position as officer in command would come to the fore, so for the assistant squadron commander to announce that he would set things straight gave me an uncomfortable feeling. I was the one who was supposed to set things straight with that man, and with the assistant squadron leader too, for that matter. Probably there were many other bureaucratic details of which I had not been informed, but even when I was informed, they had gone in one ear and out the other. So, when the assistant made this comment, I could do no more than smile. What persisted like a thorn in my breast was the sight of that man from the village standing all alone in the very midst of the squadron, with his back to me. That same man, who one day before had affected a modest stoop and an ingratiating smile, the very next day had come all by himself, rowing his little wooden boat through the inlet right up to the base in order to get matters settled. On his face was no vestige of yesterday's smile; what it displayed instead was the confidence of self-sufficiency. There was even something that made one suspect that this self-reliance was no different today than it had been the day before. I was still wearing my military sword, and he was certainly not concealing a dagger in his clothes.

I had no idea what would become of the squadron now, or what would happen to the control over our environment thus far afforded us. Since the operations of our squadron were a military secret, we had sealed off the inlet, but the legality of this action was highly questionable. We had unilaterally staked out sufficient territory for our base and did what we wished with the land, but if the owners were to come and challenge our rights to it now, how would we be able to defend ourselves? Until just a little while ago, at least on paper the land had officially been "purchased" by the Ministry of the Navy; the conditions for payment were under deliberation. Now, however, it was obvious that the whole idea would be abandoned. Though the responsibility would ultimately not rest on my shoulders alone, I bitterly regretted having thought it so perfectly natural to entrust matters to the discretion of the assistant squadron leader who seemed so able and decisive. It was only an accidental blind spot on my part, but I hated myself for not having noticed it. I felt surrounded by regulations, like a thick wall, in the new life that bore firmly down on us. Regulations, which until yesterday might just as well not have existed, the minute wartime conditions were lifted, spread their roots firmly, turning a stern countenance toward those who had ignored them. Anxieties concerning a future that would be determined by the cease-fire agreements and the peace conference, as well as anxieties concerning the attitude that would be assumed by the enemy, stole up on me so suddenly that I felt I had no place to stand; into this blurred field of vision came that man from the village, wearing his ragged clothes, barefoot and empty handed, all alone.

* * *

Now that the perpetual waiting was over, the weariness that follows a relaxation of tension began to spread. The possibility of a casualty resulting from a freak accident continued, however, to weigh on my mind. I would have the detonators disconnected in the warheads, from which the fuses had been removed; then I would order the removal of the warheads from the boats. After that, all that remained was the dangerous operation of loading the fifty-odd warheads into a larger boat and dumping them into the ocean. This job eased the tedium some-what. It seemed unlikely that anyone would attempt to hinder the operations, and my assessment of the men's reaction when I informed them of the Imperial Proclamation of unconditional surrender gave me considerable boldness. The senior commissioned officers and senior petty officers could not conceal a certain smoldering resentment but took no apparent steps to muster collective resistance. Not knowing how long this tensionless, monotonous life would last produced anxiety and the hopeful swell of a life just out of reach. At morning inspection I suggested to the squadron of one hundred eighty-four men the possibility that they might have to continue living on this base indefinitely, relying on their sense of touch to grope their way through. Maybe I had learned some-thing from the previous night's experience of sleeping with my hand on my sword. I had been thinking there was something wrong with me—I had been so agitated and reckless ever since the war ended. When the report reached the officer's room that Petty Officer O had become violent, I ran out alone to see what was happening. There he was in front of the First Flotilla boathouse, on a sandbar that jutted out in a curve into the inlet, so drunk he could hardly stand, brandishing his sword and wailing at the top of his lungs,

"Damn you. Japan lost the war. The Great Imperial Navy no longer exists. How can you tell us just to sit tight here? Damn you. Why don't we attack? You have no guts, any of you. That's why we got into this mess. I'll show you, I'll cut them all down."

Nearby, a young petty officer of the same flotilla was circling around behind him, gradually closing in on him; I said in a cool, low voice,

"Petty Officer O. Cut out the histrionics. Of course Japan lost the war. By order of His Majesty the Emperor, hostilities have been suspended. But no peace agreement or official treaty has been signed yet, so there is no telling what will happen. It's not your place to make statements like 'the Imperial Navy has ceased to exist.' That is a question that concerns the whole of Japan. If one small group does something rash it will just make matters worse. But if your faith and your samurai spirit can't put up with these difficult conditions, then dispose of yourself as you see fit, just don't go taking others with you. If you want a torpedo boat, I'll give you one. I'll put the fuse in it so you can set out to your death whenever you please. Or if you'd prefer to rip open your belly, I'll be your witness right here and now and collect your bones when it's over."

The words came with almost disconcerting ease, one after the other, as though I were possessed. I thought O might fly into a rage and come after me with his sword, but there was nothing I could do to stop him if he did. Instead, O limply threw down his sword, knelt formally on the ground, and promptly began weeping loudly. In my zeal I had turned into hatred itself (directed at what I do not know), until an unexpected reversal made me realize suddenly that moderation had come to take its place. The long months during which my fastidious nature had kept too tight a rein on them had created a countercurrent, I thought. Why could I not just leave them to dispel their own gloom and humiliation, each in his own way? Last night Ensign S, the senior commissioned officer, had spoken raptly of carrying out the original suicide attack mission. I had silenced him by the question, "I suppose anyone who had truly resolved on a certain course of action would keep quiet about it, wouldn't he?" There was a hidden trap in my words; if you fell in, it became impossible to answer, so I could use such tactics with impunity.

"It's hard on all of us. But to lose your head and start swinging your sword around is inexcusable. If you have something to say, I'm perfectly willing to sit down and listen. But let's not drink when we have our talk. Drinking just makes matters worse. For now you'd better go back to the barracks and go to bed. We can talk after you've had a good night's sleep."

I returned to my own room at headquarters. An enlisted man, O had always been one of the overly serious, know-it-all petty officers who had often been difficult to deal with. Things might change to some extent later, but right now, the end of the war had left us with a futile antagonism, as if the psychological conditions for battle were at last being fulfilled.

The commander of the reservists came to inform me that they had begun to repair a damaged boat, and I remembered the accident. I had not ceased to wince at the idea of having to report that damaged torpedo boat, but the thought lurked somewhere in my mind that perhaps I could put some of the blame on the unusual circumstances. Had we taken off on schedule the night before last, the damages would hardly have been limited to the bow of that one boat: all fifty boats, to-gether with their crew, one man per boat, would have disappeared from the face of the earth. But now that we had pulled through the crisis and lived on to the next day, we could not simply discard or disclaim the errors that had occurred. The conditions of defeat having been added to our lot, eventually we expected some change in policy, but this idle waiting was disquieting. Neither our special suicide attack mission nor the unconditional surrender had permeated our lives in any palpable way, and the authority necessary to change the daily operations of the unit was lacking.

What sort of incident was it that had occurred in the Fourth Flotilla on the night of the thirteenth, immediately after the order to prepare for battle? Even after a space of two days, no one really knew. Petty Officer R's boat had exploded suddenly during maintenance. Strangely enough, though the warhead exploded, scattering its two hundred fifty kilograms of explosives in all directions, the boat into which it had been fitted had suffered no damage except that the bow had been split. How was such a thing possible? R, who had been working on the boat, escaped without a scratch; the captain of the Fourth Flotilla, who happened to be nearby, had his eyebrows singed, but that was all. Though the torpedo fuse had exploded, the steel plates encasing it had split, and there had been enough force to obliterate the bow of the boat, the fire had not reached the detonator. The men escaped with nothing worse than those two hundred fifty kilograms of yellow explosive powder scattered over the area. No one could have predicted this new turn of events; even so, now that normality of some sort had been restored, we could not very well simply abandon a damaged boat. Almost as if we were starved for some undertaking that was in no way out of the ordinary, we sought out inconspicuous chores. The job of repairing the damaged boat fulfilled this condition, and besides, it seemed a reasonably good way of preparing for seizure of weapons by the enemy; the hammering echoed deep within my body.

* * *

The village of O—I could hardly contain my impatience to find even a small opportunity to leave the base, cross the mountain pass, and walk along the beach to that village. But that unrestrainable desire gave way, as if my nervous tension had wandered out onto a dull, sluggish desert of lifelessness. We could not keep on forever enforcing rigid restrictions on men leaving the base. After the system that granted autonomy to the secret base lost its support, all that remained was to wait for demobilization of the unit. For the time being, we would have to continue as heretofore, groping our way through an area that gave no clues, offered no resistance. I was able to slip outside the base freely in the past because of my position as commanding officer. Strict controls made the desire all the more apt to gush forth, and besides, there was the expectation that our inevitable departure would sooner or later wipe out all traces of my misconduct. But to persist, now that all support had suddenly been obliterated, might be to aggravate the symptoms, and I was afraid that what I had been covering up would come to light. There had been a necessary tension for both of us in my nightly meetings with Toë, meetings from which no fruit could be expected. But after the yoke of self-immolation had been removed, a more relaxed daily life seemed about to move in, with the intention of taking over; something whispered to me that I must watch out for elements of destruction that still might come bursting forth from anywhere. What had impelled me with such desperation toward those secret rendezvous with Toë suddenly seemed to have faded. Many things that had remained undone now resurrected themselves—so many I did not know where to start—things that were necessary in order to return to the everyday world.

* * *

In the early afternoon of that day, an old man from C village brought his boat right up to the waterfront below headquarters and announced that he wanted two carp returned. My recollection of the day the old man had brought those carp to the squadron was not so distant. The guard at the inlet had not noticed him, and then, as now, the old man had been able to row right up to headquarters, saying that he had brought something to present to the commanding officer. Followed by a youth a full size larger, the diminutive old man had come in his dirty undershirt and trousers, barefoot, a serious expression on his small face burned black by the sun. Carrying a basket containing the carp, he timidly climbed the path lined with palmtrees that led up to the headquarters and said that he would like the carp to be put into the newly dug pond in front of the main building. He added in a strong local accent, in an earnest yet straightforward monotone, that just once before he died he would like to meet a high-ranking officer of the Imperial Navy (he used a Meiji term). Somehow sniffing out the smallest incidents within the division, as if with foreknowledge of the fate of the division that had mistaken the road ahead, the old man now appeared before me for a second time to say that he wanted his two carp returned while they were still alive. What the old man foresaw was absolutely true: sometime in the not too distant future the carp would have been abandoned, and at the bottom of a dry pond he would have seen the corpses of two fish.

You would think I could understand exactly how the old man felt, but I was unable to rid myself of a needling dissatisfaction. The dazzling interest he had once shown in me as an officer of the Imperial Navy had disappeared without a trace, and his expression now suggested that he was talking to some young boy unschooled in the ways of the world. Having scooped up his carp in a bucket he had brought along for the purpose, the old man hurried on down to the waterfront, his shoulders seeming to say that he had no further business with me. Leaving behind only the sound of oars hitting the side of the boat at regular intervals, eyes fixed straight ahead of him, he furiously rowed away toward his own village.

* * *

The work load of the assistant squadron leader in charge of liaison for the base seemed to have increased. The reason was that while the torpedo-boat crew, having lost their special destination, had no other job than to grow potatoes, dealing with the aftermath of their previous entanglements had suddenly become a pressing problem. Early that morning, in fact, when he was supposed to be occupying himself with the business of locating the rowboats that had disappeared during the typhoon and returning them to the villagers from whom they had been borrowed, he had come into my room with yet another new dispatch,

"Lieutenant, we have a problem," he was saying. "In O all the villagers are starting to leave the shelters where they've been living until now and flee even deeper into the mountains."

"What's going on? That'll make it inconvenient for you on your little trips to O, won't it now," I said.

His tone parried my joke, but his face was full of affability as he spoke, "Someone has been putting strange ideas into the villagers' heads. They seem to have been told that when the enemy lands, they will do all kinds of violence to the women and children, so everybody should run away and hide in the mountains. The village is in a total uproar. They're going as deep as they can into the valleys and rebuilding their shelters. What should I do? All those guys can think of is what they themselves did in China, so they spread preposterous rumors," he said, but his manner lacked its usual openness.

"You keep saying 'somebody,' 'they.' *You* did it, didn't you?"

He looked crushed. "What a terrible thing to say, Lieutenant. Is that what you think of me? I see. But what shall we do about O village? Wouldn't it be better for the base to take some action? I will assemble the villagers, if you will say a few words to them."

"Is it really my job to handle things like that? Still, if somebody from the squadron spread those rumors, I suppose I'm responsible for dealing with the results."

"In any case, the villagers are in quite a commotion."

I wondered if it was simply my imagination, or did I see in the assistant divisional officer's expression the embarrassment of one who has played a prank that has gotten out of hand?

"Well then," I said, "I'll go to the village and read them the Imperial Proclamation—how would that be? There aren't any radios in the village, so I suppose no one has heard an accurate version. O village has provided us with vegetables, and we are in their debt in other ways as well. Perhaps it is, in fact, my duty to inform them; it should have occurred to me yesterday. Then I'll just add the comment that they might as well come on down out of the mountains."

* * *

Toward sunset the assistant divisional officer and I went through the eastern guard post in the pass and down to O village. At the far end of N inlet that had been taken over by the squadron were about ten private houses; there were about a hundred on the neighboring inlet O. Not only were there many more houses, there was a town hall, an elementary school, and a police station in O, so that there naturally was considerable give-and-take with the base, whose assistant squadron leader was always setting out for O village. I remembered my own midnight visits there, constricted by my regulation death uniform: the red earth on the pass, the banyan tree and the growth along the roadside, the color of the sea viewed from above, the layout of the village, then the cluster of thatched roofs, the cries of frogs and owls, the smell of the trees and flowers, all vividly made their presence known. I, for whom ill fortune had closed off the road ahead, had felt the dubious intensity of being in a vacuum, a desire to burn myself out in a single instant. But now that things had gone back to the way they had been, the scene shifted to one of monotony, and I was apt to stagnate in weariness and repetition. I hoped to gaze again some day, after many years had passed, on the path over the mountain and the village below.

When I reached the square toward the center of the village, I could see only a few scattered children in the streets; there were no other signs of life. The houses, surrounded by hedges, were hushed; the lively confusion in the village suggested by the assistant squadron leader was nowhere visible. I even wondered if I might not have been somewhat hasty in coming without having first checked on the situation. How had they informed the villagers that I was coming? I had expected to find the small square thronged to overflowing with people. Presently, the dim, heatless rays of sunlight, entrusting all to darkness, folded the village gently in the clear blue air. For some reason, the rims of my eyes burned, and the faces of the people gathered there began to blur. Little girls stood in clusters and watched me, and there were other children and old women. I did not see any men. Without a few men there to listen, how could I dissipate the zeal with which I had come? I waited for a while, and more people gathered, but still they were mostly housewives and young girls. Standing in front of them made me feel silly, but I was also worried that if I waited until dark, I would not be able to read the words of the Imperial Proclamation. I was, in fact, relieved not to see Toë. But now, with no sign of urgency, as if they were going out to see the local perform- ance of a traveling troupe, the villagers left their homes, slipped on their wooden sandals, and came. What was going on? I thought that families remaining in the village were supposed to be the exception—almost everyone having evacuated to shelters in the valley—and that they were all now in a state of panic trying to hide in the mountains. With the helpless feeling that perhaps I was the only one who was concerned, I took a piece of paper from my pocket and looked at it. Unable to explain the situation or make a personal emotional appeal, I thought it best just to start reading.

"Yesterday at noon, the Imperial Proclamation was broadcast over the radio; this proclamation I shall now read to you." Having said that much, I began immediately to read.

To our good and loyal subjects, after pondering deeply the general trends of the world, and the actual conditions obtaining in our Empire today, we have decided to effect a settlement of the present situation by resorting to an extraordinary measure.[1]

The darkness of the evening seemed to intensify with each word; the ink blurred and was difficult to read. I had thought I would be able to read it through without difficulty, but the sentences were long and full of unfamiliar language, word endings and punctuation unclear or missing; I was unsure of the pronunciation of many words. I had not bothered to read it over first, and like it or not, here I was.

To strive for the common prosperity and happiness of all nations as well as the security and well-being of our subjects is the solemn obligation which has been handed down by our Imperial ancestors, and which we lay close to heart. Indeed we declared our war on America and Britain out of our sincere desire to ensure Japan's self-preservation and the stabilization of Southeast Asia . . .

I had been reading only a short while when the number of people in the square increased, and there were some men among the newcomers.

. . . But now the war has lasted nearly four years. Despite the best that has been done by everyone—the gallant fighting of military and naval forces, the diligence and assiduity of our servants of the State, and the devoted service of our one hundred million people, the war situation has developed not necessarily to Japan's advantage, while the general trends of the world have all turned against her interest.

Suddenly something welled up in my breast and thickened my voice, making my eyes fill with tears. It was totally unexpected; I did not understand what had happened. Having set out intending simply to communicate the facts to the

---

[1] English translation of the Imperial Proclamation quoted from William Craig, *The Fall of Japan* (New York: Dial Press, 1967), pp. 210-12.

villagers, I was now in such a state of agitation that my voice was shaking and I had to pause and steady my breath before I could read on.

> Moreover, the enemy has begun to employ a new and most cruel bomb, the power of which to do damage is indeed incalculable, taking the toll of many innocent lives . . .

After hesitating for a minute trying to decide how to pronounce the first word, I proceeded, but all confidence had deserted me. Once again, I bitterly regretted not having read the document through in advance. I prolonged some words unnaturally, my throat was choked, and I could not keep my voice from quavering; finally, I just kept reading. I had not wanted to do it this way, I thought, with a twinge of resentment, but I could not help myself. I had simply received from the commanding officer of the Defense Forces a summary of the contents of this important document—I had not actually checked the text myself, and having had the signals clerk make a copy of it for this evening, I had not even bothered to look it over. Everything that I had done in my months as first officer of N base, the unconditional surrender, and the meek submission of the villagers, in the space of a single instant eddied and foamed, flowing in the direction of the wording of the Imperial Proclamation. Unfortunately, I had had no forethought and was being swept away unprepared, ricocheting off difficult vocabulary words along the way.

> . . . an ultimate collapse and obliteration of the Japanese nation . . .
> the total extinction of human civilization,

I read,

> those . . . who have fallen in the fields of battle, those who have died at their posts of duty, or those who have met with untimely death

The rhyme and parallel construction of the lines was thrilling, almost painful; when I reached

> . . . enduring the unendurable and suffering what is unsufferable

there were tears in my voice. The powerful language, the familiar rhetoric, formed a strange contrast with the silent, innocent faces of the villagers, and I wept. Soon, one could hear weeping in the crowd as well. For some time now the assistant squadron leader had been shining his flashlight on the paper—otherwise, it seemed unlikely that I would be able to make out the words. When the last clouds of sunset wavering in the western sky had completely disappeared, I puzzled out several more lines before I finally came to the end. Shifting my gaze to the people, I saw Toë among the young girls. Wearing a kimono with a flowered motif at the shoulder, she stood peering out from behind a wall of people. Her unusually large, round face, with her cheeks flushed crimson, virtually shone. When I had finished reading the Imperial Proclamation, the lump in my throat dissipated, the sobbing in the crowd subsided, and, feeling that we had all pulled through the difficulty together, I was able to continue easily.

"Japan has surrendered unconditionally to the Allied Armies."

The old women, the men, and the young girls stood perfectly still, and I thought they were looking at me with pity.

"Unfortunately, Japan has lost the war. But please do not abandon yourselves to despair. True, we lost the war, but we have not lost our way of life. As the Imperial Proclamation says, shall we not think of building the future? Through many days of continual air raids, the fields and rice paddies have fallen to ruin. Starting tomorrow, go out and work in those fields. Preparation for life to sustain the future is of the utmost importance. At night, remove all the shades and let the lamps burn bright. From now on there will be no air raid sirens and no bombing."

The lingering light in the western sky suddenly melted away as if erased, darkness gathered, and I could no longer distinguish one person from another.

"I earnestly entreat you, do not be misled by groundless rumors. There is no longer any need for you to stay in your shelters. Go back to the village and lay the foundation for the years to come. It is unthinkable that the Allied Army will land on this island and do violence to your women and children; relax and return to the village. Should the Allied Army come to this island, it will be for the purpose of demilitarization, and it will occur only after their conduct has been prescribed by agreement among the nations involved and a peace treaty has been concluded. These are problems, moreover, for the two armies to deal with. They do not concern the civilian population directly. Please be calm and begin working."

When I stopped speaking, heads gently stirred in the darkness. Actually, I had no way of ascertaining that things would indeed proceed as I had indicated, but in leaflets dropped from enemy planes, I had read the articles of the Potsdam Declaration, the spirit of which was perhaps somewhere in the back of my mind. I could not absolutely guarantee that some enemy pilot, seeing the lights of the village, would not drop one capricious bomb. But the words arising from my limited experience seemed to arrange themselves for me, leaving me only the latitude of individual personality as I summarized the prospects for the future. I had no way of judging the reactions of the people; they all seemed to be going back to their homes. The only evidence was the distant echo of footsteps muffled by the sandy beach road. Reluctant to leave the spot, for a while I stood still. But no one seemed inclined to speak to me; they avoided me as they receded. Prompted by the assistant squadron leader, I began to walk, but I could not bring myself to go directly back to the base. After he excused himself, saying that he had some business to attend to in the village, I went by and paid a visit at Toë's house. As I entered the front gate and walked up the low stone steps, so familiar from my nocturnal visits, the dead leaves muffled my footsteps, and the house in its garden overgrown with weeds and flowers stole my heart. Who had removed the tree branches that had been placed on the roof for camouflage? In the tatami parlor that looked out on a garden filled with the sweet, pungent scent of *hamayū*[2], whose blossoms loomed in white clusters in the darkness, for the first time in a long while I saw Toë's father, who had returned from their shelter. He wore a freshly washed yukata, and his countenance was serene.

"Now that the war is over there is no more fear of air raids," I said. He had removed to the shelter when the air raids became intense, but Toë had stayed behind, all alone in the empty village. Long white whiskers completely covered his chin and cheeks, complementing nicely his wide forehead and prominent nose. His large frame gave him a calm, masculine assurance, and there was an unworldly quality about him that made it hard to guess his occupation as a young man. He was quite emaciated, perhaps because of the constraints of his evacuation existence, and he seemed physically debilitated. Now that the war had ended, whenever I came to call he would be here, I supposed. Toë left me with her father, then reappeared, crossing the breezeway to the detached parlor from the main house with tea and brown sugar candy. Watching her approach noiselessly over the tatami, I remembered how on my first visit she had been summoned by her father to greet me. Sitting behind and to the side of her father, as if to hide in his shadow, she had kept an unobtrusive eye on me without looking at me directly. Her long, deepset eyes gave off a pure and somehow helpless impression. I had not seen her since yesterday's news of the surrender; we had many things to talk about, but I did not feel the usual sense of urgency that it must be tonight. Earlier, when I saw her face in the public square, I had sensed an understanding between us on this point. After a brief exchange of casual conversation with her father, I felt better, and when I got up to leave, he did not protest. Toë looked off into the distance, and what her thoughts were I could not tell from her eyes.

Outside, everything was cloaked in darkness; within their hedges the houses were hushed and dark, and it was impossible to tell whether the inhabitants had returned from their shelters or not. The abundant trees and shrubs absorbed all

---

[2]*Crinum asiaticum japonicum.* An evergreen perennial herb bearing clusters of fragrant white flowers, common in sandy coastal areas of southern Japan.

sound, and it was quiet enough to hear the ringing in your own ears. An owl hooted, and with each cry he seemed to push his beak into the pit of my stomach. The cry must have been audible from Toë's house too, but I had not noticed it. Walking among the rice paddies on the edge of the village, I was assailed by the croaking of frogs that resembled the sound of rough sea. The tide had risen almost up to the roadside, and had it been daylight, I would have seen the red dirt road to N inlet winding its way at an angle up to the pass. Coming down that road, and when I left the village and went back to the base as well, the expanse of paddy fields redirected my inward-turned spirit, and at the chorus of frogs my body and mind were gently lifted and carried away in an unexpected direction.

* * *

That night I made the rounds in place of the officer in charge. I had become so carried away with my job since the war had ended that even I found my new zeal excessive. Laxness in the squadron that until now had escaped my notice began to get on my nerves. Things had changed since yesterday: some men wore their caps far back on their heads, and the smartness had gone out of their salutes. The tendency seemed to be particularly strong among the fifty-six reservists. They were militiamen, physically not as strong and less familiar with military language than others on the base, and they gave off an aura of the onset of old age. Even so, there was something relaxed about them. They began to seem less wretched as they followed, with a stoop, after the veteran soldiers, and one began to sense their greater experience in the world. These changes had been gradually apparent when enemy plane patrols had intensified to the extent that we had been unable to conduct our flotilla drills even at night and the emphasis shifted to daytime work in the fields.

It took probably a little less than half an hour to make the rounds of the barracks of the various flotilla that dotted the southern bank, built in the shelter of small valleys and hollows in the cliffs. Turning left from the barracks of the First Flotilla, closest to headquarters, I checked off the maintenance corps barracks. When I approached the barracks of the Fourth Flotilla, nestled in some rocks that jutted out onto the beach, I heard someone playing a guitar.

"Stand to," I called out, meaning to warn them, but the guitar did not stop. The guard at the entrance to the barracks said,

"Fourth Flotilla, all secure, sir."

As he stood at attention and saluted, I said, "What do you mean, all secure? Can't you hear that?"

Taken aback, the guard relaxed his posture. It did not seem that he had heard the guitar and tried to cover up; perhaps the sound had simply not entered his consciousness. I felt as though I were reviewing in my head the inspection rounds of all the officers in charge since we had come to the base, though I had never in fact witnessed them. Shining my flashlight into the barracks, I saw that most of the men lay apparently asleep under their blankets, but two men, sitting crosslegged by their bedsides, fingering guitars, caught my eye. "What are you doing in the dark?" was all I could say.

They were not regular members of the flotilla but had been sent to my squadron from G Squadron after K island had been bombed and their boats destroyed along with their base; the recollection of this fact may have given me pause. In addition, the fact that these men were the youngest class of officers to have graduated from Flight School was admittedly apt to influence my attitude. Their commanding officer, G, had been a classmate of mine in Officers Candidate School. Just as the two of us differed in personality, a thin membrane that always stubbornly peeled itself off had formed between them and the men in my squadron. As slowly, sluggishly, they turned their heads to look at me, hidden by the circle of light, I saw in them no sign of the agile readiness to react when addressed by an officer, a readiness that I had come to expect from my own men; I felt as if I were face to face with a couple of impudent school boys.

"Don't you know what inspection means?" I said weakly, but I seemed to ooze an incompatibility irritating to the skin of the men come from another squadron. I couldn't understand why they should have guitars, and I asked myself whether such things had occurred among the men of our squadron before. Since I knew absolutely nothing about what had gone on inside the barracks, I could not be sure that they had not. Among the rows of sleeping men were here and there empty spaces, squares cut out from the pattern; I could not tell whether or not I should make an issue of those things that were not as I thought they should be. I lacked the experience to distinguish between what had been allowed before and what had not. Having suddenly become belligerent and deciding to make the inspection rounds for the first time, I now could not evaluate my own observations. Unable even to find the proper words to admonish the men for their impropriety, I merely left them with the parting remark, "Playing the guitar during inspection is unacceptable behavior. Just because we lost the war is no reason to relax military discipline."

I reminded myself of one of our teachers in Officer's Candidate School who, with a distracted air, lectured us ineffectually when the class misbehaved, but the more I strove to avoid giving such an impression, the worse it got. I was afraid that my authority with the rest of the men might be undermined, but I could do nothing now to offset my loss of dignity. I listened dispiritedly to the slap of the oars as the man on duty rowed me across to the Second Flotilla on the opposite shore. Had they found the other missing rowboat, I wondered. Once, I had been awakened in the middle of the night by the sound of a flute and a lively commotion in the vicinity of the Second Flotilla barracks; I prodded the petty officer on duty to go with me across the inlet and check, but they had all pretended to be fast asleep. Furious, I had sounded reveille, but when that did not wake them up, I kicked their pillows and made them assemble outside the barracks. They insisted they had done nothing. Feeling as if I had fallen into a trap, I went around hitting them as hard as I could. They staggered in the moonlight, some falling forward on the sand. Though they offered no resistance as I hit them, their bodies seemed to exude some unspoken protest. The Second Flotilla was the only unit on the other side of the inlet from headquarters and the other flotillas, and it had seemed to me earlier as well that they displayed a strong tendency to isolate themselves. What was this murderous hatred seething in me? On my way again to the far shore I felt a chill down my spine: the senior officer in charge of the Second Flotilla had built a little bungalowlike affair in the valley behind the flotilla barracks and spent most of his nights there. Even now, with the demobilization of the squadron imminent and everything about to come to an end, I could not contain my impatience. As I reached the Second Flotilla, I felt as though I had set foot in enemy territory. I passed through the barracks without incident, and when I went around to the latrines, one of the reservists assigned from each flotilla was on duty there. Without straightening the dirty cap he was wearing shoved back on his head, he reported, "Second Flotilla latrines in order, sir," yet there was no evidence that special care had been taken in cleaning them. Not only the door and the walls but the toilet itself was crudely constructed of wooden boards; I leaned over abruptly and ran my left hand along the inside of the toilet. Because the toilet had not been thoroughly rinsed, something dirty stuck to my fingertips, and with the shudder of repugnance that ran down my spine, I felt a strange budding pleasure at having been able to commit this act. In the back of my mind was the memory of the instructor in Officer's Candidate School who during inspection had done this without so much as wincing, and when I saw the latrine I had felt an irresistible urge to imitate him.

"I would hardly call this clean." Even when I thrust my finger in front of his nose, the man on duty did not grasp its significance, he just stood there looking at me uneasily, an ugly expression on his face.

"And what do you mean by wearing your cap like that? Discipline must not be relaxed," I said, giving his forehead a hard shove with the back of my hand so that he staggered and fell against the wooden door of the latrine. Struggling to regain his foothold, he looked at me with fear in his eyes, and I began to feel like a bully. He stood there, his body smoldering with resentment, not comprehending why he should be subjected to such treatment. From his babyish stagger a minute ago one would not have guessed that he was in fact an aging reservist; the thought oppressed me. Unable to deal with the obstinacy that raged within me, the desire to stand firm, to rebel against the softening current I felt beginning to rush through me, I returned to the other bank, and by the time I had made the rounds of the Third Flotilla at the mouth of the inlet, I had been driven to an inertia past caring. Returning to headquarters, I suddenly realized I was exhausted, and my own squadron seemed as alien to me as if I had never seen it before; that I had in fact spent my days here seemed no more than a figment of my imagination. The regulations that until yesterday had been obeyed were a matter of precarious balance predicated on our suicide mission. I wondered helplessly how long I would be able to uphold them now. With conditions as they were, if demobilization of the squadron were delayed, the crumbling would become more conspicuous daily. What if the reservists, who had patiently borne the menial jobs, should band together to direct their excess of energy at the seven senior officers—I had no contingency plans to block attempts of this sort. And what about the latent misunderstandings and subtle collisions of temperament among men from various regions of the country? These differences had been smoldering underground all along. Because of the conditions under which the squadron was formed at Sasebo, men from the jurisdictions of three area commands—Sasebo, Yokosuka, and Maizuru—had been put together; men of similar temperament from the same region tended to gravitate toward each other and to vie with other such groups. The situation had not seemed important to me, and I had let it pass. But from now on there was no telling when their differences might burst forth into pitiful public incidents that would come to the attention of the authorities. As one who finally realizes the weight of an object he holds casually in his hands, I was at a loss how to deal with this atmosphere of tension in which the four flotillas, the reservists, plus the maintenance corps, the paymaster's men, signal clerks, and sanitation corps stationed on the base—in total one hundred eighty-four men—might at any moment all spring into independent action.

The previous night I had gone to bed with my hand on my sword, but tonight I decided to sleep with it beside me in the bed. My nerves were frayed, and little by little I had begun to adopt a blatantly belligerent posture with the men. The war had ended, with no exposure to battle. The suicide squadron's mission stood poised for an instant, its back turned, on the opposite edge of a chasm, then went away. While waiting for sailing orders, I had been oppressed by the fear of battle, but now, reinvigorated by the surrender, I was overeager and could not keep myself from becoming more fastidious and tenacious with the men. Muttering to myself, "I'd better not go *there* now," I hit on the idea of O's house instead. It would not do to burn up all at once what lay in the many days ahead, I told myself, so the thing to do was to take it slowly. I could not say that I had fulfilled my duty until I had led the squadron safely to demobilization.

* * *

The next morning, I conferred with the commander of the reservists and removed the detonators from the warheads they had defused the day before.

Stripping the power from these dangerous weapons one by one seemed like the first step toward disarmament, and the sadness and insubstantiality of new vulnerability clung to the event. But ultimately, I opted reluctantly for our physical safety. There was no one visibly advocating resistance, but to leave the weapons intact was dangerous because it invited accident, and it had begun to seem important to bring the squadron to the stage of dissolution without a single casualty. One reservist, whose thigh had been shot through by a pistol, did not have free movement of his leg even after treatment, but otherwise we had managed to come this far without serious mishap. Even when the torpedo fuse had exploded, we had weathered the incident without a single casualty. The statistic of that one wounded man, therefore, was sure to bother me for a long time to come. But the dazzling summer days passed innocently on, and as the men assigned to working in the fields laughed cheerfully, the captain of each flotilla, as a fisherman might improvise a net, removed the canvas from the extra beds to make knapsacks. Despite the jokes and the insults that were heaped upon them, they refused to give up, and gradually the knapsacks took on the proper shape. The men talked to each other of carrying their personal effects home to please their wives when the time came for them to return to civilian life. Except for the captain of the Fourth Flotilla and me, all of the senior officers had been married throughout their naval careers, and now they seemed to be making plans in anticipation of life with their families.

Having received an invitation from the deputy mayor, in the evening I went alone to O village and proceeded directly to his house, built by the waterside, at the mouth of a small river that ran through the village. The tide came all the way up to his stone wall, and the house itself was filled with the smells of the beach. The host said he had intended to invite all the officers in the squadron, but because we seemed to be so busy, he had asked me to come alone. The mayor was absent, having evacuated to his native village, and why the deputy mayor had issued the invitation I could not imagine. Perhaps because the house had stood empty since they had removed to a shelter in the valley, it seemed moldy and dilapidated. The official had been sitting beneath the hanging lamp, all alone and bored, with the door to the front room shut. But as soon as he saw me, his face lit up, and he rose and opened the door. Apologizing because the rest of the family were delayed in closing up the evacuation shelter, he added that he wondered if it was all right for the room light to leak out. I answered emphatically that, in fact, the brighter the better, but he looked dubious until he saw the lights of the town of Y on the island across the straits, where there were both Army and Navy command posts. I secretly shared his anxiety—the deputy mayor still could not rid himself of the fear of enemy attack. As he apologized uneasily for the inept preparations, I found myself feeling slightly suspicious of his motives since I did not know the reason for his invitation.

"Please make yourself at home," he said, but there was no way to be comfortable; all I could do was sit cross-legged under the lamp, as though I had been given a zen kōan on which to meditate. Almost imperceptibly, there was a new familiarity in his attitude as he said,

"You are so young, and yet you did a good job. That you were never arrogant I suppose is an indication of your good character. I probably shouldn't say such things, but you know Lieutenant I—he speaks to us with no respect at all, you'd think we were his servants. It is extremely humiliating for us being treated like that by someone not much older than a child. Oh well, I suppose there are all sorts of people in the military, just like everywhere else."

It was hard to believe he had brought me here just to tell me this. I did not put much faith in this old man's rough words, spoken with a strong local accent. He said that dinner was to be prepared and served by women from the town hall, and two or three times he went out into the garden, seemingly preoccupied, mumbling something to himself.   Just as I was beginning to feel like going home, I heard nearby the gentle voice of a young woman,

"I couldn't find the soup bowls."

"Oh, thank goodness. The commander came early, and I was getting worried," the deputy mayor said, showing his relief. Accepting with a flurry of eagerness born of impatience the tray brought by the young girl, he placed it before me and began filling my cup with mash liquour mixed with hot water. He apologized for the rudeness of the girl, who had brought all three dishes, which according to local custom should have been produced one at a time. The girl was diminutive but lively, brimming with cheerfulness and an open familiarity, and she resembled the other girls of the island in the way she walked with her toes pointed inward so that her legs seemed to cling to each other. Her sharp chin, conspicuous eyebrows, and deepset eyes were typical as well. The cramped life in the shelters had dragged on, and the days she had spent there unable even to bathe seemed to have taken their toll.   Eventually, when the paralyzed affairs of village government were back on track, she would emerge from her baggy work trousers and begin to dress again like a young girl, prattling on with the innocent confidence of youth.

I had let myself drink too much, and I began to tell myself over and over in my drunkenness that the war had ended. Before I knew it, I had relaxed, and for no apparent reason I seemed to have clasped hands with the deputy mayor. He was saying that as a result of my talk in the public square, people had finally been convinced, and that he was grateful to me. Someone from the base had been telling them to hide deep in the mountains, and they might very well have had a riot on their hands; the words were pleasant to my ears. We had believed in victory and sacrificed everything for it, he continued, and now that Japan had lost, he didn't know what to do. What were the prospects for the future? I wonder how I answered him, my head thick with drink. As the room swayed around me, conscious of the girl modestly refilling my empty sake cup, I talked on and on. By the time I realized I had drunk too much, I had lost the impetus to stop by Toë's house. Filled with bitter self-reproach, I said good-bye to the deputy mayor. When I reached the outskirts of the village, once again I was surrounded by those croaking frogs, like angry waves, all over the fields. Suddenly, I could hear myself saying "Victory and defeat at war is a matter of historical record. Losing does not mean the end of the world, so for a while our most important task is to rebuild our lives." I felt like vomiting. The life to which I had submitted in total earnest, obediently surrendering my body to preparations for a suicide mission, now seemed like a counterfeit, a phony. The croaking of the frogs overwhelmed my body and passed on, as if washing away the various toils and obligations of humanity.

* * *

The next day we set to the task of removing the warheads, each filled with two hundred fifty kilograms of explosive powder, from the bows of the boats. They were so heavy that they could not be lifted without constructing a scaffolding of logs and hoisting them with a chain attached to a screw jack. The tall, square-shouldered commander of the reservists could be seen directing operations, making the rounds of each flotilla.

Toward noon I received a telephone call from the Joint Special Attack Forces commander, Captain H. He said I was to designate one man to return to Sasebo ahead of the rest, on a plane departing soon for the main island. He said this man was to act as liaison, to inform the Area Command of conditions in our squadron and to facilitate the demobilization process. My automatic reaction was to choose the senior commissioned officer, and as I walked down to the beach to look for him, I was reminded of how I had felt when I received orders to stand by for attack. At first, only one flotilla had been called for, and I had fought the strong impulse to designate the Second, commanded by the senior commissioned officer, finally naming instead the First Flotilla, of which I myself was the commanding officer. The situation was different now, but I could not deny that in my heart I anticipated with pleasure a bitter reaction on his part. He was standing on the pier, looking at the far bank. His sunburned, correct profile rebuffed me; I could discern no sign of receptivity in it. He looked at me with eyes that showed his many years of discipline and training, as if to say he might go along with me for the sake of regulations, but he would never be in sympathy with me. These days he seemed to have given up. His expression overtly displayed a stiff aloofness. Not that he neglected his duties as senior officer, but he spent much of his time on the far shore with the Second Flotilla, which was directly under his supervision, where with the determination of one sharpening his own sword he concentrated on the training of his men.

"S," I called to him. Approaching the hard face that turned its gaze on me, I continued, "It looks as though I'll have to send you back ahead of the rest. There is a plane leaving for the main island. You are to take it and go to Sasebo. There is no need to come back here. Captain H says he wants someone to report on conditions here and act as liaison later. I would like you to go. How about it?"

Something seemed to be crumbling inside him, and then, loosening his strong, resigned mouth as if to spit out angry words, he said clearly, "I see. In that case I shall go."

"You are to report to the Defense Forces," I added.

When finally, shouldering his handmade canvas knapsack, leaving his own torpedo boat to be taken care of by his men, he rowed away from the inlet, there was no sendoff by the men; only the very few who happened to be on the shore saw him off. As if setting out on a top secret mission, he hurried away without looking behind him. Leaving me with the image of his resolute back, he disappeared.

* * *

Night had come, and there was no one in the main office except the guards. Perhaps everyone had gone into the village—the thought that I could not stop them made me irritable, and without taking off my clothes or even my shoes, I lay down on my bed. I could hear the deep mountain stream that ran beside my room and the hoarse croaking of frogs under the floor boards, but the stillness deepened until presently it invaded my ears, ringing on and on. Suddenly, I got up with the thought of slipping out to O, but the inclination soon withered. Ah, the dizziness: everything starting to return to the past, the sensation of reverting once more to those distant days. Then those days once again sidled up to the war, whirling around and around without cease; there was no possibility of survival—but the war had now ended. No matter how short the interval, for a while death had looked away and I could let myself do as I myself wished. What was there to be so obstinate about? If I just sat tight and waited, I would eventually find myself liberated from the squadron. The cry of frogs, like the sound of hard, dry walnuts rubbed against each other—it was a soft, gentle, low sound, sinking off into the distance, marking off and protecting the area within its range as a comfortable hidden village. I listened, abandoning myself to those tremolos that made me desperately want to live, until I was no longer sure they were frogs. They might be insects hiding in the earth; it was like something I had heard before, yet somehow different, like something one heard only in the warm night air of the southern islands. There was no sign of anyone returning to the main office—the very minute the senior commissioned officer was out of sight! My heart pounded, but eventually I fell asleep. Once, the sword guard hit my back and I thought of taking it out of the bed, but sleepiness made my hand heavy, and with sword guards whirling around in a mist inside my head, I again fell fast asleep.

* * *

The next morning I slept late. The daily routine had not changed, and we continued the practice of morning inspection. Each morning when I awoke, I thought I would like to line up behind the ranks. I very rarely actually did it, and this morning as well, I did not leave my bed. The practiced, rythmical commands of a petty officer trained in Gunnery School, directing the exercise drills, could be heard from the assembly area near the beach, riding the clear morning air. Eventually, the commander of the reservists, who was the officer on duty, took over, and I could hear his decisive voice assigning various duties and delineating the operation of loading the warheads onto a boat borrowed from the Defense Forces and disposing of them in the ocean. What was this dark cloud hanging over my head? The attack mission was to have bleached everything to transparency. Now that I could no longer anticipate such an effect, the past resurrected itself and began going through all its paces. I could not prevent the fat from collecting on my indolence and my various infractions—the spread of selfishness. Ever since that day, we had had fair weather, and as soon as the sun crossed the mountain ridge, we were suddenly in the realm of broad daylight. When I thrust open the plain board window, a white explosion of seething tropical air forced its way in, and I saw the commander of the Fourth Flotilla, F, his back to the inlet and the far shore, slowly climbing the path up to headquarters. In his student days he had been on the track team; his body was slender and had a smooth resiliency. In his profile, as I watched him unnoticed, was a vague shadow of fatigue, but when he suddenly turned full face, his eyes met mine. He repressed some natural inclination, as if in an effort to reassert self control and mount an attack.

"Lieutenant," he called out to me. Regaining his youthful, bright expression, he quickened his pace and came to my room.

"Lieutenant. Something terrible has happened."

When I said nothing, hoping to deflect his zeal somewhat, he went on: "Yesterday evening T attacked the elementary school teacher's house, Miss Ōhira's."

"I don't know what you're talking about, but 'attack' is a rather strong word, now, isn't it?"

"I wouldn't take it so lightly if I were you, Lieutenant. T got himself completely plastered and then went wild and stormed into her house. It seems like a serious matter to me."

"That's quite something. Tell me, were you with him?" Since we were both graduates of the same training program in Officer Candidate School, I always found myself addressing him in familiar terms.

"Oh no, sir. I went and got her away from there in a hurry."

I started to ask him how he could have known that T was going there, but I changed my mind and said instead, "Nothing very serious happened, then."

"T got mad and broke the high heels of her best shoes."

Though I tried to control it, my fingers trembled and my voice changed, "You are sure about this."

"Absolutely sure."

"I'll ask you one more time; you are positive that T went to Toë's house, is that right?"

"I heard T shouting, so I took her with me and fled toward the mountains. I was afraid something might happen. It was T—there's no question about that."

"Don't you think maybe he was just a little drunk and decided to drop in for a chat?"

"No. When he got really smashed, he started saying he was going to the elementary school teacher's house and sow some wild oats."

I called the orderly and said, "Tell the captain of the Third Flotilla to come to the commander's office on the double."

At the time of the formation of the unit, Petty Officer T and I had been assigned together, just the two of us, to training the men, and he invariably treated me with generosity. Now that mutual trust had collapsed: I felt my face grow pale in an atmosphere of distrust, dark anger, and conflict. But I could not suppress my zeal for uncovering what had been hidden. Presently I heard footsteps hurriedly approaching, and I was just wishing I could refuse to see him when he entered headquarters and came up to my door.

"Petty Officer T reporting," the formality of his words struck me as odd. Heretofore he had always called out from outside the door something like "Lieutenant, did you want to see me about something?" in a familiar, casual, friendly way. Perhaps he had an inkling that something was wrong.

"Enter," I said, much more stiffly than usual.

Opening the unlocked rough wooden door, he came inside, then pushed the door closed with both hands, bowed, and stood at attention.

"Petty Officer T at your service, sir."

I made it a practice, when addressing this petty officer and the special duties ensign, to use their titles. They were both older than I, and it was after long and devoted service in the Navy that they had been assigned to my squadron. I had left matters in their fields of specialization entirely in their hands; perhaps one reason I saw no need to change this policy was that we were a demolition squadron. Now, suspicions were arising, and my confidence in the practice was beginning to crumble—all as a result of something so insignificant.

"Petty Officer T, I understand that you went into O village last evening, is that correct?" I said, feeling as though I were leaning out over a cliff.

"Yes sir."

"If you had a quarrel with me, I wish you had brought it directly to me."

"I am afraid I don't understand, sir."

Slowly as if forcing open my reluctant mouth, I told him: "You went storming into Toë's house, didn't you?"

"Me, sir?" said T, his eyes wide, incredulous. His luxuriant moustache, his youthful complexion, his short, plump body brimmed with friendly charm. "It is true that I went to Miss Ōhira's house last night, but she was out so I left immediately."

"According to my information, you got smashed and set out claiming you were going to sow wild oats."

"Me? Why would I do that? Do you think I would do such a thing, Lieutenant?" T asked, his cheeks flushed, looking aghast. Suddenly, I felt my aggression falter. This had happened before, hadn't it? I never succeeded in interrogating anyone; it was tantalizing how I never quite managed to come up with the right phrases to parry those of my opponent and attack. I was inevitably struck with the apparent validity of the other person's claims and took back my accusations—the pattern was obvious even to me, but somehow I always allowed myself to be driven into the same familiar corner. When you venture a step forward, then feel unsteady on your feet, there is no wiser policy than to withdraw, but it isn't always so easy to do in practice. Moving feet are reluctant to stop, and words once said pitch headlong into degradation.

"For one thing, they say you ruined her shoes."

"I had a little to drink. I am not proud of having gone to Miss Ōhira's house in that condition, but the idea that I 'sowed wild oats' is preposterous. I have been totally devoted and loyal to you, Sir, and I have been under the impression that I had your good will and trust. I am devastated to learn that you have such a low opinion of me. Who did you hear this tale from—that I went to Miss Ōhira's house and sowed wild oats?"

Hoping to check the rapidly spreading flames, I said, "From Ensign F," whereupon T turned to F.

"Ensign F, where did you hear me say a thing like that?"

"I didn't hear it myself—the reservist commander told me," said F, his dark, skinny face twitching.

Apparently unable to suppress his rage, T broke in huffily, "I have no recollection of having said any such thing."

I had the man on duty summon the reservist commander, and Petty Officer R appeared immediately. He, too, sensing unusual tension in the air, marched briskly into the room and stood before me at attention. Basically, he was the sort who would not relax his posture in my presence even when he cracked a joke; right now his thin broad shoulders seemed almost squared for a fight. All three of these men seemed unusually tense, visibly shrinking before my gaze. My own mood softened, I said in a normal tone of voice,

"R, we seem to be having a disagreement. They say T got drunk last night and announced he was going to Toë's place to sow wild oats. Is that true?"

"I'm not sure what you mean. I had a drink or two with T yesterday evening, but I didn't hear anything like that."

"Ensign F says he got the story from you."

"Absolutely not. I don't remember saying any such thing."

Turning to F, I said sharply, "That's not what you told me." I had heard that phrase somewhere before. Someone had been saying just those words in an overbearing tone. I couldn't recall where or when I had heard the words, but they had come from my own mouth.

"There is no question about it: I heard the story from Petty Officer R," said Ensign F.

"I'll thank you not to go around making irresponsible statements," said R, fixing his sight on F out of the corner of his eye.

"For the record, I have something to say. Ever since Ensign F came, relations among the officers in the squadron have been difficult. Before that everything had been going smoothly, as you know, Lieutenant. I can understand perfectly well why you should be fond of Ensign F. You were both students and led the same kind of life before coming here. But as a result, we Petty Officers are no longer able to approach you as freely as before. For some reason, Ensign F is telling you tales about us, not all of them true."

F walked up to R. "Liar," he said fiercely, then raised his right arm threat-eningly and hit R in the face with his fist.

"What do you think you're doing?" R drew himself up ready to fight and grabbed F's arms.

"How dare you," F gasped, and he tried again to knock R down. I intervened:

"Cut it out, Ensign F."

Reconsidering, F pulled back, glaring at R with a terrible expression.

"There is no excuse for such behavior. If you want to pick a fight, it's all right with me. I'll go get out of my uniform and be back," R said, his hands trem-bling, his eyes bloodshot with the rage of humiliation.

F simply repeated, "How dare you, such impudence."

"All right, all right. I get the picture. This has been an illuminating con-versation and I intend to remember it, so you had better watch it in the future. I wish all this had happened earlier. Now, when the war is over and we're just waiting around for demobilization of the squadron, I've finally heard how you really feel, yet before I have a chance to make use of the information, we'll all go our separate ways. At least let's not fight among ourselves in the short time remaining. I want you to forget about what happened today. I shouldn't have gotten so carried away myself. But after all, maybe it was a good thing to clear the air."

As I spoke, I was thinking that I would like to end the matter as quickly as possible. Petty Officer T still stood perfectly straight, his lips tight in angry silence, his feverish cheeks and eyelids flushed and swollen.

"You may leave now, all of you. But I don't want any more scuffling. And if you have anything to say, I want you to come and tell me directly. I am always ready to listen."

When I had finished, the three men, dissatisfied, went off in different directions, leaving their chilly backs in my mind. It was as though a film that had been running suddenly burned and curled up at the edges so that the screen scat-tered sparks of light. I was left in white emptiness, thinking I was simply reaping the seeds I myself had sown. And I could not rouse the energy to do anything. I removed the stick that propped open the little hinged window and planted my elbows on the unpainted wooden desk made by a carpenter from the maintenance corps. I looked through the darkened room and stared for a long time, face to face with my own image reflected in the bare mirror nailed to the wall in front of me.

* * *

Shortly before sunset there was a telephone call from Lieutenant H saying that the suicide pilots from A and G squadrons on K island were to be transferred temporarily to our base. My squadron had been assigned to accept G squadron. In the near future all the suicide pilots were to be shipped back to the mainland, and I was the first to be assigned as officer in charge of transport; he himself would remain behind to take part in concluding arrangements and disarmament.

I had made up my mind to stay on the island after seeing the last of my men off to the mainland. Even were I to go back, my house had been burned, and I had a feeling that my father, the only other member of my family, was dead. Despite my resolution, though, I could not refuse to be transport officer, and since I had received no communication from the senior commissioned officer, I did not know what was happening at Sasebo Command and would have to go there at some point. Suddenly, as if a dam had burst, I wanted to go home. After I had discharged all my duties, I could come back to the island by myself. The strange incident of that morning faded like an old photograph. A desire to jump for joy welled up from the depths of my being, and I could hardly wait for the authorities to fix the schedule for our departure. But in that case, I thought, I must go to see Toë's aged father and convey to him my intentions.

EVERYDAY LIFE IN A DREAM

I had gone into the building of a certain charitable organization in the slums. Having heard that a gang of juvenile delinquents lived on the roof of that building, I had decided to become a member of the gang myself. Not that I thought I could enter into the spirit of things and live like this new generation of boys more than ten years younger than I. It was just that I had recently defined my identity and was under the illusion, one might say, that I had lost all other ambitions. In short, I had succeeded in convincing myself that I was a novelist. Society did not, however, accept me as such, since I had not yet published a single work.

One could say, though, that for a long time I had been working on a story. It seems I had been such an eccentric since junior high school days that those around me found it terribly irritating to stand by and watch. That, too, was because I was embarrassed to declare myself an aspiring novelist. I deceived myself with the optimistic view that I still had plenty of time. When I realized, however, that I was past thirty and still had acquired not a single employable skill, I felt like an abstraction. It even seemed to me that, in this modern age of progress in all fields, it was actually criminal not to possess a skill. To ease my anguish I hit upon the idea that since I had lived in this world for almost thirty years now, I must have mastered some kind of skill. And thus I decided that I had been trying to write "novels," and I set about completing a work. But "verbal expression" became so heavy a burden that I almost abandoned my trade. Although I occasionally mouthed the word despair, in actuality I ate, slept, performed my bodily functions, and, in the meantime, managed to pile up pages covered with handwritten characters. I put up with that life for one year. The end product was a mere hundred and twenty pages. Reading back what I had written, I found that it was extraordinarily unclear. I had simply strung words together; there was no sign either of divine guidance or of satanic inspiration. Even for an accumulation of words it was rather paltry. But, as it turned out, I sold those hundred and twenty pages. How could such a thing have happened? I wondered if it might not be some kind of joke. Then someone pointed out that publishing is really no big deal—it's a mere glass of soda pop. And someone else passed on the word to me. Gradually I began to believe it. I'm not sure what the connection is, but at the same time I began to have visions of myself as a "novelist." I would receive such and such an amount of money for my manuscript, which would win brilliant acclaim from the critics, and I would be recognized as a person with a skill, as a real personage, first by close relatives and friends, gradually by the world at large. But having taken everything I had to say and sold it off cheap in those hundred and twenty pages, I realized I had nothing more to write. So I was now in the position of having, one way or another, to develop something to write. Not that I was deluged, like some big name, with requests from publishing houses and magazines, but I had begun to be impatient. Just when I was in precisely this mood, I saw a certain movie that seemed to have a special significance for me. It was about a "novelist" who had just published his first work and had nothing more to write. Unable to bear the embarrassingly futile efforts of honing his prose, the man slipped into the sake cup of alcoholism. Such a thing would never happen to me, I thought, but the attractions of laziness snuck up on me, and at times, when I was powerless against its allure, alcohol came to seduce me. And so it was to resist this attraction, one day when I was in a good frame of mind, that I had come to this slum.

What I intended was to become a member of the gang, to actually try my hand at picking pockets and burglary, to make friends with a twenty-year-old girl (the most blatantly bad age group since the end of the war), to snatch from her willy-nilly the acrid flower of her adolescence—I was shrewd enough to arm myself with such prurient interests. I was convinced that I would have psychological security: with the gimmick of being a novelist, I myself could not be hurt no matter what happened. This double-edged blade drawn, I had also provided the backup snare that I might thus be considered a practicing "humanist." What is more, the account of my daily activities and the "fiction" based upon it would become my second literary work. Not yet embarked on this way of life, I had various expectations, plans, and glorious aspirations, so that even before I had written it in vivid detail, I gradually began to feel as though my masterpiece were already completed, though I was intermittently knocked flat by the prospect of the vast, insipid task of putting it into words.

On the roof—actually on the third floor of the building—as a result of bombing during the war, all that remained was a bare shell of reinforced concrete; the inner walls dividing the rooms had been blown out, leaving one hollow space like a huge lecture hall. Exposed steel girders dangled from the ceiling, bits of concrete lay everywhere about, and the large, now glassless windows, like gaping holes, looked out over the harbor and the sea. Here the gang leader conducted his meeting of some twenty boys. I supposed the topics under discussion would include plans for the next undertaking, denunciation of weakness in the group, methods of evading a tail. I walked gloomily up the crumbled staircase and waited at the very back. I had permission from the leader to join the gang. I was to be a sort of guest and had received assurances that I was free to incorporate any part of their lives into my "novel." I was not some sort of missionary but, in fact, felt quite close to them in mental outlook, the only difference between them and me being that I was considerably older and had once received a formal education:

such was the ingenious status I was able to demand of them. I was able to accomplish this for reasons that had something to do with the character of the charitable organization that had taken them in. I found it difficult to get a true sense of this organization. I had a pretty good general idea, but nothing was crystal clear. I was on extremely familiar terms with the two or three administrators whom I knew, but, to tell the truth, down deep we more or less hated each other's guts. So I was, like the gang, merely using their facilities.

* * *

The leader was a handsome young man apparently not much past twenty. His attitude was one of deliberate rudeness, always keeping people at an arm's length, and when he opened his mouth in self-criticism, he related with embarrassment how he was always weak and passive and could not bring himself to violate rules of courtesy and convention.

The gang leader was just about to speak when the receptionist downstairs came up to say that someone was asking for me and that I should go downstairs immediately. It seemed a bad omen: I had been called back by the receptionist just as I was to take the plunge into a new way of life. I went downstairs.

At the reception desk was a friend from elementary school days. It wasn't someone I had been especially close to; we were never good friends. Even so, I was disconcerted at the sight of him. Why should an elementary school buddy have such an unsettling effect on me? To make matters worse, I had heard a rumor that he was suffering from a terrible disease. I remembered having passed him on the street two or three times after learning that he was ill. Out of consideration for his illness, I had taken special care to act as though nothing had changed and we were still friends as always. It did not seem likely that I would be able to deal with him brusquely today. The terrible disease was leprosy; he had leprosy.

"I hear you've embarked on some great things these days," he said nervously, as soon as he saw me. "And they say your story is going to appear in a first-rate magazine."

I completely lost control. I couldn't stand having my work talked about by an outsider who knew nothing at all about my mental life. Besides, there was something extremely vulgar about the way he pronounced the word "story." On top of everything else, that he was an elementary school friend completely flustered me.

"You said you wanted some of these, didn't you?"

He took a bag out of his pocket and showed it to me. His right hand was unnaturally hidden in his loose sleeve, the bag dangling directly from the sleeve. I knew what it contained, a certain article made of rubber. I wondered when I had asked him for a thing like that, but I couldn't swear that I had not.

"Oh, yes. Thank you for going to all the trouble. How much do you want for them?"

I wished he would hurry up and leave. He was clammily persistent, however. Fidgeting all the while, he opened the bag and took out one of the rubber articles, holding it between his thumb and forefinger. I felt a dull anger spread steadily through my stomach. Why weren't people with his disease kept in isolation? And what would bring him to touch something like that with his contaminated hands? Worst of all, faced with that situation, I had not the courage to censure him for his conduct. It was because I was daunted by my lack of courage that I could not rebuff him.

As he played with the rubber thing, fingering it and stretching it, he said, "They don't make them like they used to. Better watch out, they might break, you know."

Then he began to examine them painstakingly, one at a time. How can I describe my state of mind at that point? Steeped in humiliation, I simply waited for the time to pass.

Eventually, he put them all back in the paper bag, which he handed to me. I took it by the very edge so as not to touch his diseased fingers. Then I produced a hundred yen bill, handling it, too, by the edge, and held it out near his hand.

"Here you go, take this. If you happen to find some high quality articles, let me know. I might be interested." Grimacing, I forced myself to flatter him.

With affected carelessness he tried to put his hand over my fingers as he took the bill. Sure that I sensed malice, I added, this time with less care to conceal my impatience, "Well, see you around. There's a meeting I have to go to today, so I'll be taking off now."

I slipped away from him like lightning. What was the moisture that seemed to ooze from his whole body? I went into the office, poured some corrosive sublimate solution into a metal basin and diluted it with water. Then I thrust both hands, and the bag, into this disinfectant. The action was almost instinctive. Just then a door opened with a creak. I shuddered and, without removing my hands from the basin, looked around at the door. There stood my leper friend, rigid, a seething jealous rage in his eyes. What could it mean? Whereas a little while ago his face had shown no sign of his illness, the area around his eyes was now shaded with dark flesh sores. For a while he continued to stare unpleasantly at my hands submerged in the disinfectant, then he wailed in a high-pitched voice, "You too, you too, you're just like all the rest."

He came close to me. "Damn you. You're nothing but a phony. I'll give it to you, I'll infect you with my incurable disease!"

I moved away, using the table as a shield. He came after me, black with rage and disease. Just then the receptionist, who had heard the commotion, came into the room. Furious, he turned around and saw the young girl standing there looking apprehensive.

"Shit. I won't let anybody get away. I don't care who I infect," he said, and went over to the girl and grabbed hold of her with both hands.

I kicked the floor and fled. I escaped, leaving the young girl to die.

* * *

I wonder what happened to them after that, or what happened to the building, or the members of the gang, for that matter. I do not know. I never went near the place again, even though it always pricked my conscience that I did not.

I was walking through the streets of the town. I was always walking. Ever since that time, planes had been flying overhead. Countless planes flew above me, and I trembled in fear. The very idea of metal flying through the sky alarmed me, but I was even more frightened at the thought that something might fall out of them. So whenever they came, I would look up at the sky and plan what to do in that event. From time to time aluminum gasoline barrels would be dropped. They struck the earth with a metallic thud and lay motionless. This was reassuring, but there was no way of knowing what would fall from the skies next. The planes gradually increased in number. At lower and lower flying altitudes, they buzzed around the skies over the town like an invasion of locusts, their hard bellies gleaming in the sunlight. I began to feel that the end of the world was near.

One day I was unreasonably restless. Everything seemed strangely insubstantial and in suspended animation; so I decided to call on a certain famous "novelist." The issue of the magazine that was to carry my story had not been printed yet, but something urged me on. Besides, as the days passed, the details of my meeting with the leper became fuzzy. Had I actually touched him that day, or had I not? Had I succeeded in completely disinfecting myself, or had I run away before I could use the disinfectant? I tried to recall from the context the precise order of events, but I simply could not remember. I lost confidence in my own flesh—and there were all those planes flying overhead. My story had not yet appeared. I had had no reaction to my work. My plans for the next work were at a total standstill. For all I knew, having my story printed up in many copies and distributed to the public at large would turn out to be no more than a figment of my imagination. Or else the editors of the magazine might inform me that, for practical considerations, my story would not appear until the following issue. Or that the printers had lost my manuscript. If that happened, would I be able to rant and rave? Would I not, just as I had fled from the leper, simply run away? Staggering under my own weight, I began to move. And everything around me lurched and swayed.

I cannot explain my motive for going to see the famous novelist. I could not shake the feeling that at the moment I might just as well not have written my story at all. When I introduced myself to the famous novelist, I would probably look like an idiot. Faced with a complete stranger, he would feel uncomfortable and annoyed. I was sure he would find it unbearable if I were then to bring up the subject of his fiction. Whereupon I would cleverly interject, "I happen to have sold a story myself." "Really, to whom?" "The magazine in which you yourself have published. Except it hasn't come out yet."

Just how much in awe I was of that novelist even I do not know. Perhaps, in a way, I looked down on him. I mulled the project over in my mind until it began to seem like too much trouble to go see the man.

When the final day approached, what exactly would I want to do? What would I desire? I would not wish to use one of those rubber things. Where had I mislaid them, in fact? Since the day of the unpleasant incident, I had not gone near that building, which was my sole link with human society, so by now I had not a single friend in this town. Where were my father and my mother, I wondered? I had lost track of them both. Perhaps that is something of an exaggeration. I had not been able to discover my father's whereabouts, but I had a pretty good idea where my mother was. She was supposed to be living in a town in southern Japan, said to have been largely destroyed during the war. The newspapers had in fact reported that it was completely obliterated, but I would have to see for myself to know for sure. Therefore, I had an idea where my mother was, I just did not know whether she was dead or alive. And I thought my father was probably looking for my mother.

Suddenly, I decided to go to that southern town and see. It was not so much that I wanted to see my mother, I think. I just swung my heavy body about and headed in that direction.

*   *   *

Here, without question, was that southern town. What had once been so familiar seemed a little different now, but it was clear that I had walked into that once familiar town. It had not been destroyed after all. I walked around. My mother had been born here, but her family had died out long ago. I, too, had lived here for a while. By now, however, there was apparently nowhere for me to rest my bones. The families I had known slightly had passed into a new generation. Even so, it seemed perfectly reasonable to expect that I would find my way to my mother's house.

After wandering about the city, I found myself at the very edge of town, at the last station on the train line. Whether because it was evening, or already night, everything was ridiculously dark. I stood still. Then all at once various things came back to me. On intuition, I walked through cheerful buzzing crowds of people around a department store, a barbershop, and so on. Then, sensing the backdrop of houses built up on slopes surrounding the dark terminal, I remembered something: I knew where I was going. All I had to do was to take a train for the suburbs and go to a certain place. And that place was the very spot the newspapers had said was totally destroyed.

There seemed to be train tracks heading into the darkness northward, away from the terminal. I had no idea where those tracks went or what kinds of towns they strung together, but it seemed to me that if I went in that direction, I would find that place, in a district flattened where the hills and the buildings had turned to ashes and crumbled, virtually melted, to the ground. And I felt twinges of budding worry in the area round my heart. I had to get there fast.

* * *

As I bought a ticket from an old woman on the roadside by the terminal, a strong wind arose. At the top of a nearby utility pole a bare bulb, loose at the socket, swayed as it spotlighted the boxlike stall of the ticket seller. As if I were her last customer, the old woman began hurriedly to shut down her stall, so I rushed onto the train.

The train was crowded, but I was able to push my way through the passengers. As I was hanging on to a strap toward the middle of the car, gasping for breath like a fish, I began to feel certain that I would get a seat. And just then, in fact, I did. Directly in front of me sat a girl in the prime of maidenhood, a young girl with a good figure, wearing an inexpensive silk kimono. Her wide, flat nose bothered me, but I was subtly attracted to her plump body. She looked as though not so many days had passed since she had come from the surrounding countryside. I tried mentally dressing her in the showy, bright-figured kimono of the mistress of a small bar. Whereupon, like an unrestrainable child, I felt an overwhelming desire. I showed a persistent interest in the seat next to her, until she finally moved over to make room for me. Her languid movement was in fact ugly, but I was extremely aroused. I felt as though I held a little bird in my hands, at my mercy.

I sensed the resilient warmth of the body of another human being. At her slightest movement, I was keenly aware of the contours of my own flesh, distinguishing clearly the boundary between my body and the woman's. Then, as though I had been smoking a little too much, my vision blurred. Suddenly, I sensed that since that day my flesh had begun to give way and was no longer sound. At the same time I was certain that the woman was perfectly aware of all this and was having a feast. I lost the ability to think of the future: the seconds piled up, at each instant the past moved into unknown time. I began to count the various contracting muscles in my legs. Just then the girl moved her leg away from mine. Oh no. I panicked as though I had been slapped in the face. I pitied my own involuntary nervous system. I was sure that the girl had, in a cool and calculating way, sized up my penis and then abruptly withdrawn the warmth of her leg. I was furious, I wanted war. The first step was to look deeply insulted and turn my head away in a huff. Then—as I was half hoping she would—the girl began to look flustered. At that I lost some of my momentum, and I looked at the girl out of the corner of my eye. Since I had been sitting with my body slightly away from her and my knee firmly up against hers, the girl's knees had been forced into an un-ladylike position. She had meant to put her knees together and straighten her kimono. Bringing her body close, the girl said, "Sorry. Don't be mad at me. I couldn't help it."

Her tone was extremely intimate. I felt I had lost in this strange competition until I heard the girl's voice, and then I was disgusted and came back to my senses. I decided then and there to snap the thread of that little imaginary dalliance. With the lingering saccharine sensation of total laxity, suddenly I found myself in a certain house.

* * *

It was in a section of the area I had expected to find totally destroyed. By some whim of fate, the house, my mother's house, was still standing. Then I realized that I had forcibly dragged my father with me. That's right, I had forgotten—on the way here I had felt somehow physically hampered. Someone was with me, following me like a shadow. It was my father. As soon as I entered this house I realized clearly that it was my father.

Having already decided to move into this house, I walked around on the tatami, looking into the various rooms; standing out on the veranda at the back, I looked over the wooden fence at the house next door. In the unkempt little garden grew a single loquat tree. I could see too clearly it's darkish leaves, plump and heavy as if made of rubber. The dusty, spongy tatami bulged; the floor boards were loose and creaked when you walked. The ceiling boards had all been removed, exposing the ugly sight of roof beams full of spiderwebs and electrical wiring. True, it had escaped extinction, but I saw that, in that instantaneous flash, the entire house had sustained unhealable wounds. The rooms were terribly gloomy and depressing, and I wondered how my mother managed to live in such a place.

"The tatami are really dirty, aren't they? I hate living like this. If I'm going to live here, I'll fix it up right," I said loudly, rather pointedly, stressing the word "right."

My own words suddenly engendered the thought that my mother was unclean. I had had an ulterior motive for making this statement in such a loud voice. In so doing I was purposely taking my mother to task for her loose living. That way, I would curry favor with my father and, at the same time, help my mother to lose some of her defensiveness with respect to my father and to relax a little. As far as my father was concerned, the results were excellent; it seemed to have worked a little too well on my mother, however, which plunged me into sadness.

I had thought my mother was older. Looking at her now, I noticed that she had retained a surprising bloom of youthfulness. With her narrow undersash carelessly tied in a jaunty asymmetric bow, her hips were even seductive. On her back was an illegitimate child of mixed blood. I remembered having seen that albino-like little boy, every now and then, in the town where my mother was born. The child was big and plump for his age, and I didn't understand what would make my mother want to carry such a big child on her back. Come to think of it, it seemed to me that as long as there was no way to hide the child—since my father was alive—she had decided to go the whole way and carry him on her back. That the Eurasian child I had seen playing in the streets was the result of my mother's misconduct I had not realized until I came to this house. Even so, I was not in the least surprised. I felt as though I had had all along a general idea of how things were. In fact, the thought that I possessed this truly "novelistic" background mysteriously encouraged me. I felt I held my own will in my bare hands. Don't forget, I had defined my identity as a novelist.

My mother seemed to be acting sulky and irresponsible out of desperation at my father's sudden appearance. She looked as though she might very well lash out and answer back if my father said anything at all. And yet, to my eyes, she seemed a woman at wits' end, the pale foreign child on her back, by nature and habit unable to go against her fate as a woman. Carried away by sentimentality, I found myself saying, "There's nothing to worry about, Mother. After all, this child is my little brother."

In an instant I was moved by my own words, my chest swelled, and I even felt heroic. My mother and the Eurasian child would have tears in their eyes, I thought. I had it at the back of my mind that even if my father should object, I was secure in my own determination. I had resolved to put no faith in my spontaneous emotional reactions. It had been that way ever since the day of that incident.

My father looked on in silence. He seemed extremely annoyed by it all, including my eccentric self-confidence. I had no physical sense of my father's existence. I had brought my father here to my mother's house, but my father had almost nothing approaching a position there. Moreover, it was clear that, mentally, I had awarded him a position with respect to my mother. His fatherliness resided in this position. And this "fatherliness" looked annoyed.

My father spoke. "Besides this kid, there are two girls," he remarked simply. That is all he said, but more than the words themselves, the suggestion of what he did not say—You wouldn't know about such things—stung me to the quick. It was what these words implied that was engraved so vividly on my heart. I shrank unbecomingly from my father. A normal family, safe and sound, had been my reality until the war. But what about now? Think how adversity comes, one misfortune after another in such thick profusion. I no longer know what I am. How wonderful! All this is my reality. As the feeling spread over me like pox, I was stung by that simple comment from my father. To me, father seemed like the immovable iron wall of society.

Forcing a poor imitation of a smile, I managed to answer back to my father, "That much I figured out a long time ago." I would do anything to restore my mood of sentimental generosity, so ruthlessly taken to task as if for an inexpiable sin. "Father, the truth is I have leprosy": I wanted to satisfy my vanity, to state that no reality could startle me. But the only result was the realization that, faced with the all too human disharmony between my father and my mother, I was utterly powerless.

My father said something. These were terrible words. When I heard them, I wondered if my mother's skin were not also my own. Those words gave that skin a glimpse of the brothel.

My mother tried to answer. If my mother did not say something, the balance of the whole world would be upset; I was in extreme suspense. My mother had to hurry up and say something. The gaseous substance emitted from my father's mouth must be neutralized by more gas from my mother's mouth, or it seemed the entire nation would collapse around one certain piece of ground strangely left intact in the midst of the ruins. My mother took what looked like a tray and set it down on the tatami. Apparently, whenever my mother wanted to say something to my father, it was agreed that in order to prove there was no falsehood in her words, she would perform a sort of *fumie* ritual, trampling on a sacred image. I suppose there was a portrait painted on the tray. It happened to be upside down so I could not see it; I wondered whose portrait it was. I felt an unnatural curiosity to see. Lifting high her skirts, my mother stepped on the tray. The sight was so bewitching that I could hardly believe she was my own mother. Intuition told me that this extremely critical, taut moment was the best possible chance for reconciliation. I felt almost like praying. But what in the world. The words my mother finally blurted out were an expression of her true devotion to her Caucasian lover.

My father bellowed with rage, and the waves of his emotion spread to me. I became furious along with him. At the same time, however, my father's psychological unraveling gave me no small satisfaction. My father picked up a whip and raised it to flog my mother, whereupon I felt that sentimental generosity well up within me again. I told my father I would receive his punishment in place of my mother. At first, my father was reluctant to agree. His face was pale and serious. When I saw his expression, I repeated even more insistently that I would take my mother's place. Even I found something compelling in my zeal. My father finally agreed. There was a faint, chilly smile on his lips.

I took the flogging from my father.

It was a formidable flogging. I all but lost consciousness. My father stood like a stone at the extremity of hatred. I was brutally made to realize that I had taken too indulgent a view of things, but I was determined not to cry out in pain even if it killed me. After the whip, he beat me roundly in the face with a club.

*   *   *

Eventually, I was outside the house. Several of my teeth were missing. No matter how many times I reached into my mouth with my thumb and forefinger, I could not get rid of the grit of pulverized teeth that clung to my tongue like dry cement. My mouth felt like the mouth of a grasshopper or a katydid.

Where was I walking, I wondered. I had totally lost track. This was supposed to be the place that had been obliterated. But where I was walking now, the streets were lined with houses, and there were people about.

The streets smelled of sulphur. And the row of houses sloped. Apparently, a valley stream ran alongside the houses. Only I couldn't see the stream, it just seemed to me there was one. The road was lined with rows of trees. What kind of trees were they? Perhaps cherries. I supposed when springtime came there would be pink blossoms drifting overhead like a sleepy cloud. But right now there did not seem to be any flowers. The houses were covered with what looked like steam, and I smelled sulphur. Why was I on this road? Was I looking for another night's lodging, checking out inns and rejecting them one by one? The road gradually began to go downhill. Increasingly there were lots of stones. People passed by; they all seemed insubstantial, had pale shadows. It was dark, but it was certainly not evening. There was the sun, high in the sky, and it was dark. People walked by in droves. Oh, give me the thick heaviness of lying on a beach in the blazing, glaring midsummer daylight I once knew.

So thinking, I walked on. Was I intending to pay a call at *that house*? I was walking as if to nowhere in particular, but surely I had a destination in mind.

The houses became sparser. Presently, I went by a long, narrow, three-story wooden building. My mood darkened, as if clouds had covered the sun. Tilting my head back, I looked up at the top of the building. Suddenly, I saw faces filling every window. They seemed to be the faces of school children. My whole body burned with humiliation. Still, there was no reason to think that all those students were staring at me. I tried taking another good look—rather, I turned my face in that direction, lacking the serenity for careful observation. What appeared to my feverish eyes convinced me that only two or three of the children were looking at me and laughing. I walked away.

(You're cheating. You're a fake) my mood whispered.

(You know, the trouble with you is . . .) my mood whispered again.

(This isn't "Nothing ventured, nothing gained." It's venturing something after losing everything.)

(And just what do you mean by that?) I challenged. (Suppose you tell me exactly what it is you are trying to say?)

Whereupon my mood answered me in an intimidating singsong, (These days you've been making such a big deal about NO-thing VEN-tured, NO-thing GAined.)

(What would I make a big deal about a dumb thing like that for?) I shook my head. I was walking. I began to smell sulphur.

(Don't trust your mood.) I wonder who could have whispered this?

(I know where you're going, you know.)

Somehow or other I was standing in the doorway of that house.

"Please put me up for the night."

I was shown to the woman's room.

(This is your specialty. Here we go. Let's have your usual superb performance.)

Hanging on the lattice, looking out the window was a child.

"That kid isn't going to make it," the woman said announcing her presence behind me.

"How do you mean, not going to make it?"

"The doctor has given up hope."

I went up to the child. What could be wrong with him? He didn't look sick at all. I spoke to him,

"What are you looking at, kid?"

"I'm looking over there," the child said in a perfectly clear voice. I sensed the view outside the lattice window. It was an expanse of rice paddies in which nothing had been planted. The earth had been tilled and then left that way to harden and freeze. These fields extended as far as the eye could see; about a mile away a sparse pine forest was just visible, a little fuzz dancing at the horizon. And I could hear the roar of the sea. When I looked fixedly in that direction, through the pine forest I seemed to see white caps.

"Hey kid, you can see the ocean from here. Want me to pick you up so you can see?"

I picked the child up. He weighed almost nothing. My heart sank. Then, as if he had just been waiting for me to pick him up, the child went into convulsions. Gently I set him down.

"I see what you mean," I said to the woman.

My head itched terribly. I stuck my fingers into my hair and scratched and scratched my scalp. Then I sat down at a vanity stand at one end of the room. And there lay the latest issue of a magazine. The woman was sobbing quietly. Wasn't this the magazine in which my first story was to appear? Hurriedly I picked up the magazine and opened it to the table of contents.

Hey, it's really in here. My name is in print. But why didn't they send me a copy, I wonder? Surely I have the right to see this before any one else. My head itched. Then the back of my neck began to itch wildly. So I scratched and clawed where it itched.

"Where did you get this magazine?"

"What? Oh that," the woman said as she came up behind me.

"Besides, is this the title I gave it?"

"Look," said the woman as though she had had a start, "What's the matter with your head? It's full of something peculiar."

I felt my scalp with my hand. Big sores, like calcium rice crackers, had formed all over my head. I shuddered and was assailed by the unpleasant sensation that all the blood in my head was freezing and withdrawing to the center. I tried peeling off the scabs. They came off easily. But afterward, the itching was completely out of control. Able to stand it no longer, I began to scratch and claw uncontrollably all over my head. At first, it felt intoxicatingly good. But immediately, a violent itching returned. This time it was not just on my head, but an itching that seemed to well up all over my body. There was nothing I could do to assuage it. It was a horrible sensation, as if my body were submerged in ice and slugs were crawling all over my neck, like the lukewarm shampoo you get at the barbershop after a haircut. Whenever I stopped to rest my hands, the sores grew like mushrooms. With the strange feeling that I might at any moment be about to abandon the human race, I scratched and scratched the sores on my head.

At the same time I felt a violent pain in my stomach. Like the wolf who had his belly stuffed with stones, I seemed to reel, and I felt unable to walk straight. Gathering my courage, I thrust my right hand into my stomach. Then, still madly scratching my head with my left hand, I tried forcibly scooping out what was in there. I felt something hard adhering stubbornly to the bottom of my stomach, so I pulled at it with all my might. And then the strangest thing happened. With that hard kernel uppermost, my own flesh followed up after it. So desperate at this point, I was beyond caring what happened to me; I kept pulling. Finally, I had turned myself completely inside out like a sock. The itching on my head and the pain in my stomach were both gone. On the outside I was like a squid, smooth and blank and transparent. Then I realized that I was submerged in a pure, murmuring stream. It was a shallow stream, apparently in the open fields. Still steeping my body in the murmuring stream, outside I saw an old tree—what kind I do not know—completely bare of leaves, on each of whose thick bare branches perched a crow holding on with its wide open beak. Looking more carefully, I saw that on each and every branch were not one but swarms of crows with their beaks open wide. They looked as persistent as plant parasites. I had the sense that these crows would remain just as they were, in that position, for ever and ever. The only sign that they were alive was the way they occasionally moved their upward pointed tails and softly spread their wings. But they kept right on clinging fast with their beaks to the thick, dry, leafless branches. Still bathing my body, I thought how much I wanted to strip those crows, those scale insects, from the tree.

THE STING OF DEATH

On the following day, I noticed that the alarm clock on my desk, which had stopped long ago, was running again. Since I had not fiddled with it, or given it a shock of any kind, I have no idea why it decided to work again. In the past it had not responded even to vigorous shaking. But there it was now, ticking away diligently. My first thought was that my wife's will had lodged itself within.

All day long it rained, and as I listened to the pelting on the wet clay soil in the garden, I envisioned another scene on some other day: All the shutters are closed. Without stopping to remove his muddy shoes, someone comes into the house and examines the bodies of a family suicide.

The income from teaching night classes at a high school two nights a week was not enough to support a family of four. I had to find other work, but after three days of relentless cross-examination by a wife determined to expose the secrets of my past, I was as thin-skinned, vulnerable, as a shrimp that had shed its shell. I was defenseless against the slightest blow from society and did not see how I could venture out in public by myself. Since I had no special skills, I had no other recourse than to look for an editor who would commission me to write a story. My wife was aware of the situation, but somehow, subtly, she had changed. I could no longer expect her to make every sacrifice, to devise ways of supplementing our income or scrimp to make ends meet. Were I to face absolute ruin, she would probably sit by, arms folded, and gaze at her husband's distress as though it were somebody else's concern. I could only think that a deep-seated change had occurred the day I had given her such a shock. If I did not succeed in finding work, she would probably blame me; I could hear her saying that the whole disgusting mess was my fault. There remained no trace of the old trusting, clinging gaze with which she had fixed my eye as she followed me around from place to place.

Trying to find a publisher basically meant waiting around for an opportunity to present itself. Still, if I kept up my relations with other writers, something might turn up that would lead to a job, and I could hardly stay home all the time if I wanted to give it a chance. But, under the present circumstances, going out was not easy. Even if I could bring myself to break my resolution not to go out alone, I would be consumed with anxiety at leaving the house and my wife unattended for any length of time. Just going out to a movie and coming home slightly late for dinner, I was assailed by a fear that made me shudder. My whole body was wracked with a lonely sadness.

As I wondered how I could go on this way, time passed. There were days when my wife remarked that Daddy's gloomy face had brightened, and days, too, when my wife's eyes seemed wetter, softer than they had been since that day. At such times I wanted to believe it was a sign that we had finally emerged from our ordeal; I wanted it to be such a sign. But there was the worry that as soon as we returned to normality, something would set us off again, and our temporary progress would crumble, leaving us right back where we started. I could not expect to find a sympathetic observer ready to concern himself with what had happened within our own family. As the days went by, I was quietly invaded by the hopelessness of waiting, shut up at home. Partly because of the seasonal change from summer to fall, I began to feel as though the two of us were huddled close together under the heatless rays of an eclipsed sun. How long would we be able to remain hidden there, face to face in that cold air? A voice whispered that in order to return to our normal routine, we would have to venture out into the mire of society. In moments of weakness, that voice would assail me.

* * *

But after feeling depressed and claustrophobic for a while, I made up my mind to leave the house. Come to see me off at the station, my wife stood Shin'ichi and Maya on one of the turnstiles, and the three of them waved good-bye as they always did. Looking back at them, I stepped onto the train; the doors closed, and it began to move. Maya was looking not at me but off in some other direction as she mechanically waved good-bye, and my wife was still managing a smile. As soon as the train was in motion and the station wall had once again become a barrier that hid from view the ticket-taker's turnstile and the faces of my wife and children, my wife's smile, lingering before my mind's eye, suddenly clouded over, and the air seemed to force itself up through my throat—just as it always had before. Outwardly, my bearing was in no way different from all those times when I had waved a cheerful good-bye to my wife and children and slipped out of the house to go to visit the other woman. Perhaps inwardly I was like a fish freed from the small hatchery into the open sea. What was my wife thinking as, aware of the implications of my departure, she took one last look at her husband smiling at her from the other side of the door as the train carried him away? I felt the strength leave my arms and legs like a receding wave. At the thought that she, too, seemed the same as always, I felt a sharp pang in my breast. The train was not crowded, possibly because it was an in-between time, before noon and after the morning commuting-hour crush, and no passengers were standing. Though there was an empty seat near me, I couldn't bring myself to sit down. Instead, I went from one car to the next; crossing, one after another, the platforms between cars, with their overlapping steel plates, I went toward the front of the train, telling myself all the while that my wife had endorsed this expedition.

In the very midst of our three-day ordeal, I had received a telegram from the editorial board of Q magazine asking me to do a documentary article on a certain factory, but since it came at a time when I couldn't let my wife out of my sight, when one slip might bring my life crumbling down around my ears, any thought to the future was a luxury. I simply could not accept the job.

I climbed a steep wooden stairway to the editorial office where the Q staff was working, each absorbed in his own job. No one looked up when I came in. Once I had refused the job and expressed my deepest regrets, there was nothing more to talk about. Perhaps I had expected as much. Outwardly, my appearance must have seemed no different from the way I had looked, say, two weeks earlier.

"Thank you very much for your understanding." Just as I got up to leave, Z, a member of a group from which I was trying to withdraw, came into the room.

"Oh, I didn't know you were coming," he said, adding quickly, "Are you finished here? Wait for me—I'll be done in a minute. We can leave together."

He was being more forceful than usual—besides, I thought, even if I did intend to dissociate myself from the group, there was no reason to do it abruptly. I waited for him near the door, impressed by the brisk way he spoke to the editor, getting right to the point.

"I got the reporting job you turned down. You just did me a big favor." Z invited me to lunch.

"I'm glad," I said.

When he asked after my health, I remembered how recently I had been telling everyone I had tuberculosis. I ran a low-grade fever, had a slight cough I couldn't seem to shake, and was depressed for days on end. All that was a mere two weeks ago. I was undergoing chemotherapy; I had even been afraid I might start coughing up blood. But now all that seemed so distant, like something that had happened to someone else. It was woven into a past when, if I complained of not feeling well, my wife would go to any extreme, make any sacrifice—a past to which I could not now return. My wife seemed to have completely forgotten that I had been taking medicine at all. Swallowing my impulse to complain, I said quickly, "We've been having psychological problems. It's all right now, but for a while I didn't know whether we'd make it. No, it's not me, it's my wife—but she'll be all right now. The worst seems to be over. It's just that it's dangerous for me to go out the way I used to. This is the first time I've been out of the house."

Suddenly, I realized he must be more interested in hearing about another side of my life. I was reminded of how I had given way under my wife's cross-examination, confessing all my past misdeeds. I felt guilty for telling Z so much, but I was unable to restrain myself. Becoming increasingly impassioned in my eloquence, and thinking all the while how dangerous it was to talk to him, I realized this was the first conversation I had had in days.

"But tell me how all this came about," Z asked. Once again, I consciously suppressed the unconscious urge to talk. "Don't look so innocent. Do you know what your friends are saying about you behind your back?" I remembered my wife's cool gaze as she had said these words.

"I guess I just put her through too much."

I would not be able to avoid going out alone from now on, but I was determined never again to respond with such openness to simple expressions of good will. Even so, when he told me, "Today it's on me—I've just been paid," somehow I went along with him. But even if I could not pick up the whole tab, I must pay my own way. I must catch hold of the will I felt slipping through my fingers and hold it up for my wife to see. The wife whose image had quietly stuck by me had now changed beyond recognition. And now it was I who felt disposed to try this and try that in an effort to show her I was someone she could trust. During those three dark days and nights, I had found something in my wife that I did not want to let go from my grasp. This feeling was different from the blind infatuation I experienced when first I discovered her. The ecstacy I sought elsewhere had not yet been completely purged from my body; I was troubled by the thought, and frightened. The fleshly odor of secrets from my past unexpectedly rose to the surface, like foam on the polluted water of a canal. By force of will alone, I could not stamp out the memories that kept reviving, nor could I simply blot out the long months when my body and soul were held captive by the other woman. The guilt I felt about those months began to assume the face of vengeance.

Not knowing when, if ever, I would be able to get away, I could not go home empty handed. I wanted to find some work to keep us going, and to be able to smile at my wife and say, "What did I tell you—I found a job. It was a good idea to go out and look." As the time passed, I began to be aware of a budding anxiety in the pit of my stomach at being away from home so long, but my conversation with Z had left me with an unpleasant sensation, like being covered with a wet rag; I had to do something to remove it.

Hadn't my wife warned me? "I'm not going to mention any names, but your old friends are making fun of you. I don't know what they say to your face, *but*."

That sort of observation was all too obvious—and yet in my vulnerable state, every little thing got to me.

* * *

Next, I dropped by to see another group of writer friends. The confession I had so far managed to hold back overflowed.

"The inevitable has finally happened," I blurted out.

"That's awkward," A sympathized, but I kept talking.

"I have to be with her all the time—the minute I take my eyes off her she's liable to commit suicide. Even sitting here like this I can't relax for a moment." I began to talk so glibly and cheerfully that even I was embarrassed. But then, at his house I always, with very little ceremony, like emptying a glass of water, spilled whatever bottled up emotions I had brought with me.

"B and C are supposed to be coming over later," A said, and I began to feel that with all those writers together I might get a lead on a job. "They should be here any minute." The irresistible magical power of A's words was soothing, but I sat poised on the edge of my chair, uncommitted. While I was fretting that it was past two and I really should go home, the bitter taste of time spread over my tongue. Then B came in.

"Sorry to be late."

C arrived almost on his heels, coming in without saying a word. I took advantage of the change and started to get up. I was ready to burst with impatience.

"I'd better be going," I said, rising.

A objected, "Why? Just when everyone's finally here."

"Suddenly I'm worried about what's going on at home," I said, looking him in the eye. Then I excused myself to the other two, "I have to be getting along." B responded, "See you again," but C said nothing.

* * *

Outside, a feeling lingered that I had closed up shop and sneaked away, but for some reason or other I felt surrounded by an atmosphere of brutal defeat. The three men who had stayed behind had probably made a few remarks about me. They probably wondered why I left in such a hurry and why I seemed a little different from my normal self, but they would soon move on to the topic for the day. Even if they had not settled on a discussion topic ahead of time, they would find subjects of common concern and enter into a typically intense conversation. I realized for the first time that all three of their careers were in the ascendant, amidst irrefutable popular acclaim. At the thought I turned red with shame, and when I felt calmer, the rays of sun above my head seemed to flicker and dim. I looked up, wondering if a bank of thick clouds had just appeared, but apparently not. I wished I hadn't come. What had turned my steps in this direction was the unpleasant aftertaste of my encounter with Z. That such coincidence had lain in wait for me at the Q editorial office was the real disaster. Had I been one or two minutes earlier I would have been spared the meeting with Z, and I would have gone directly home. Only one errand at a time. At present, it was not a good idea to see all sorts of people just to maintain friendly relations.

At the nearby national railway station, the boarding platform was built alongside a moat; when you went downstairs to the platform from the ticket gate, the bridge to the other side of the moat was overhead, giving the illusion of a subway station. A concrete wall rising above the platform roof on one side put a chill in the air. Wishing to avoid the stares of others who were waiting, I went to the far end of the platform.

I could not shake the feeling that I had been exiled from humanity. Apparently, other people could get by with just about anything while I myself was forbidden a single transgression. As the train approached, its lithe body undulating behind its proper square face, my anxiety blazed up and spread like fanned flames. Despite my impatience, whenever the train stopped, I had to wait while the doors opened, people got on, and the doors closed again. Worse, they had to go through the routine of opening and closing the doors two or three times, as if they were testing them, before they finally shut them tight. Even then, there was an interminable interval in which the train seemed glued to the spot. With a slight impulse passed on from one car to the next, the train started to move, and at last we were back on course. But I was impatient with our sluggish pace and walked through the cars to get as far forward as I possibly could. I felt exactly the same going home as I had coming out. When I thought of all the overpasses, trestles, factory smoke stacks in between, I wondered when I would ever reach Koiwa Station.   After inching forward like this bit by bit, there still remained an intraversible distance ahead.   When I had reached the front of the car, as I had done on the trip downtown, it would be unbearably frustrating to be able to go no further. It occurred to me to push my way slowly up to the forward doors while the train was in motion and then leap out the minute it stopped and get back on in the next car. I kept repeating the process; each time we ticked off a station, I was unmistakably one car closer to home.

The tickling optimism in my abdomen was overcome by a sensation of gradual collapse, and when I finally reached the front of the train and looked through the glass windows out at the cliff that overhung the tracks before us, we were approaching the familiar temporary overpass for waterworks construction. I looked ahead and saw the Koiwa Station bridge. Vacant lots, planted fields, and little streams began to give way to the city; each time we passed one of the many railroad crossings, we would slow down, the steel wheels would resume their cruel sluggishness, and the tired faces of housewives and delivery boys waiting impatiently behind the crossing gate would catch my eye. With a slight curve, the train slid alongside the station platform, which seemed longer than I had remembered, until finally it creaked to a halt. I could hardly wait for the doors to open, then I leaped out and began walking in long strides, soon anxiously breaking into a run. Once my anxiety was in motion, it grew and grew, gathering speed until it was out of my control. If I was so worried, why had I left home in the first place, I asked myself, as I scaled the stairs to the bridge over the tracks two at a time, taking them five at once going down on the other side. I wondered briefly if my wife wasn't waiting for me at the exit with the children, but when that hope proved vain, I cut across the square in front of the station, turned into a narrow street by the movie theatre, and after two more turns, our decaying, falling-down bamboo fence came into view.

* * *

Why were the gate, the front door, and the sliding glass doors to the hallway all wide open? My wife was an ardent housekeeper. When the weather was good she would often open all the doors and windows to let in the fresh air, and she would do laundry as if it were the most important thing in life and hang the bedding out in the sun, draping it over the neighbors' fences—the Aokis' on one side, the Kanekos' on the other—as well as our own.

But now the sight of the front gate standing ajar struck terror into my heart. Trying to sound as cheerful as possible, I called out, "I'm home," and went inside. But there was no answer; Shin'ichi and Maya, who apparently had just come in from play, were bent over rummaging around in their toy bin. ("Miho isn't here!") Everything seemed to go black before me, and my arms began to shake. So as not to startle the children, I asked as off-handedly as I could, "Where's Mommy, Shin'ichi?" Without looking up from his toys, he said, "I don't know." Maya, apparently sensing that something was wrong, dropped her toy and looked up at me. I forced a smile. "How about Maya—do you know where Mommy is?"

"Don' know," she said, giving the same answer as her brother.

"Shin'ichi—look at me. This is important, OK? Tell Daddy, did Mommy go out someplace by herself?"

"Unh-hunh."

"To the bath house? To the store?"

"Unh-unh."

Even so, I checked her towel and hand basin the kitchen. No, she wasn't at the bath. I looked in the lavatory, and all the closets, and the little alley between our yard and the factory behind us, but I knew very well it would be no use.

"Shin'ichi, were you home when Mommy went out?"

"Mm-hm."

"Didn't she say where she was going?"

"Hm-hm."

"Did she have on a kimono or a skirt? Was she all dressed up?"

"She had a kimono on."

"That's funny. Did she seem angry or anything?"

"I don't know. She didn't say anything."

"Maybe she went to see Ujikka," I suggested without conviction.

As soon as I said the children's name for my wife's uncle, I began to feel that, having no other relative to take her in, she must in fact have gone to see "Ujikka." She had probably decided to go to her uncle's house and then think about what to do next. I pictured my wife sitting there talking cheerfully to her aunt and uncle, not breathing a word of family discord. It began to seem that if I just went to call for her, she would say "How nice, you came to pick me up," as if nothing had happened, and we would buy lots of presents for the children and go home together. I couldn't control my impatience.

"Shin'ichi, I think I'll go see Ujikka—I'll bet that's where Mommy is, don't you think?"

I knew they were used to being home by themselves, but I felt particularly sorry for them under the circumstances. I thought of Ishikawa, whom I really hadn't known very long, and went to his apartment behind the pharmacist near the train station. He agreed immediately. The first time Ishikawa had come to the house with his friend Suzuki, they were both wearing cotton kimonos and wooden sandals, which gave me no clue to what they did for a living—I thought perhaps they were simply young men leading a life of ease. Even when they pressed me to tell them how I had written my short story entitled "Truth in Illusion," I didn't know how to answer. I later learned they were both elementary school teachers. My impression of Suzuki was that he was slightly reticent, so I decided to ask Ishikawa. I didn't approve of dragging outsiders into family problems, but I was desperate. I brought him home with me; then, leaving the children in his charge, I got back on the train.

* * *

After the train I took a streetcar, and as I walked from the trolley stop and neared Ujikka's house, it began to occur to me that my wife, having always absolutely refused to discuss family matters with outsiders, would now hardly go to see her uncle, who would know immediately that something must be wrong. I wondered why I was going there. I turned onto a street that branched off from the main thoroughfare. This road was disproportionately wide for the traffic on it, creating the impression that streetcar tracks from an earlier, more prosperous era might have been removed. Mixed in among the shops that lined the streets were temple grounds and vacant lots overgrown with weeds, and the area had a deserted feeling that suggested I was leaving the city entirely. But around our uncle's house were shops and businesses, and a public bath with a large smokestack. I began to feel like a lonely traveler who had left the main highway for a lively post-town after a long day on the road. The moment I caught sight of the glass doors of the familiar entranceway, however, I felt like turning around and going home. But I made myself walk on by the house, like an ordinary passerby. At the glass doors of the room facing the road, the curtains were drawn, and the lights were out; apparently my wife was not there. Like a suspect on the run, my heart pounding, I turned around and walked by again, checking the house to make sure there were no signs of a guest. Then I quickened my steps and went back the way I had come. Suddenly, out of the blue, it occurred to me that my wife had snatched a butcher knife and gone to see the other woman, and I seemed to see her expression as she held up the brand new carving knife and threatened to use it. How did I know she hadn't had one of her attacks and, not aware of what she was doing, run straight to the other woman's house—for all I knew tragedy had already struck. Why hadn't I thought of that in the first place? It wasn't as though I had been under the delusion that my superficial expression of moral reform, my new resolution alone, would make everything all right, but shouldn't I have realized before now that the matter would not be concluded without the spilling of blood? Despite the fact that no solution was even in sight, I had been going on convinced that if I just assumed an air of contrition and maintained a low posture for awhile, a secure, stable future would present itself to us. It had occurred to me that the other woman might put up a struggle—but I did my best to put the thought out of my mind.

While I was hesitating, hadn't the worst possible thing happened? Sooner or later I would have to confront the other woman and inform her of my change of heart, but I had hoped to postpone that eventuality until my wife's hysteria had subsided. From my wife's point of view, gradually unraveling our difficulties must seem an unbearably drawn-out process, and I could well imagine her suddenly wielding the butcher knife. I couldn't shake the image of my wife out back of the kitchen, crouching all alone in the alley between our house and the factory behind, a faraway look in her eye as with her left index finger and three fingers of her right hand she very quietly wrung a chicken's neck. Startled, at first the chicken had looked blankly around him, but as my wife twisted harder, he expired without a squawk.

Was it that going outside had opened my eyes so that I began to feel the imminence of the possibility? The scene flashed before my eyes: the knife in my wife's firm grip, she thrusts it horizontally into the enemy's belly; the cramped rented room fills with pools of blood, the woman lying there, already expired. My wife would make sure she had finished the job and would not leave her there to die. But I had absolutely no idea what she would do then. Would she rejoice, having killed her enemy face to face—or had the woman resisted; for all I knew, with the help of another gentleman caller who happened to be there, she had wounded my wife. My wife had informed me, without revealing any names, that the woman had not one but several other men. All I could do now was to prevent the stabbing before it happened. My ego having been obliterated without a trace, what finally came to sustain me was simply the idea that quite possibly I myself had been deceived; but there was no changing the fact that I could not stand before my wife and children and deny their view of me as the actual deceiver. Even granting that my wife had not really been deceived, that she on her own initiative had been secretly investigating her husband's movements, there was no hiding the fact I had not told her everything, that I had lied to her. The burden of guilt for the lies made me feel justified in my choice; with the ulterior motive of breaking off completely with the other woman, I began to feel I should take advantage of my mood and go there right now.

Back on the familiar course I had taken so many times in the past, each transfer strengthened the desire that now stirred again and pushed far into the past the ugliness of the last few days. The crowds of people, strangers going and coming, jostling each other, brushing shoulders and going their own ways, seemed about to pull me forcefully back into the excitement of my former life. A slight logical leap, and it began to seem that I was free, that there was no reason to restrict myself out of deference or consideration for anybody. I got off at a station in the outskirts of the city, and when the train had disappeared into the distance, its noise gradually diminishing, I heard the cries of numberless autumn insects in the weeds of the dark, deserted area. Picking out in the darkness the irrigation pond, the stream, the earthen bridge as I walked, I could not keep my heart from pounding faster and faster. I was afraid that my wife was lying in wait, about to jump out at me at any moment, or that I would reach the home of the woman with whom I had supposedly cut off all relations only to be met with a scene of indescribable violence. I was beginning to feel a certain anticipation: I was about to see the woman I had been infatuated with for so long, to hear her words, her voice. But even if at the very base of consciousness I clung to a secret

I could not easily abandon, my head was filled with an immediate fear that contained the germ of a horrible thought: if the sort of scene I had been imagining indeed awaited me, the present state of stagnation would at least be remedied. It contained, as well, the thought that I still ought to be able to prevent bloodshed, the feverish resolve that I must at all costs prevent it. Without considering what I would actually do if faced with such a crisis, I approached until—there was her house.

I had been preparing myself for the worst, to the point of asking myself if I was willing to take the blade in my own abdomen if necessary, but when I caught sight of the house where the woman rented a room, the strength left my body as the difficult implications of the conduct on which I had embarked and the memories I was supposed to have wiped from my mind enveloped me: the reassuring light shining through the window, and the familiar scent of the flowers in the garden. There seethed within me something that resisted, that told me I must not succumb to the power of such memories, and an abnormal excitement raged within me. But there was no place for it to go—no commotion, no sign of a disturbance. Suddenly bereft of the nervous energy with which I had launched out so vigorously, I stood there, wavering. What rushed in to fill the vacuum was the memory of my former self—spending night after night here for countless months; all sense of the legitimate reason for my having come seemed about to desert me. A voice ordering me to withdraw echoed in my ears like raging waves, but unable to restrain myself, I approached the entrance. My wife might be lurking amid the thick foliage of the garden, watching me. I had to use this opportunity to sever relations with the other woman, but no matter how urgent the reason, it was inconceivable that my wife would agree to my seeing her. If I didn't take this chance to declare my intentions to the other woman, the present unstable condition would simply continue. Not knowing what to do, I was left with a feeling of blankness, frozen, as if I had exhausted all my body heat. Apparently the woman was not alone; she seemed to be talking with someone in a low voice, and, strangely unsettled, I called out her name from where I stood near the entrance, as I had done so many times before. There was the familiar answer and the sound of things being put away as she straightened up the room before the sliding doors opened and she appeared. She was alive! No blood had been spilled. Why all of a sudden I should be assailed by a strong sense of disappointment, I did not know. Doing my best, however futilely, to resist the desire that welled up at the sight of the woman, I finally managed to speak:

"My wife wasn't here, by any chance, was she?"

"What are you talking about? Has something happened?"

Suddenly I started babbling incoherently:

"I won't be coming here any more. My wife might come and kill you."

"What is going on? First you stay away completely for days, then you show up and talk about your wife."

"My wife has left home—I can't come here any more. I don't have time to tell you the whole story, but my wife knew about you all along. My life is in total chaos. While I'm standing here talking to you, there's no telling what's happening at home. We're on the verge of total collapse. Maybe she's killed herself."

"Hold on a minute. Collapse, suicide, what is going on? At any rate you'd better come inside and tell me about it."

The woman, who had thrown over her shoulders an extremely becoming coat I had never seen before, spoke quite calmly, but I insisted that something terrible would happen if I went inside and refused to budge from the entrance hall. I thought the voice I had heard a minute ago must have been the radio—or was someone hiding in the closet? As my imagination carried me away, I began to think my wife was about to leap out and scare me. But, impatient to get away as soon as I possibly could, I launched into a recitation of cliches:

"We have been seeing each other for a long time—I just want you to know that I won't be coming from now on."

"I don't know what you are talking about. Didn't you get my letter? Why didn't you come?"

"In any case . . ." In order to keep from falling under her spell, I hurriedly repeated my lines. "I cannot come any more. My whole life is on the brink of collapse. I won't come again."

Whereupon the woman interrupted, "You keep saying that, 'I won't come again.' Something's happened, hasn't it? Somebody must have been telling you stories. That's it, isn't it?" A shadow of gloom passed over her face as she said this. Strangely stirred, I said,

"No, this concerns my family. It has nothing to do with what I may or may not have heard. I have no idea what people say about me behind by back, and I don't much care. But I can't come here to see you any more." I was sounding a little stiff and formal, but I couldn't help myself.

"Wait a minute. Please tell me more about what's going on, at least. Come inside, for a minute anyway."

"I can't, I'm leaving. I won't come any more."

"Oh, I see, you don't have to tell me. You don't want me any more."

"It's not that at all."

"You still love me?"

"I love you."

My own words surprised me, and I couldn't hold back the tears. Then the woman took my hand and, weeping, said, "I love you too. Couldn't you come just once a month at least?"

"I can't."

"Then write me."

"I can't do that either."

"Can I write you?"

"It'd be better if you didn't."

During this rapidfire dialogue the woman's eyes moved back and forth in pursuit of mine, and after a pause in which she seemed to be sizing up the situation, she said,

"If there's anything I can do, just ask—I'll do anythng. I want to help you."

"Hurry. No time to lose," said a voice inside my head, and my whole body was anxious to leave. When I withdrew my hand from her grasp and declared my intention to leave, the woman said she would see me off. I said no, but she repeated that she would see me off. I refused again, but finally let her have her way. On the road back to the station, I still had the feeling that I was being watched; several times I conjured up the pain of the butcher knife plunged into my side. Having curtailed the usual order of events when I went to see the woman, all I could think of was I wanted to get away from her as fast as I could. The bitter taste that remained on my tongue was, in fact, the residue of my own selfishness, and though the other woman, and my wife, must have their egoism too, I could not point a finger at it. The woman again brought up the subject of writing letters, so I said,

"I can promise you this much. Every time I write a story, I'll send you a copy of the magazine it appears in." The woman was silent.

"Good-bye. Take care of yourself."

Briefly I held her hand, then set her free like a little boat leaving the shore for the high seas. I went up to the boarding platform of the nearly deserted station. In the shadows just beyond the circle of light from the bare electric lightbulb at the railroad crossing, the woman was standing, darkly. She had a cigarette in her hand, and every time she took a drag on it, the red tip swelled and I could just barely see the outlines of her face. On the platform I smoked a cigarette she had pressed on me at parting, and the woman's tiny glow looked like a firefly hovering, glowing in the darkness. This light, which went on and off at regular intervals, began to resemble the woman's will as she tried to think of a fitting punishment for the man who had beaten such a hasty retreat when the going got rough.

* * *

On the train on the way home, my mind was in a fever: though I had set out with such power and resolution, charged with a mission to prevent imminent disaster, the net result was that I had seen the woman. There my resolution to avoid deception had turned into something highly doubtful and insubstantial. There was no changing the fact that I had once more done the very thing that I was forbidden to do under any circumstances. I kept telling myself that I had made my intentions clear to the woman and put an end to the affair, but I began to be uncertain of the actual results: how explicit and definite had I been, and was there any proof that the woman had acquiesced? After the intoxication of adding one more to my many visits came a certain lassitude; the smell of tobacco clung to me, and I wished the train were not getting closer and closer to Koiwa Station. What had become of the unshakable conviction with which I had set out? Thinking impossible thoughts—if only I could go back to the point where I'd asked Ishikawa to mind the house and start all over again—I reached the house. Maya was in bed, and Ishikawa was teaching the alphabet to Shin'ichi, who would be starting first grade in April; my wife was not home. Though there was an immediate relief (I was safe for the moment), my anxiety then mounted all the more. I simply must not tell my wife that I had been to see the other woman, which meant that I was adding another secret to my past, just when she was determined to ferret out all my lies. I was still hiding a few things and quite willing, if possible, to let sleeping dogs lie—but I was not pleased with my own attitude.

Turning a weakened, unsightly face to Ishikawa, I asked him to spend the night, and when he agreed, I felt like kneeling before him in gratitude. No matter how many times I told myself that having made the woman understand the situation and conveyed to her my intentions, I had done what was fair and re-established a normal position with respect to my wife, I could not wipe away the stain. I resembled my father in that whenever I found myself at a disadvantage, my voice got hoarse, and though I didn't admire that side of my father, confronted with a similar situation I looked and acted exactly like him. Without consulting Ishikawa, I decided that he would sleep in my four-and-a-half-mat study, and I repeated my trip back and forth to the station exit. Presently, however, the rows of shops lining the main street by the station all closed, and people on the streets began to dwindle; it would not be long before the last train of the night passed through. I had absolutely no idea where my wife had gone, but when I thought that in days past my wife had waited for me as I was waiting now, I seemed to hear a voice saying "Vengeance, vengeance." Every time I returned, the front gate creaked damply, and Ishikawa raised his eyes from whatever he was reading so intently. Funny, I don't remember Ishikawa's wearing glasses, I thought. Unable to sit home and wait, I soon headed back to the station. When I was away from my wife, I thought of her as she had been, remembered her way of calling out to me with a bright smile, and I simply could not understand why she was now persisting in such dangerous, fruitless behavior. Couldn't she just call out "Let's not do this anymore," as one might end a game of hide-and-seek, seal off the past and thrust it aside?

When the last train had come and I realized my wife wasn't on it, I had no inkling where else she might be, and my strength left me. As I retraced my steps along the utterly deserted main street, various thoughts ran through my mind: How nice it would be if just the two of us could eat some Chinese noodles at the little noodle stand in the station plaza—I remembered, too, how my wife had said she had mistaken the howling of a dog for the sound of my weeping. It occurred to me that perhaps my wife had come home while I was out. Holding my breath, I approached the dark back street house and opened first the gate, then the glass doors in the entranceway, but there was no sign of my wife inside.

Ishikawa looked up from the book he had been reading in the back room. That was all. I had no idea what to do at this time of the night; it began to seem that I should wait for morning and reluctantly direct my steps toward the police station. In any case, being sure I couldn't sleep, I decided to send Ishikawa to bed —there was no point in keeping him up too. Just as I was getting out his bedding, he tiptoed up to me and said, "Your wife seems to have come home." I hadn't heard the door open or close.

Confused, I asked, "Where is she?"

With a characteristic expression, he pretended to think for a moment, then answered, "There's no question about it, it's your wife. I had the feeling for a while there was someone outside the hedge trying to peer into the house, but now she's passed by that window and gone around back. It's all right. I'm sure it's your wife."

"Can I ask you to come out with me?"

I was unsteady on my feet as I fumbled for my *geta*, but as carefully and quietly as I could I walked around back to the alley between our house and the factory: there, in the shed piled high with bags of coal, stood my wife in her best kimono. Without thinking, I grabbed her shoulders and tried to embrace her, babbling, "Miho. You're home, thank goodness. Thank goodness." Stiffening, her arms full of bundles, she elbowed me away. I could hear a little toy bell jingling in one of the packages.

"Don't touch me, get your dirty hands off me, you beast, you miserable bastard." Her eyes flashed with hatred. Recognizing her expression even in the dark, I began to shiver. Her words had an even stronger effect on me because I had been to see the other woman. Still, I could not fathom the drastic change that had occurred in my wife since she had so cheerfully seen me off that morning. She was in a state much more hopeless than that of ten days earlier, with the result that everything was getting worse instead of better. We stood there for a while face to face, both of us shivering.

"Anyway, let's go inside."

"No. Today, once and for all, I have made up my mind to leave you. I'm never coming home again."

"But why?"

"You have a lot of nerve asking a question like that. Ask your own con-science why. I've said all I have to say. I thought you'd really reformed, and I felt much better; I was practically a living corpse, but I was managing to hold on. But you, you're just a good talker. You promised you'd be home by two, but did you come by two? You haven't changed one bit. It's no different from when you were seeing *her*, is it? There is no way you can stop me."

Ishikawa, who had been standing over by the henhouse, approached hesi-tantly and said, "I think I'd better be going home."

"But it's so late. Please stay the night. You're welcome to use the bed in my study."

I wanted him to stay, thinking his presence might lighten my wife's cross-examination somewhat.

He refused, however. "No thanks. Don't worry about me. Now that your wife's home I'll just take off." So saying, he walked away, leaving behind only the sound of his *geta*. I had no recollection of having said I'd be home by two. Finally I explained lamely,

"After Q editorial office I stopped in at A's place and then came right home." There was no other way to defend myself. I tried to convince myself that sometimes, in order to avoid total disaster, I would have to feign insensitivity.

"Today of all days I was determined not to come home at all—I'm such a coward—I'm hopeless." As if my wife had recovered her senses, she started be-rating herself and suddenly burst into tears. "I'll never see my children again—

tomorrow morning please give them these toys. I kept seeing Shin'ichi's and Maya's faces, and I couldn't bring myself to walk out on them like that, without a word. Why did I have to go and have children? But none of that matters now. I've lost everything that means anything to me. Please. Let me go. This is for you, a bottle of scotch," she added, picking up a slim rectangular package that she had set down on the ground and handing it to me. "Get out of my way now. This time I've really made up my mind to leave."

"Where in the world are you going?"

"That I can't tell you."

"How can I let you go if I don't even know where you're going?"

"I don't want to see you ever again. Just the sight of you makes me ill. Let me go—stop it, you're hurting me!"

Immediately I loosened my inadvertent iron grip on my wife's arms. I had never seen her this way, her whole body so totally full of defiance. Until now no matter how furiously she might grill me, I had always been able to see that she was still strongly drawn to me and that she was resisting that impulse. But tonight she was entirely different. By the time I realized what was happening, it was too late to do anything about it. Until this morning, however slowly, our wounds had been healing gradually; now, in the events of merely half a day, the situation had worsened dramatically. Whenever I tried to deal with people, somehow or other I would be drawn into an awkward situation, complications would arise that exhausted me and drove me to despair. When my wife called me a miserable bastard, I would mentally assume the proportions of one. If my life had any value I was convinced it lay in restraining my wife so bent on committing suicide. Even if she was not amenable to reason, though I had to stand before her physically blocking her way, I began to think that the only way of justifying my own existence was to stop her. The futile determination that until then I had harbored in secret had collapsed utterly. But when the words "beast, miserable bastard" were flung at me, accepting them, I found surprising new strength. I picked up my wife and carried her inside. Suddenly, she was a different woman: she became submissive, and there was no trace of the fervid, seemingly immovable defiance of a moment earlier. What was I so worked up about? "You haven't the guts to kill yourself." I blushed with shame at the thought, but as I kept repeating these words under my breath, inexplicably I felt calmer.

* * *

We were awake all night. It was exactly as though that three-day ordeal had returned. Only now, the situation was more serious, seemingly hopeless. Over and over my wife would berate me.

"You said you'd be home by two but you broke your promise"; the only thing that kept her going was the hope that her husband would never again deceive her. "No matter how trivial," she said, "if you break a single promise, how do you expect me to forgive your many deceptions in the past? I was not worried in the slightest until two o'clock. But as soon as the clock struck two I was so overwhelmed with suspicion I couldn't sit still a moment longer. It's a perfectly reasonable reaction isn't it? Considering that for ten years you were deceiving me. I wonder if you really went to the Q magazine office."

"I did."

"What were you doing all that time at Q magazine?"

"After I left there I stopped by at A's house, as I always do, you know."

"I checked there," my wife's speech became animated.

"They told you I'd been there, didn't they?"

"They said you'd just left. There was one guy—I didn't like the way he looked at me. Who is he? I suppose he's another one of your disgusting, dishonest friends. Then where did you go?"

"I came directly home and you weren't here."

"Really? I think you went to see *her*—didn't you?"

"No, I came right home."

"I can't believe a single thing you say. You talk sweetly, but who knows what you're doing behind my back."

"What good would it do me to go on hiding things at this point?"

"Then I wonder why, when I question you, it always comes out that you have been lying to me?"

"There are so many things sometimes I don't remember them all, sometimes something doesn't occur to me until later. But fundamentally I am telling the truth. If I were still lying to you I wouldn't be here."

"I'm sure you wish you weren't. You're a strange man. Tonight for instance, why did you try so hard to stop me? Why don't you leave me alone and do what you want to do? You can butter me up all you like; it won't wipe out what you have done."

"I'm not trying to hide what I've done."

"I should hope not. It won't do you any good, since I know all about everything anyway. I'll bet you didn't know that woman was going around advertising
your relationship."

"No, I didn't know."

"You really are something. How dumb can you get? She's even telling
people you're impotent. She tells your friends that you never bring her anything
but a package of cigarettes, and they all laugh at you, you know."

Pause.

"I envy her, though. I'd be happy to get a package of cigarettes. I wonder
if I've *ever* gotten a present from you."

Pause.

"What else did you give that woman? I want you to list every single thing."

"I never took her anything special."

"There you go again. That's another lie. All right I'll tell *you*. Then I
suppose you'll say you'd forgotten. I've done a thorough investigation, even of
her. I paid that man seventy thousand yen to investigate. Now I wish I hadn't
burned his report. I suppose you won't believe me, but she's a formidable woman.
I'm sure you thought of her as an innocent twenty-year-old. Don't you wonder how
I managed to come up with seventy thousand yen? Do you want to know? Take a
look in my dresser. Not a single one of my kimonos left. But I haven't touched a
thing that belongs to you, not so much as an undershirt. Do you know why I did
something so extreme? All for you—all for you. I thought I'd investigate that
woman's background, and if she seemed all right, I was going to leave quietly. But
after I investigated, I changed my mind. If I'd left you in her hands, she'd have
killed you. You think I'm lying?"

"No, I'm sure you're right."

"After all, I'm not a liar like you. She's quite a woman, that one. 'That
woman'—every time I say 'that woman' you make a face. Forgive me for referring
so rudely to your precious girlfriend. But she doesn't deserve any better. I could
see how it would all end—you wishing you'd never gotten involved with her, sooner
or later driven to suicide. Come on, think: what did you give her besides
cigarettes?"

"I took her some chocolate."

"How many times?"

"How do you expect me to remember every single time?"

"If it's inconvenient to remember, you just forget, don't you? You're very clever at that sort of thing. You went to Nakamuraya, didn't you? What did you buy there?"

"Oh. That's right, ice cream."

"For whom?"

"I took it to her place, and we ate it together."

"That's the life. I wish you'd treat me the way you treated her, just exactly down to the last detail as you did then. Isn't ice cream a present? You never took her anything special—how can you say such a thing? Do you know how much you were giving me a month for household expenses?"

"I think it was fifteen thousand yen."

"Do you think a family of four can live on that?"

"You never complained."

"Oh, so if I don't complain you assume it's enough? Then on top of that you kept telling me to give you five hundred yen, or a thousand yen. What did you do with that money, I wonder. How much were you giving her a month?"

"I didn't give her money."

"That's another lie. You withdrew ten thousand yen from our savings account, didn't you? I saw the passbook. But I never saw a red cent of that money. What did you do with it?"

Pause.

"Out with it. I hate liars. You swore you wouldn't lie. Actually, I know perfectly well what you spent it on. Isn't it amazing how much I know? But I have to hear it from your own lips."

Pause.

"If you're determined to go on hiding it, I'll tell you myself. You used it to pay the woman's hospital bill, right? You put her in Shibuya Women's Hospital. That's right, isn't it?"

Pause.

"Right, or wrong? Which is it?"

"It's true."

"Damn you." Suddenly she slapped my face. I had decided I would have to sit there and take whatever she did to me, but instantaneously my hand slapped her back.

"You hit me. You actually had the nerve to hit me. Toshio hit me. Toshio hit me."

My wife glared up at me wtih blood in her eyes, then lunged at me. My automatic reaction was to get up and run to the front door. The lights were still on in the house next door, on the side facing the kitchen and the tiny room next to it. The neighbors were probably up listening to us. Maybe they were annoyed at us for keeping them awake with our interminable arguing. But I could hardly stop now. I hadn't particularly intended to leave, but finding myself in the doorway, I thought I might as well run down to the railroad tracks. My whole body filled to overflowing with horror and rage, I stepped barefoot on the cement floor in the entranceway, groping for some kind of footwear. My wife, who had been looking on with indifference, as if to push me away, suddenly shouted, "Get up Shin'ichi. Get up Maya. Your father's leaving us. Get up, hurry." She came and clung to me. "Over my dead body, you'll leave. I'd run away myself before I'd let you leave," and she grappled with me to keep me from unlocking the door.

The children, startled from sleep by their mother's shouting, took one look at their parents struggling in the entranceway, hair flying, clothing torn, and burst into tears. Seeing the terrified look in their eyes and hearing them cry as they had never cried before, I realized what horrible demons of the night we must seem to them, and I came to my senses. I had been using hysteria to escape from my wife's grilling.

The strength left me. "I've had enough. I won't run away or hide; just please stop it."

If I had chosen to do so, I could probably have flattened my wife on the spot. Why had I simply struggled with her, showing just enough strength to match hers? As we grappled, the smell of my wife's body came to me, and I couldn't help feeling that she had become gentle: holding on to my limp arms, she kept trembling, ever so slightly.

"Don't cry, Maya, Shin'ichi. Daddy's not going anywhere," I said, trying to calm my breathing.

What a relief it would be if this were really the end. It often seemed as though the violence of our passionate outbursts would simply burn up all the trouble between us, but when the attack had passed and we had cooled down, there were just as many unsolved problems as before, and I still did not know what to do.

"On top of everything else you try to push the children off on me and run away. I will not let you do it," said my wife, gasping for breath.

"From now on you raise the children. I've been doing it practically single handed all these years. You never even held them when they were babies. Every time they cried you looked so annoyed—do you know how careful I was not to displease you? And I took such good care of you—you don't know what good care I took of you." Her arms still around me as one would hug a pillar, she suddenly slipped as if she were shinnying down a pole and sat on the floor.

"These arms and legs wouldn't be so healthy if it hadn't been for me."

Half crying, my wife spoke deliberately, as if she were rehearsing lines from a play. Seated on the concrete floor, she rubbed her husband's feet then pressed her cheek to them and wept on and on—suddenly, I was reminded of the wartime. I was stationed on a naval base near her home town and would go to see her late at night; she was then still plump and girlish. She would touch my uniform, running her fingers over its insignia in the dark, then stooping to rub my boots. The memory made the scent of *hamayū* flowers come wafting over us, here in our tile-roofed house in the heart of Tokyo. Somehow, in the midst of the confusion after Japan's defeat in the war, one thing led to another until eventually my wife and I had become physically estranged. Now, looking at her frail little body as she crouched sobbing at my feet, I could not help seeing in her my own irreplaceable past.

"Miho. I don't want you to cry. I won't try to leave any more. I'm sorry. I was wrong. If you and I and the children don't learn to live happily together, I don't know what I'll do. Who'll take care of us? Let's stop this stupid fighting. Just please do this one thing for me, please. You call me a liar, but the trouble is everything I have done in the past has been wrong. Call me a beast, there is nothing I can say. I don't deny what I've done in the past, I couldn't bear to choose one over the other, and I hated having to pretend I was in the right. But now I've wakened from that directionless nightmare. Now I want you to forget all about the past. I'm not trying to play the good boy. No matter how deep you go into a past based on lies, all you'll come up with is more stale lies. From now on, I won't ever lie to you, even about the most trivial matters. So please—I'm asking you to stop digging up the past and concentrate on the future. Otherwise you get upset, and I lose my balance completely. Let's make an agreement. I've made you suffer for ten years. Now I will serve you for ten years. You can do anything you want to, anything. But please, I'm begging you to stop asking questions about the past. The two of us are alone together in a tiny boat. I may be a terrible skipper, but if you start panicking and rocking the boat, it'll turn over and we'll both be drowned. What are you dissatisfied about now? Just tell me, and I'll do anything to correct it, or if there is anything you want me to stop doing, just tell me and I will."

My wife clung to me in silence. I put my arms around her and led her back into the room. The children climbed back into their beds; they watched their parents for a while but soon fell asleep. The air stirred with the signs of daybreak, and as we began to feel against our feverish foreheads the cool breeze of dawn, we heard first the clinking of milk bottles outside, the screech of bicycle brakes, then two or three times the opening and closing of milk cases; gradually the noise receded into the distance until finally we could not hear it at all. These were the first signs of the daily activities of the townspeople, but in our list-lessness after the incident, we were plunged into introspective musing. Finally, we dropped off into a deep sleep. My wife clung to me, and I, wary of my own body so sensitive that it reacted to the slightest change, could not disentangle myself. Totally exhausted, next to her husband's body stiff with tension, my wife fell asleep, a tremor running through her arms and legs. I could hear her regular breathing, then I, too, felt relief. With my sleeping wife beside me, separated from me almost as if by a temporary death, I felt at last that I had regained some freedom of action, however fleeting. Trying to embrace that freedom, chasing it, presently I, too, drifted off to sleep.

*   *   *

What had led me to awaken I did not know, but the reality from which I had been cut off until just a moment before now formed a continuum from the instant of my awakening to the reality that existed before I went to sleep. Remembering what I had been doing when I entrusted that section of reality to sleep was painful. But to one who has awakened, reality comes back to life completely unabridged. I would have liked to bury everything that had happened until yester-day, but our problems were not about to come to an end of their own accord, nor could I hope to resolve them immediately. For some reason I had not been pressed for the details of what had occurred when I went out to look for my wife, but without a doubt those details would now put further restrictions on my life.

From the following day, a subtle, indefinable change was born in my wife. I could not open my eyes in the morning without first calculating her mood; an excruciating life now began for me in which, from the very boundary between sleeping and waking, never relaxing my guard for a single moment, I had to wear full armor. Never was I allowed the leisure of climbing to a high place and sur-veying the path I had just walked, then looking to check out the road ahead. The only method granted me was to deal with the days from moment to moment as situations developed and changed.

* * *

And so began a life whose continuity I could not perceive. Ishikawa stopped by on two or three occasions, and I took Shin'ichi to call on him. But no sooner had we gotten there than I began to feel preoccupied, and we left almost immediately. Hurrying back along the sidewalk in front of the station, I ran into my wife. She looked troubled and was wearing an old kimono that had been put away at the bottom of a drawer since we were married. After that, I stopped leaving her at home to go visit Ishikawa. We had to do something, my wife and I both, but we did not feel like doing a thing.

"Can we just go on like this? Shouldn't we be doing something?" said my wife with a shiver after many chilly days had passed. Without a request from my editors, it was difficult to find the impetus to write a story, and at the moment, even if I were to accept an assignment and agree on a deadline, it was doubtful whether I could get down to work. In order to write, I had to stick my head once more into tangles of personal relations with society and my friends in the immediate past, and when I was emotionally in an unsettled state, struggling to escape from memories of the past, it was painful even to think about my fiction. Assuming I did manage to write something, it was clear that every word of that concrete verbal expression would produce a violent reaction in my wife. Fear would restrict my movement, tie my hands. But now that I was barely eking out a living by my writing, I had no idea where else I might turn for work if I abandoned that.

My wife's restlessness seemed to increase daily.

"Daddy, see how well I am? Aren't you pleased? Today I feel just fine. I'm just going to go on getting gradually better and better. I'll be the old Miho again, you'll see."

No sooner had she said this than she suddenly took the rice she had been washing and threw it all around the room. When, startled by the ominous sound, I went into the kitchen, my wife glared at me fiercely. Feeling my spine freeze, I had to ask what I knew to be a useless question:

"What's the matter?'

"Nothing's the matter."

"Then what are you doing throwing around the rice you've just finished washing?"

"The *Unima* is coming. The *Unima* makes me remember unpleasant things. The *Unima* tells me things. The *Unima* is coming! The *Unima* is coming!"

Then she stooped and started to pick up the rice she had spilled. There was nothing I could do but withdraw quietly to my study and sit at my desk; the splattered ink over the desk top and the wall was still there, a graphic reminder. Just as I had feared, in a few minutes I recognized my wife's footsteps tiptoing up:

"There's one little thing that has been bothering me. Can I ask you just one thing?" she says.

"The trouble is, no matter how I answer you won't be satisfied. We'll get into the same mess all over again. What's done is done. I wish you would forget it," I answered very cautiously.

"I just want to clear up one thing. I won't ask anything else."

"As soon as one problem gets cleared up you think of something else."

"Oh. I see. Then I won't ask. Why are you so determined to hide things from me, do you suppose? You hate me, that's why, right? You told *her* everything. I understand. I will never ask you another question."

"OK, OK. Go ahead and ask."

"How many pictures did you take with her?"

"I can't really say exactly how many, out of the blue like that. I thought I handed them all over to you—though I have no way of knowing what you did with them."

"Not those. The *rest* of them. There are more, aren't there?"

"I think that's all of them."

"There should be more—think harder. Take your time—just so long as you remember every last one."

Pause.

I realized I had once again fallen prey to the very trials I had subjected myself to I don't know how many times before. It was essential that I avoid such situations, and yet somehow I kept succumbing. Even when I meant to tell my wife the truth, I always wound up leaving some things out. It was strange—when what initially passed unnoticed surfaced later, how hard it was to add the missing details and put everything out in the open. I should just state the facts, but I somehow always pretended ignorance or tried to cover up. There were, in fact, four or five photographs that I had kept hidden from my wife. Perhaps I had thought of them as material for my writing—I no longer remembered. Now, I wished I could erase anything and everything that might start a quarrel, but I was under a spell that prevented me from being able to alter the slightest detail of the present situation. My wife's tenacity and her abnormal sensitivity meant that I had to assume that she had positive knowledge of every single fact surrounding her husband. If I changed the position of some little thing I had been hiding, she took it as a strategy to keep her from discovering something else, which simply made matters worse. To defend myself was utterly impossible. The only approach was to confess completely, but instead, I tried to obfuscate, as usual.

"I think I gave you all of them. Why would I hide them when you'd give me such a hard time if you found one? How could I hope to keep anything hidden from your sharp eyes?" But my wife, who was driving her husband into a corner for a purpose, was as calm and unhurried as a scholar in singleminded pursuit of knowledge. Her cheeks paled, but her every word was spoken with care; like a veteran fisherman, she reassured me as she drove me into the area of danger. When I was totally exhausted, I awkwardly disclosed to my wife, as though I had suddenly remembered, the hiding place of some pictures there had basically been no need to go to such lengths to hide in the first place. My wife, once again, assumed the stance of the relentless inquisitor.

"Aren't you secretly writing to her?"

Startled by her question, I hastened to answer, "No I haven't written to her."

"I'm glad to hear it."

With that my wife returned to the kitchen, and I could hear her washing the dirty laundry that had been accumulating. Whenever she did laundry, she plugged the drain in the sink and turned on the faucet so that the water from the tap sounded like a little waterfall. In the past this had always seemed like the sound of a stable family life, but now it was a precarious sound that might stop at any moment and signal the onset of another attack in my transfigured wife.

Presently, mixed with the sound of the running water, I heard my wife singing, and just as I began to think she must be in a good mood, I realized there was something odd about the words to the song that reached my ears.

> So what the hell
> I'll just drink sake,
> get drunk and
> forget my cares

It was true that I hadn't written, but I had slipped out—telling my wife I was going to the bookstore—and bought the latest issue of P magazine that had just appeared on the stands two or three days ago, carrying my latest short story. I had wrapped it at the post office and sent it to the woman. I wanted to think of this gesture as a signal to her not to expose our past, but whether she would take it as such was questionable. If I defended myself on the grounds that though I had sent the magazine, in fact I had not written any letters, I couldn't expect my wife to understand. It was terrifying the way what had seemed a good idea when I was with the woman turned afterwards into unavoidable commitment. "Just don't lie to me," my wife was saying over and over.

> Though I gave my very life to him
> The love he gave me was a lie.

Every line my wife sang contained a needle of spite, and the popular melody that cloaked the words made my breast boil.

> Like the flower of the black lily
> How pitiful and lonely the sight
> Because of a heartless man . . .

I was on the verge of screaming "All right, all right. Enough. I get the point," but I was afraid of bringing on an attack. "When Tama the cat died, Daddy wasn't around. Where do you suppose you were? When M brought her American friend to the house, where were you I wonder." My surroundings were full of eyes peering into my eyes, ready to pass judgment, piercing me, biting into me.

"Daddy never gets mad at Mommy, but Mommy's always mad at Daddy. Maybe I won't love my Daddy any more," said Maya, looking straight at her father. The image of our son Shin'ichi getting rough with his neighborhood playmates hovered and refused to leave my mind.

I remembered how suddenly Shin'ichi had let out a yell, grabbed a stone, and waved it threateningly. The other children, all older than he, beat a hasty retreat, and after chasing them into an alley, Shin'ichi threw his rock against a wall and came home deflated, all alone. And I remembered Shin'ichi's precocious remark, "When my parents have their domestic *exigencies*, I get so worried that Mommy's going to run away that I lose fights with the kids."

                                    * * *

We had run out of money to live on, but for the present there was nothing I could do but go to collect payment for the short story that had recently appeared in P magazine. I didn't have even the roundtrip train fare, so my wife borrowed sixty yen from the Aokis next door. Just in case they wouldn't pay me today, I was carrying two books that I might be able to sell for a high price. I set out with the whole family; the children were wearing their best clothes: used American overcoats that my wife had patched, and playsuits.

Without thinking, I took the shortest route to the P Magazine office, but when we got off at Suidōbashi Station, my wife's step began to lag, and she dropped her handbag. When I picked it up and tried to give it back to her, her fingers wouldn't grasp it firmly. Each of us held one child by the hand, but my wife wasn't paying attention. When I asked her what the matter was, she didn't answer but just stood there at a distance staring at her husband, her face contorted, piercing darts in her eyes. I had not noticed the receding figure of her husband, on his way home from teaching night school, sitting on the train platform, anxiously waiting: with gleaming eyes he watched the train coming in, and when he finally saw the woman, his face broke into a smile, and he walked protectively beside her down to the exit. I had paid no particular attention to the agitating effect this imaginary scene was having on my wife. But I hated having to drag the three of them through such a place and wanted to get out of there as soon as possible. I was convinced that my wife was being intentionally perverse, and I could not conceal my irritation. But when we had left the station and were standing by an overpass waiting for the streetcar, lifting my face to broad daylight, I felt somehow ashamed. I thought, here stands a man who is trying to decide how to dispose of his past misdeeds, and a white film of sand seemed to coat my tongue, and any idea that might allow me to stand alone turned its back and went away. The newspaper headline "Family Suicide" came to my mind and, like an indelible stain on my retina, assumed the contours of a face I saw all the time. As I stood with the children on the crowded streetcar, my back began to ache, and my mood grew ruthless. Watching me disapprovingly out of the corner of his eye, Shin'ichi picked up the handbag his mother kept dropping and tried to give it to her, but her grasp was completely limp. I watched, but I simply could not bring myself to reach out and help.

P magazine was in a large concrete building. The receptionist called my editor for me and directed me to the waiting room. I led my wife and children down a linoleum floored corridor to the elevator, saddened to see that they showed no simple childish pleasure at the prospect of riding it. Fortunately, the editor paid me immediately. I headed for Ikebukuro to have the check cashed at the specified bank.

"I want money. If only I had money I could take this worn out body of mine and get it fixed," my wife had said with a sigh. When I received a stack of thousand-yen bills from the teller—though it was only enough to keep us going for a little while—relief made me forget my dangerous mood earlier at Suidōbashi.

Virtually everything about our life from now on would be a new experience for me; my task at the moment was to go along patiently with my wife's shopping. It was clear that if I showed the slightest sign of annoyance, she would launch out on another rehearsal of my heartless conduct in the past. I took my wife and the children to lunch in a department store restaurant and let them order what they liked; I walked around patiently selecting what my wife had wanted for so long, the lampshade and the paper to cover sliding doors. But my family was not yet comfortable with the new role of the reformed husband. Despite herself, my wife pictured the other woman walking next to me and wandered dangerously on the dark edge of an attack.

Afterwards, we took the train again, got off, walked up one flight of stairs and down another to catch the next train, which we rode for a while longer, then returned home exhausted. I noticed the fence in front of our house, the bamboo thoroughly rotten, on the verge of collapse, exposing its seedy self so like conditions inside the house. And when my wife said, "It's so old it's beyond repair—we had better replace it with a board fence," I could only agree; even if it meant spending more than half the money I had received today, I could hardly suggest that we put it off to another time. If my past extravagances were to come to light, I would be utterly defenseless, and besides, she had ceased to show concern over the family budget, as if determined to flee as far as possible from her former thriftiness. She neglected cooking meals, and especially when we had all been out for the day, the children and I had to wait with bated breath while she got dinner ready, hoping against hope that the Unima would not come to attack her. But it invariably did come. Even if she was in a good mood, there was no telling when she might let out a horrifying shout and glower at her husband, dark shadows under her eyes.   226524

"Did you take *her* to Ikebukuro?" So began the cross-examination; one suspicion gave rise to another, and a seemingly interminable game ensued. Nothing more was done about dinner.

"Domestic *exigencies*, domestic *exigencies*," said Shin'ichi with a knowing look to Maya; then showing the whites of his eyes he yelled out frantically, "Stop it!" but there was no way of stopping us now. My wife asked every question that occurred to her, pressing me for detail after detail, until finally she remarked,

"Now that I know how little you love me, I can only think that I have lost my love for you. Please let me die."

"Let me die, let me die. You keep threatening me with that," the words slipped out.

"You think it's just a threat?" She got up, a new gleam in her eye, whereupon Shin'ichi threw his arms around his mother's waist and screamed,

"Don't do it! I've got you and I won't let you go."

Unable to restrain myself any longer I shrieked, "If you're going to die, I'll die before you," and headed for the front door. This time it was my wife and Shin'ichi who grabbed hold of me and refused to let go. During the struggle that ensued my wife's expression softened, and she began to look pitiful. I realized that she wanted to end the bout there and then, but by this time, I was so agitated myself that I couldn't respond immediately.

"Please, please don't run away. It's because I'm afraid of that that I think up all those dreadful things."

Somehow our positions had been reversed. When I retained my sullen expression, my wife yawned conspicuously. At this Shin'ichi and Maya jumped around in a frenzy of delight,

"Mommy yawned. It's over, it's over, domestic *exigencies* are over."

Despite myself, I smiled, and when I looked at my wife, I saw another face smiling back at me. We hugged each other and patted each other's back.

"Thank goodness." No sooner had I said this than the tears welled up. "Don't cry, don't cry," my wife said, her own eyes filling with tears. Then we sat down to the dinner that was so long overdue. The temporary calm was sweet as a drop of water to a thirsty man.

"When Daddy tries to run away, Mommy and I are too strong for him," remarked Shin'ichi, "and when Mommy tries to run away, Daddy and I are too strong"; my wife and I smiled at each other again. After the quarrel we were physically tired; my wife went right to sleep, and when I heard her even breathing, my feeling of relief grew and I drifted off to sleep.

"I'm sorry about last night. Forgive me. I'll be a good girl now," my wife said when she awoke next morning, her expression still cheerful. My eyes, now so susceptible, immediately filled with tears.

"I forgive you."

Whereupon Shin'ichi, who was already awake, piped up, "That wasn't a fight yesterday. It was a discussion, right Mommy? You had domestic *exigencies*, right?"

We all got up together. While my wife was fixing breakfast, it was my job to fold the bedding and straighten up the room. I had to abandon all thought of an independent schedule apart from the daily activities of the family, for fear of arousing memories of my former lifestyle. Instead of centering our family life around the husband's job, we focused on my wife and children; my job was to act simply as support for them. This was the policy we had adopted among us. Since the cat died, the mice had been running rampant. So, while putting the bedding away, I took a good look at the hole in the closet ceiling and discovered stains on the extra bedding and that reserved for guests. I called my wife, and we took out every quilt. They were chewed full of holes and covered with traces of urine. My wife said she had inspected them and had begun a year ago resewing them and replacing their covers so that she could die at any time with a clear conscience. She had finally just finished. Her memories seemed about to drift back again, and her expression began to darken.

"We'd better get another cat," I suggested hopefully, adding, "Instead of putting them away for some hypothetical future guest, why don't we just use the good ones ourselves?" trying to divert my wife's attention. I could almost reach out and touch that hard-working wife always busy with the laundry and mending the bedding, the wife who had remarked, "Just think how much more work I'd get done if I didn't have to sleep at night."

But now my wife immediately looked suspicious: "You're not secretly writing to her, are you?"

Once the inquisition had begun, no matter how I answered, I would not be released until the entire process had run its course. I couldn't help feeling that her barrages were becoming gradually more frequent. According to my wife, she was in unbearable pain herself at such times, but it was frightening how I lost my presence of mind and became as agitated as she. As soon as she fixed me with her obstinate glare and began grilling me about the past, I was overcome by a strange rigidity of my own, and instead of trying to soothe her anxieties, my first incli- nation was to run away from home or scream at the top of my lungs. As the days went by, the number of things I was forbidden to do increased. Don't blow smoke rings. Don't turn on the radio. Eventually, not only blowing smoke rings but smoking itself became a curse. Unless I succeeded in creating a new role for myself, there was little hope that I would be able to rebuild my life.

*   *   *

I could not go on indefinitely cancelling my night school classes, so, on the next evening I was scheduled to teach, we had an early dinner, and all four of us, wearing our only respectable street clothes, boarded the train. I was especially careful to stay away from women over forty, but my wife, as if drawn to them, invariably tried to go in their direction. She called my attention to one in particular:

"Did you notice her? Look closely."

"Let's go over there," I suggested, trying to move away, but she kept at me:

"Come on, just look at her. The spitting image. Look at her eyes and her mouth. I never saw such a strong resemblance." Noticing that my head was stiffly turned away, she said: "Look. Look, will you?" her tone of voice changing. Reluctantly, I looked in that direction: Come to think of it, there was a slight resemblance, but it seemed to me she was making a fuss over nothing.

"I don't really see the resemblance," I answered lamely, feeling the strength leave my body.

"I suppose you mean *she's* much prettier—Sorry. How could I compare your precious darling to an unattractive woman like that?"

Pause.

"They still look alike to me." My wife's lips were trembling. Inevitably, whenever we went out, half the people we saw were women; most of the time I'd have preferred not to see any women at all, and with my wife at my side I felt like wearing blinders. The feminine qualities every woman radiated bore right through me in my oversensitive state, leaving me with an unpleasant sensation, as if I'd had an attack of food poisoning. Once, watching a train coming in at the opposite platform, my wife cried out,

"I saw her. There she *is*. There she *is*. I saw *her*," and began running toward the stairway. I had to chase her and grab her, to soothe her agitation, but at this point my wife could only see me as an ally of the other woman; I simply fanned the flames of her hysteria. The children clung in apparent desperation to their mother with whom they could no longer communicate, their faces resigned in the knowledge that no one would come to their rescue. If they just stood still and waited out the unpleasantness, eventually their mother would yawn and the domestic *exigencies* would be over: it was the children who understood this; I had no patience.

As a last resort, I could leave my wife and children at Ujikka's while I taught my classes, but I would have to avoid the most direct route there, which would take us through Suidōbashi. Going from Akihabara via Ueno and getting off at Tabata would arouse few memories of the past, but it was a long way from Tabata Station to Ujikka's house. Walking behind the young children along a twilight road lined with stone walls that completely blocked the view, I considered the fate of the two children who could not relax and enjoy themselves because of their troubled family. As I watched the backs of these children who, despite everything, were holding on with all their might and main, my mood was dismal. Our road took us to a busy intersection where the streetcar ran and all sorts of stores were lined up vying for shoppers' business, but I could buy nothing for my family. So that their parents would not catch up with them, Shin'ichi dragged Maya roughly by the hand and broke into a trot, but Maya soon tired and began to be unsteady on her feet, whereupon Shin'ichi got annoyed and peevish:

"Come on, Kitten. Walk faster."

Maya started to cry, so I let her ride on my back. Across the intersection the road went uphill. As I gazed at the Jidō temple halfway up the hill, smoke from the incense stick offerings rising unceasingly, there flashed before my eyes a vision of the same neighborhood as I had never seen it, back in the days when it was heavily wooded and there were few passersby—a dark, deserted, uphill road. My wife seemed to have recovered her spirits.

"Daddy, for the children's sake let's do our best to make it, shall we? Looking at Shin'ichi's little back somehow makes me feel stronger."

"Mustn't let Daddy get tired," she said, and she tried to shift Maya to her own back.

"I'm OK, I'm OK," I said, but she wouldn't listen.

*   *   *

As it happened, the day I taught was the day my wife's aunt taught flower arrangement, so we could use the excuse that my wife wanted to join the class. Whenever she met people outside the immediate family, the clouds lifted from her countenance. Concern for her husband and children restored her former state of mind so quickly and dramatically as to be disorienting. Perhaps because they understood this, when someone other than the four of us entered our group, the children seemed to come back to life, and at such times, they paid no attention to their parents' reprimands. I was finally able to relax, temporarily at least, and set out for the night school not far from Ujikka's house.

It was my job to teach "World History" and "Social Studies" to one class of freshmen and one class of seniors, but as I walked through the male and female students gathered by the school store and mounted the stairs to the classroom, it seemed a staggering burden to have to throw aside my fatigue and begin teaching a class. My chest was hollow, and I found it harder than before to tolerate the thought of garnering my uncertain knowledge and imparting it to others. Informed by the program director that the student body had issued a complaint because I had cancelled so many lectures, I feared I would not be able to hold my head up in class. The students had their own bosses and jobs during the day. Just looking at them, I could not distinguish them from ordinary high school students. Among them, however, were policemen and nurses, as every now and then I was startled to realize. Even though I stood at the lectern, the students were still immersed in their own conversations; they would not settle down until I signaled for class to begin. With the rollbook before me, for a while I stood there feeling ineffectual and out of place, listening absently to the students' conversations. When, finally suppressing the impulse to turn around and walk out, I began calling the students names one by one, somehow or other I felt more comfortable with my role. But then I pictured myself meeting the woman at Suidōbashi after class and submitting, with a grimace, to my wife's cross-examination. The strength suddenly left me, I felt dissociated from reality, and I lost track of what I was saying. I'd taught senior World History three or four times before, so I had developed a comfortable lecture style stringing together individual episodes, and the students listened quietly. In the Social Studies class, however, I exposed my half baked knowledge in an uninspired delivery, so I began to lose the students. Remembering they were freshmen, I tried to put things simply, but my explanations got even more disorganized until I sensed hostility from the students. When I began to suspect that it was this class that had lodged the complaint against me, my manner stiffened. Hoping to lessen the tension, I tried making sarcastic remarks of the sort that elicited conspiratorial laughter from my class of seniors; no one laughed, and I was met with faces full of antipathy. In the end, I walked out of the class without being able to fill the period and retired to the teachers' room. The teachers there, who happened to have no classes this hour, were busy at their own various tasks and paid no particular attention to me; still, I could not shake the feeling that they were all watching me. Telling myself that I was only part-time and under the pressures of a crisis situation, I turned my name plate to "out" and left.

Cutting across the dark schoolyard, I went out the front gate and, instead of taking the sidewalk, crossed the street. Suddenly, my wife came up to me out of nowhere and asked in a voice that betrayed suppressed agitation, "Where are you going?"

"Oh, so you came to meet me? What do you mean, Where am I going—I was about to go home."

"But you were heading in the opposite direction. Besides, class shouldn't be over yet."

"I was tired today, so I decided to end a little early." I started to defend myself, but I soon realized it was useless, and I no longer felt like speaking at all. In her black coat with Mandarin collar, she looked like a bat.

"You went behind my back and arranged to meet her, didn't you? A minute ago a woman who looked like her went by," she said. The remark sounded ominous.

"I was going to cross the street first. All right. Let's agree on the route from now on. You walk straight down the street in front of Ujikka's house, then when you get to the streetcar tracks, walk on the lefthand side of that street, because I'll cross the street right in front of the school. That way, if you come to meet me, we won't miss each other along the way," I said.

She nodded her assent, and apparently an unrelated matter immediately came to mind:

"Shin'ichi and Maya's shoes are coming open in front—it's hard for them to walk, the poor things." We stopped at a shoestore and bought a pair for Shin'ichi, whose shoes were in much worse shape than Maya's. Then we went back to Ujikka's house, where we found the children carrying on as if it were a holiday. I realized that taking care of them must be a bother for my wife's aunt, but I could think of no alternative. She urged us to sit down and have a cup of tea before we left, but, saying it was already late, I put the children back into the coats that had been so hard to get off. As I squatted in the entranceway to put their shoes on for them, my wife said, "Me too," so I put her shoes on for her as well. Then she said, "Toshio, I'm a little tired tonight. Call a taxi, will you?" so I went out into the wide street and hailed a taxi.

"Miho, I got one, I got one," I told her, and the children were all excited about their first ride in an automobile. My wife's aunt, who had come out to see us off, listened with disapproval to my wife asking to have her shoes put on for her and addressing her husband in such disrespectful terms.

"How long have you been calling your husband by his first name like that, I wonder?" she said with a suspicious look on her face. "You're really luckier than you deserve, to have such a gentle, understanding husband." My wife seemed quite satisfied at these remarks; remembering her complaint, "When you go out with *her* you take a taxi, but you always make us walk," I looked at the floor.

*   *   *

The train to Akihabara, where we had to transfer, was not crowded, and we found seats easily. The reflection of the family of four in the window opposite us looked like any family coming home tired after a holiday outing, but after we transferred, we were just barely able to stand up, squeezed and jostled by other passengers. This train had come through Suidōbashi; there was already a shadow on my wife's brow. When I finally managed to find a seat for her and get her seated, Maya leaned against her mother and fell asleep.

Tired and thinking of nothing in particular, I was suddenly conscious of a burning gaze. Looking up apprehensively, I found that my wife was staring right into me. Her eyes showed that an attack was already underway. What we needed was a place to relax, somewhere we could sleep peacefully, yet what awaited us was our cramped little house, all locked up and left to the mice, where, without having to worry about outsiders, my wife could now take her time and devote all her attention to having her attack in the privacy of her own home. I felt weak in the knees, and the wife who relentlessly reproached her husband began to look like a horrible monster.

Shin'ichi gave in to the sleep goblin and started to drift off while standing up, awakening with a start when his knees buckled, but falling asleep once more, then wakening again when his knees buckled, over and over. I smiled despite myself, and the passengers around us smiled with me, but they were watching us with curiosity. I propped up Shin'ichi between my legs so that he could go to sleep, and in no time we were at Koiwa Station; my wife and I, with the sleeping children on our backs, were standing on the platform. There happened to be a dense mist, and the air smelled of earth, with a freshness that instantly eased the fatigue of the day. As we went outside, the red of the neon signs on the commercial street in front of the station blended with the heavy mist enfolding the town like an omen of disaster; even the movie theatre directly in front of us was not clearly distinguishable. My solitary fatigue returned, and the child fast asleep on my back was as heavy as a corpse.

My wife walked along in silence until we got to the narrow road behind the theatre, but there she shook Maya from her back:

"Maya. Wake up now. I'm going to put you down. Stand up, stand up. Mommy can't take it any more. See, we're home already, wake up." Then she said "Come on, Shin'ichi, get down from Daddy's back and walk," so I put Shin'ichi down, and as I moved my shoulders to wake him up, a cat came up to us and meowed. When we started to walk, it seemed to be following two or three steps behind, so that when my wife clicked her tongue, it followed us all the way home. When we turned the corner and the bamboo fence came into sight, our street, too, was filled with mist, and in the night stillness, feeling as though I had returned to the wild, open land that must have been here long ago, I heard the faint, chill sound of groping for keys. Then the gate and the front door were opened, and my wife called "Tama, Tama" (the name of our dead cat). The stray meowed once and came inside. While my wife was occupied with trying to take it captive, her symptoms abated, so that to me the cat began to seem like the incarnation of something. Without a single hesitation, the cat ate the food that was soon prepared for it.

"It might be the reincarnation of Tama. See, doesn't it look exactly like our old cat?" she said, but I couldn't remember what sort of cat Tama was. I was reminded, though, of how I had behaved after Tama died, so I was careful not to go too far into a discussion of our previous cat.

"It's true, it really looks like Tama," Shin'ichi agreed, and Maya, too, said,

"This is *my* Tama."

"There's only one cat, so you'll have to share nicely. Today it's Shin'ichi's cat, tomorrow it'll be Maya's cat. Everyday you can take turns." I tried to lead the conversation in that direction.

"But what'll we do if it's somebody else's cat? I suppose they won't like it if their cat disappears. I guess I'd better go return it," said my wife, stepping outside, but she was soon back again, still carrying the cat. "It refuses to leave. Daddy, shall we keep it?" she said.

"I guess it has chosen our family, so why don't we?" I answered, and we decided to name it Tama and keep it. The name made me nervous, but my wife was set on it. She fixed some dried bonita shavings for the cat and fed it, and since both parents and children were hungry again, having had an early dinner, we had a simple supper, after which we all went to bed in the six-mat room: the children in their own futon, and my wife and I in the double futon to which we had finally become accustomed. After folding by their pillows the clothes they would wear when they got up in the morning, the children went right to sleep, but my wife tried to initiate a conversation:

"These days my heart pounds so, it gets numb, as though I've had an electric shock or something. I wonder what's the matter?"

I tried suggesting that if we started talking after we were in bed, we always got into trouble, so we should try to go to sleep without talking. But we couldn't seem to get to sleep. My wife would try to test her husband with her body, but I was so tense physically and emotionally that I was apt to get flustered and react in the wrong way, whereupon my wife became suspicious and jealous, and she kept after me until she got her reassurance. Danger lurked everywhere. The slightest provocation sent her into another attack. There was nothing in her husband's surroundings that was not a temptation, a catalyst, but the inclination to avoid these temptations apparently did not arise. That night, just as her husband was hesitating once again in the face of such inducements to anxiety, Tama climbed quietly onto our bedcovers, and I felt the futon indent with the animal's weight. At first I tried to kick it away, but in no time at all it was back. After repeating the process two or three times, I experienced a certain unexpected sensation, so I gave up, and the cat promptly crawled under the covers. My wife didn't seem to mind, so I fantasized that the two of us had become catnip, and presently I noticed the strength penetrating every inch of my body.

*   *   *

The carpenter we had asked Mr. Aoki next door to get for us, who turned out to be his cousin, came and set to work replacing our bamboo fence with a board fence. Not only did my wife take the trouble to provide snacks and meals, but with someone outside the family in our midst, her "cloud" disappeared. For the time being I felt secure; I would have to use the time to work. I had just received a letter from the publisher of a magazine I had never heard of, asking for a short story of twenty-five pages or so. If I could manage to write it, we would be able to live for a while on the proceeds. It was not a magazine for the general public, so undoubtedly someone had given my name to the editors. It was strange how these days, whenever I found myself on the verge of total bankruptcy, I was rescued by some job. One of my friends must be pulling strings somewhere. I had been spending time regularly with three separate groups. The mere mention of the name of a member of the first of those groups was enough to produce a drastic reaction from my wife; the second group wasn't so bad, and it seemed likely to her that the members of the third would reach out and help her husband find work. This attitude reflected my conduct within the groups and was only natural, but it tore me to shreds.

                                    *   *   *

The fence was finished in three days, and my short story was written. I had not spent all that time at my desk but had cooked, cleaned, and repapered the sliding windows in preparation for winter. My wife, under tension during the day while the carpenter was around, at night was prey to emotional ups and downs. When I repapered the windows, she remembered having done the job herself, working until late at night last year as she waited for her husband to come home— and he never did; her mind leaped from one thing to another:

"Tell me every place you went with the woman," she said.

My first thought was to try to get by with mentioning one and skipping the rest, but I was finally driven to the wall and forced to confess them all, and soon the stain spread all over the map of Tokyo. As those places increased in number, so did the places I would have to avoid in the future, until it seemed that eventually we wouldn't be able to go anywhere in the city. My two days of teaching were surrounded by forbidden places, and going to the school would be walking on thin ice. One would think that, as time passed, bad memories would fade, but in our case they were being polished clean and fresh.

"Our family's no good any more. There are too many things we can't think about," Shin'ichi remarked as if to himself, then my wife said to me,

"In your notebook it says 'wife: impotent'—what does that mean?" but I had no idea what she was talking about.

The next day when I awoke, I was met with another question, as though she had been waiting for me; then the grilling started, and with the curtain to the hallway unopened, at noon we were still at it. The children had gone out to play without being fed, coming home every once in a while to check on the situation, but the domestic *exigencies* went on and on. The machinery in the factory behind us was in operation, and the house shook, as usual, from the vibrations and the noise. "You're still hiding things," she said, and her relentless inquiry reached farther and farther back into the past; "Confess all your wrongdoings since we got married," my wife said. But when she heard the facts clearly from her husband, the memories of ten years of loneliness began to expand in her brain, and she said she would have her revenge on me.

"You get your revenge every day, that should be enough," I answered, and she said,

"What do you mean? This isn't revenge. Revenge is much worse. This absolutely is not revenge. I misspoke when I said 'revenge,' and I take it back. What have you been doing to me for the past ten years? What attitude did I take toward you in return? I never even thought of any man but you; if it would make you happy, I was going to leave you. And I wasn't in the least dissatisfied. Ever since that night I've been in such a state—I don't understand what's going on myself. I feel sorry for you because I give you a hard time, but I just can't help it. It's painful for you too, I know. I'd like to be the way I was again, but I can't. But believe me, this is not revenge. You think this is revenge? Revenge isn't so mild. It's because you think this is my revenge that instead of trying to make me feel better when I get upset, you get upset too. When you start acting crazy and threaten to run out of the house, I really abhor you. What don't you like about me? Be honest with me. Otherwise, I cannot go on living with you another day. Tell me what displeased you. If I can change it, I will. On the surface you speak sweetly, but you put me off with a wave of your hand, 'I'm busy right now, later, OK?' You've always rejected me like that, haven't you? I'm a woman, after all. Left all alone for two years, three years, what wife wouldn't complain? You've never made *me* happy either, you know."

There was no way of telling when my wife's words would end. When I left her side, she said, "Stay right where you are"; when I sat crosslegged, she said, "Sit in a more respectful position when I speak to you."

Maya came in as if to check on us and said, "Birdie died," and my wife rose immediately and went out back. I couldn't bring myself to go look; sighing, I couldn't even muster the energy to open the curtain to the hall. As I was sitting there dully among the bedding strewn about the six-mat room, my wife came back and explained that one of the chickens had stuck its head in the water trough and almost drowned, but when she grabbed it and pressed its neck, it had revived. Then Tama came back from somewhere and meowed to be fed, so my wife stopped her interrogation temporarily and went to fix the cat something to eat. I thought the interruption might change my wife's mood, but as soon as she had finished, she sat down and took up where she had left off.

"As long as you keep on hiding things and hiding things, my anxiety will never go away," she said. "I can say with confidence that for the past ten years I have loved you unselfishly; that's how I was able to keep going until today, and it frightens me to think that sooner or later I will really hate you. When that happens, there will be nothing left for me. Maybe the only people in the world I have ever really loved were my poor, dead Papa and Mama."

My wife sobbed for a while as though she had forgotten the world's existence and her own. She said that, ever since she could remember, her aging parents had never once scolded her. As I watched my weeping wife, I could only think that it was all my fault. I had taken this precious only daughter, raised with loving kindness, almost worshipped by her parents, dragged her from a life of total comfort on the island where she was born, and set her down in some Tokyo backstreet to lead a lean and meager life; I had disillusioned her. My wife's body now bore no traces of the gentle roundness of her girlish figure when she was on the island.

"In your diary you wrote something about not being able to refrain from doing something or other, you were telling your wife such and such—what is that all about?" she asked. I answered that I couldn't imagine writing something like that, and that I had no recollection of having done so, but she brought my diary, which I kept in a locked dresser drawer, and showed me the place. When I saw those very words in my own handwriting, I was horrified to realize that my feelings then and now were so different that, unable to connect them, I had forgotten and denied my own actions. I hazarded a few words in my defense, and got slapped in the face. Having learned my lesson earlier, I did not slap her back this time, but I lost control and rammed my head against the dresser. I had stepped back, ready to do it again, when my wife screamed, "Stop acting like an idiot," and wrapped herself around me. After grappling for a few minutes, we were overcome by a new sensation, and we embraced. Our animosity subdued, we found it hard to look each other in the eye; just then the children came home tired, and seeing that their parents had stopped fighting, they announced that they were hungry. Outside, the sun was already setting, and I was reminded that we had spent the entire day holed up in our six-mat room. "I'm hungry," my wife said simply, and with that the children and I felt restored to life.

Shin'ichi and Maya cried out, "She smiled, she smiled, Mommy smiled," and danced all over the room. My wife took her shopping basket and started to go out to the market, so I went with her, leaving the children at home. The newly erected white board fence loomed conspicuously, rather embarrassingly, apart from the rest of the neighborhood. At the store where we bought bread and peanut butter, at the butcher's, and at the green grocers where we bought apples, my wife was so animated that one would never guess that she had been in the dismal throes of an attack all day. My wife's liveliness outside the house made her great friends with the store employees and sales clerks, who always threw in a little something extra when she made a purchase; I saw this for the first time as I walked around with her. But I had not escaped; that night there was another eruption. After dinner was finally ready and we had begun a pleasant evening meal, suddenly, my wife threw her bowl and chopsticks across the room, and as though a gloriously radiant sun were abruptly hidden behind a giant black curtain, turning everything around us into a vast ice field, our home in an instant became a chilly and desolate place.

"You always said you wanted to live away from the children and me, what were you going to do when you moved out?" she asked. I could think of no good answer. Unable to control my impatience, and remembering what I had done that afternoon, I got up without saying anything and stuck my head through one of the sliding doors whose paper we had just changed. The thin wooden frame gave way and bits of it flew all over the room. Still unsatisfied, I went to the six-mat room and bashed my head against the dresser. This time, however, my wife did not come to stop me. I was alone and deserted, as if I had been pushed off a cliff, but feeling that I would look more foolish if I stopped there, I raised a war cry and banged my head two or three more times until there was a lump on my head and my scalp was bleeding. The dresser was completely undamaged, but pain reverberated through my skull, a broken bell in my ear. Frightened, I sat down to catch my breath, but my agitation had not subsided in the least, and I felt like smashing anything fragile I could get my hands on. At the same time, it occurred to me that my wife would have to be alarmed if I was properly wounded—but then I thought better of the idea, since on me even the slightest scratch tended to get infected. My will caved in, and I looked at my wife and children sitting at the table, silently watching my idiotic behavior.

Staring unflinchingly into his father's eyes, Shin'ichi said, "I *hate* Daddy," then looking at his mother, added, "I'm fed up with Daddy. Now you know." I was devastated, and something Shin'ichi had said earlier resurrected itself like a living being, overwhelmed me, and knocked me flat: "Daddy, Mommy's slips are all torn, you should buy her a new one."

It was raining outside, and the rain pounding the earth reverberated through the house, but my wife's mood was not so easily soothed. She said to the children, "Mommy may die, so she wants you children to get your father to raise you. Instead of this awful Mommy, Daddy will get a new, pretty, nice Mommy to take care of you, and I'm sure she'll buy you clothes and give you good things to eat. You'd like that better, wouldn't you? Or else, if you really like this Mommy anyway, do you want to come with me?"

Shin'ichi said, "I've already seen too much. What's the point in living? I'll do whatever Mommy says. I'll go with Mommy, and if you die, I'll die too"—it was hard to believe he wasn't even in school yet. But his little sister sobbed, "Maya don' wanna die." Soon, however, both children fell asleep.

But my wife refused to let me sleep. "Swear you won't see the woman, swear it, swear it," she said. She brought me water and an inkstone and made me write out an oath and sign it with my thumb print; she said that, almost immediately after I first took up with the other woman, she had noticed it and had hired a private detective. As a result of his reports, she had followed me occasionally, and she herself had spent the night hiding under the woman's window when her husband was there. She had gone around asking his friends, she had picked up what

they said behind her husband's back about him and the woman—rumors and depre-
cating comments—and she had discovered with her own eyes and ears exactly what
was going on. From bits and pieces of what she had told me time and time again, I
had basically guessed as much, but hearing the details in so many words directly
from my wife's lips, I shuddered anew. Looking back on my past and my friends,
they now seemed so strangely different from what I had taken them to be; I no
longer understood what I had seen in the world, or how I had interpreted it. I felt
emotionally exhausted, empty, body and soul.

My wife was saying, "Now that Toshio has finally developed some sense, I
can die in peace," then, tired from a solid day of talking, she lapsed into sleep. I
could not follow a train of thought; people's faces and fragmentary scenes from
the past kept flashing before my eyes. My mind was cool and clear, and I couldn't
sleep. Listening to the even breathing of my wife and children, I lay awake the
whole night. It apparently rained all night long. Just before dawn, when the
milkman had made his delivery, I got up to go to the lavatory; standing there, I
looked vacantly out the window. I could see the newly erected white board fence,
which had soaked up quantities of rainwater and swelled with the moisture.

OUT OF THE DEPTHS

During the period when we were still going to the treatment room of the hospital outpatient psychiatric clinic, I often walked from the outpatient building in a wide circle around the psychiatric ward, gazing at it from a distance, and inevitably I fell into a dark mood.

I was battered, mind and body, by my wife's disturbed mental state. When she was in the throes of one of the attacks that were symptomatic of her illness, her logic was iron-tough, and if I were to submit to that relentless logic, neither my wife nor I could go on living. When she drove me into a corner, I would completely lose my head, and many times I grabbed a sash or a cord and tried to strangle myself. Whereupon my wife, like the *Kenmun*, an amphibious goblin in Ryukyuan legend, would suddenly gain amazing strength in her arms and remove the cord from my throat. When the demonic cloud lifted, my attachment to life was restored. After that, it was my wife who felt the dangerous lure to suicide. My nerves were frayed to a pulp.

At that time, for a period of about half a year, my wife and I could never be apart from each other, virtually even for a few minutes. For that reason, I had given up my teaching job, and with no leisure to do my writing either, I did not know how much longer I could continue to make ends meet.

For me society had ceased to exist. We simply went from one day to the next looking squarely into each other's face, waking or sleeping, even in the dead of night. In the exasperation of the suspicions that bubbled endlessly, like methane gas, to the surface of my wife's disturbed consciousness, one day turned into the next.

There was almost no indication that the treatment was working. Had the symptoms not already become part of her personality? My wife and I, and to a certain extent the children as well, had become unable to consider what form the future might take.

For a long time we went back and forth to the psychiatric clinic. I wonder how many times we got into an ugly shouting match on the train and bus we took to get there. On the crowded train platform my wife would suddenly slap my face, and I would lose my temper and slap her back. My wife's frenzy would increase all the more, then I would start walking through the train calling her name in a loud voice. I became abnormally persistent and kept beckoning and calling to my wife, who stood near the engineer's cabin at the opposite end of the car, forcing a simpering childish smile. (The corners of that twisted smile somehow kept haunting me, piercing my heart.) When my wife came up to me, I started walking unsteadily back toward the other end. Everyone in the car was watching us. Some farmers' wives, who had come to the city from a neighboring prefecture to sell their vegetables, poked each other and smiled. I felt as though I could no longer see what lay ahead of me.

There was nothing we could do, however, but to continue the treatment, effective or not. Might she not return to normality as an evil spirit leaves the possessed? I was not above praying to stones by the roadside. In much the same way, as a member of a suicide squadron during the war, I had wished for the Okinawan Islands to sink suddenly into the sea.

As I waited while my wife had her long session at the clinic, I passed the time in stagnant depression, like an insect crawling hopelessly around and around in an inescapable hole. On the one hand, I welcomed it when my wife's session dragged out, since at least during that time she was safely in the care of a doctor whom she trusted. But presently, we would once again be on our timid, nerve-wracking way home, the unbearable hopelessness of existing until her next appointment casting a shadow over our shoulders like black clouds descending.

I crouched at the edge of a small concrete reservoir and stared meaninglessly at the surface of the cloudy water, or I looked for a four-leaf burr clover; each moment seemed disconnected, separate. Lying with furrowed brow on a bed behind a black curtain in the treatment room, my wife, in a faint voice that sounded rapt and pleading, was continuously giving verbal expression to her free associations. Thinking about my wife's abnormal, uprooted world, I began to feel unbearably sorry for her and thought that no matter how I might be covered with disgrace, I would have to accept in silence the whip of her possessing demon.

Before my eyes the low building that housed the women's psychiatric ward loomed gloomy and weatherbeaten. All the doors were securely closed, and the windows were covered with wooden lattice or wire netting and iron bars. The inside was dark, and, as if I were looking at strange tropical fish in an aquarium, I could make out dimly, on the other side of the bars, patients' faces gathering and separating.

Occasionally, there erupted from this ward a loud laugh like that of a monstrous bird, and I envisioned a disheveled madwoman laughing raucously, running and running through the ward corridors.

And it seemed to me this was the essence of human tragedy. I supposed that mental illness was finally incurable. What did it mean, to treat mental illness? This was a dismal, stifling thought.

I considered the many female patients housed in that psychiatric ward. I pictured the peaceful everyday lives they had been able to lead before they were incarcerated there, supplementing my view with our own past and the complications that had led to our present state, and my chest constricted. We could not bring back the tranquil innocence of days gone by. Those days would never come again. Darkness, like india ink seeping from the edges of my field of vision, came and lay heavily on me.

The many innocent occupations of the world at large. It began to seem to me they were all, every one, taking place on the brink of a dark chasm from which one could never climb out again. The thought tormented me.

"Look, look. Tsuru in the West Ward laughed. Think that means rain tomorrow?"

The words of the nurses reached my ears. I didn't know that old joke—that an extremely unusual occurrence would bring rain—was still around, I thought. Certainly those nurses had not noticed the abyss. Would such days return to us? I felt driven even further into lonely isolation. I realized that I looked as though I were about to cry. There was nothing to do, however, but restrain myself.

For some reason, I wanted to go around to the other side of the ward. I didn't know what was there. The sign saying "Only authorized persons beyond this point" held a strange fascination. Perhaps I was shadowboxing with those regulatory words, with the attitude of the people who had written it, or simply with my own sense of isolation from the mental patients. I was all the more convinced that some important key was waiting on the other side. It seemed to me that over there the mental patients' ward had its mouth open wide. I made up my mind and headed in that direction.

As I drew close, I felt a chill air beneath the windows. The inside was pitch dark; I could see nothing. It gave the feeling of a storeroom or an attic. I hesitated to look at the creatures wriggling in that darkness. On the ground beneath the window I half expected there to be bits of broken pottery, knives, and razor blades, on which I might accidentally cut the soles of my feet. But I didn't see anything like that on the ground near me. Walking on tiptoe, I gradually worked my way around to the other side, afraid all the while that someone would come and reprimand me.

On the other side was another building. Beyond that one there was apparently another. Like buildings inside a maze, each was hidden from my view. There were windows up high, all with iron bars. Suddenly, a wan face moved. Lowering my eyes, I avoided the sight. Then, holding my breath, I looked at the building I had wanted to come around to see.

There were many rooms, each with a single window. There was apparently no one in the room immediately before me. Suddenly, an ominous thought occurred to me—"Oh dear. Wasn't this an abandoned building?" But when I shifted my eyes to the window of the next room, unconsciously I stopped in my tracks. A young woman was watching me, both hands clutching the iron bars. She caught my eye, almost as if she had long been anxiously awaiting my arrival. Then she started to smile slightly, silently. (I thought of my wife's wordless smile when she tried to put the best face on my misbehavior by forcing a smile for the other people on the train.) Without thinking, I retraced my steps. My face must have stiffened. Then I walked quickly back to my starting point at the outpatient clinic.

I was physically exhausted. What should I have done, I wondered. Could I not have managed to show that patient a slightly more gentle bearing? Her hair swept straight back, her brightly figured kimono, and her youth almost gave me the illusion that she was my young wife just after our marriage, when I had brought her to our old house in the countryside, so far from the city. Her tired, defenseless eyes made me think of my wife's. I was tired too, and perhaps my vision was deceiving me, but this woman's eyes reminded me of my wife's: those feverish, thin-skinned eyelids, those abnormally keen, observant eyes, slightly childish, filled with perplexity at having lost control of her own actions. What was that young woman thinking, holding on to the windowbars? And what sort of future would come to call on her?

Why had I gone around to see the other side of the ward, anyway? With a wave of my hand I tried to brush away the impression it had made on me.

Those days I often tended to think that if I did not isolate myself from my surroundings, I would not be able to stand the pain. For all I knew, however, this was but another twisted form of my pent up resistance against the uncontrollable attacks of that other wife who had lodged herself inside my wife.

Soon, however, it was decided that we were to be admitted to the hospital. Moreover, for various reasons, we were to be placed not in the open psychiatric ward but in the psychotic ward.

I was no longer making a wide circle around it from the outside; I had gone over to the side that holds the windowbars and gazes at the outside world. The only difference was that since I was to be hospitalized along with my wife, the women's ward was inappropriate, so we were sent over to the men's ward.

In the area that I had caught a glimpse of beyond the women's building, there were many more buildings than I had seen; the doctors and nurses and orderlies walked around jangling from their belts the keys to open the locks to all of them.

When you actually lived there, what went on inside was not so mysterious after all: the precipitious chasm that I had thought lay waiting there, the screams of disturbed patients, the difficulty of verbal communication, the cramped, single-minded determination, over-excitement and exaggeration, the unexpected. It was perhaps quite natural that the dense, resilient, refreshingly startling vaporous substance that surged around us when we first entered the psychotic ward should gradually lose its intensity with the passage of time.

At first I was regarded as another patient just like them. It must have seemed highly unlikely to them that a female patient had been admitted to the men's ward.

In fact, for me, not only was the emotional wear and tear of dealing with society absent, but thanks to the bolts on the doors, the many kinds of malice that encroached persistently from the outside were blocked as well. If the demon dwelling inside my wife could only be exorcised, I thought, I wouldn't mind at all living for a while, just the two of us, in the hospital ward.

By now I was able to scream in front of everyone when I felt like it, chase my wife up and down the corridor, quarrel with her all night long. And when suddenly my wife's attack (or mine, for somewhere along the line I had begun to have attacks myself) abated, I would immediately walk down the corridor beside her, helping her to the restroom and doing all the things that most wives do in society. While my wife called me by my first name and played the generous master, I cheerfully busied myself in her service.

Perhaps the outside world would find such behavior strange, but in here there was nothing to tie us to another way. Perhaps that is an overstatement. In any case, as we became accustomed to the patients' quirks, we began to understand their language and were no longer startled by their screams or frightened when they were overwrought. Although it was true that the standards of the world outside the doors had crept in here to some degree, these patients, though they looked quite normal when their agitation had subsided, all had their own uncontrollable attacks, which apparently meant that they accepted everyone else's. No matter how inured one became, this was still a place where one was understanding of the attacks of others, and it seemed to me that I would be able to live my life here with fewer wounds and more dignity than elsewhere.

There were so many patients, with so many different symptoms. I supposed this was no different from society, though, made up different people with different personality quirks; these people all shared a certain fragility that made them, at some time, suddenly recoil before some reality. Their retreat in the face of anyone else's attack gave me a sense of security. I was able to think of them as huge-bodied insects with wounds that resisted cure. Besides, they had something grotesque that one could not find in the adroit self-presence shown to all by the doctors and nurses and attendants who confidently lived their lives in society. I could not hide the relief that I felt in their uncomfortable awkwardness. Pitiful bugs that could not attend to the wounds on their own backs with their clumsy arms and legs. Pathetic, good people, always conscious of their wounds, always thinking of them as weak points.

When I walked through the corridor late at night, I was seized by an inexpressible excitement.

Patients with somewhat more severe symptoms were concentrated in one section of the building, which itself was locked. I was still in a room that allowed me to wander freely up and down the long corridors, and when I thought of those souls asleep within so many locked doors, entrusting themselves into the hands of others (of course many of them suffering from hallucinations or insomnia), I felt subdued and sad. The nurses and doctors on duty—sometimes I wondered if even they could counteract the nearly irresistible force of the giant cogwheel of fate. Was I not completely crushed, simply from struggling against my wife's attacks?

* * *

One night I had this dream.

It was bedtime, our room had been subdivided into smaller units, and the outer door was locked. I felt a faint satisfaction at this. Now I would finally be treated like the real thing. I had come to think that unless I became disturbed like my wife, the two of us would never be able to climb out of the abyss. Now at last, I would be incarcerated behind many locked doors.

Not that I didn't feel a certain sentimental sadness as one by one the possibilities for returning to society were cut off. But a place to withdraw and resign ourselves to being able to concentrate on furiously burning up our lives seemed somehow more preferable. All right now, everyone who is horrified by us, please go outside these doors. A sarcastic smile on my face, I could see the people who didn't have attacks, hurriedly washing with disinfectant, scurrying back to their homes. Nurses dressed in white, scattering rude phrases, carried dishes and cans of food inside the doors, then quickly left. "Hurry up, those who are going, go now," I chanted under my breath. Some kind of vicious bacteria had broken out inside the ward, and we would have to be isolated for quite a while; there was little hope that any of us locked in on this side of the doors would escape the disease. The loudspeakers in the corridor were informing us to this effect. I did feel some anxiety about living henceforth in a locked world with the other patients. (Priests and cold rice balls, Mr. Han'yū, mumble mumble, my friend Saitō, Mr. Wakino, our little boy, Kitten, Mr. Yumiya, delusions of grandeur, hangers on, little Susumu, university students, chivalrous gentlemen, introspective youths, loudspeakers, a hippopotamus. All these extremely individualized fond and familiar images floated kaleidoscopically before me, laughing faces with wide-open mouths.) But the more she was locked away, the more secure my wife would feel, I supposed.

Nurse C, smiling brightly, was about to lower the bolt, "I'm closing the door, is everyone out who's coming out?"

"Nurse, if you lock the door, won't you be stuck inside with us?" I asked, worried.

"That's right, I'm on duty. I'm staying inside."

"But this is no ordinary situation, you know. Why should you have to stay behind alone? The patients might very well start a riot."

C just smiled unconcernedly. Would she be made a helpless victim, I wondered. I felt sorry for her but felt, too, that there ought to be at least one such person; it ought to happen so.

Immediately I awoke.

These days I tended to forget the thread of my dreams, but I remembered this dream clearly. Strangely, it had the effect of showing me what I had to do.

* * *

How persistent, intractable, were the symptoms of my wife's illness. The various methods of treatment she underwent in order to blur her memory of the past had in fact generally succeeded in doing so to a certain extent, but the essential psychogenic memories were branded on her mind even more vividly and intensely than before, and, moreover, in an already distorted form that my wife was unable to distinguish from the original events.

That morning, too, I apparently awoke when my wife turned over in her sleep. But for a while I held my breath and observed her condition. If I called out to her and wakened her, I would have to start that day's ceaseless scuffle with her frequent attacks. There was no way to avoid that struggle, but I took fleeting respite in putting off the eventuality until the last possible minute. (The only time during the entire day when I could completely be myself was when I was in the lavatory, I thought.) So it seemed to me there was no point in waking up my wife and purposely summoning the time when her attacks were most apt to occur.

I sensed, however, that my wife was already awake and was struggling with assailing delusions and hallucinations.

So I went ahead and sat up abruptly in bed, calling out to her, "Miho, are you awake?"

"Uh-huh."

I always weighed my wife's every word for any indication of the symptoms of an attack. Even if I recognized the symptoms beforehand, however, there was nothing I could do to allay them. I simply had to prepare to wait quietly until the squall had passed (except that it was a much more lengthy process). By now it was no longer a question of watching quietly; my emotions were at such a pitch that when my wife had an attack, I got upset along with her, then our behavior began to affect each other and the situation became more and more complicated. But that morning, though I realized it was probably wasted effort, I decided to take the offensive.

"Miho, are you all right?" I immediately put out a feeler.

"I guess," my wife answered ambiguously. I was certain that her brow was tense, her eyes open wide and rolled upward, staring fixedly at me.

Whipping my body, still lethargic from lack of sleep because of my wife's attack the evening before, I forced myself to get up and, my ankle and knee joints aching as though they had been wrenched, went over and got in bed with her.

The only result was that I learned that my wife was hovering in the doorway to an attack. It was exceedingly difficult to keep from purposely allowing myself to be sucked gradually in toward what I hated, what I feared, what I should avoid. It was almost impossible for me to lead my wife away from that door out onto more open ground. When I tried to influence her mood, she went precisely in the direction I did not want her to. If I left her alone, the situation merely stagnated. If I tried to push her by too fast, she began to suspect my motives and insisted on stopping. In short, no matter what I did, we had to go through that doorway.

In nauseating disillusion I went on trying to divert my wife's attention to innocent subjects, but like being slowly but surely sucked into the current of a large whirlpool, in the end I was drawn into my wife's attack.

The slightest thing was enough to set her off. What had started it this morning was her remembering suddenly, like noxious gas fermenting and rising to the surface of a ditch, that I had never taken her to see a movie or a play.

"Why didn't you ever take me? Wasn't I worth that much to you?"

I felt as helpless as one teetering and tumbling down a red clay cliff. Movies were not really the problem; once again I was forced to try to explain myself under my wife's cross-examination, which for the past ten months over and over had taken exactly the same stubborn course. The discussion would begin to get convoluted, and bit by bit I awkwardly divulged my past until I could not put the individual pieces back together. Ah, here we go, here we go again. My mind reeled, and in my wife's head the possessing demon ran rampant. One after another, cruel, selfish words leaped to my tongue. Finally unable to stop myself, I said them:

"A husband doesn't have to take his wife to those places."

"Damn you."

Her face dominated by its angry, indignant phase, she slapped me with all her strength across the left ear.

I sprang to my feet.

"What do you think you're doing?" Wild-eyed, I felt like beating my wife as hard as I could. But, just at that moment, I recognized in her expression something familiar: the sight revived the painful memory of spanking our two children—now left with relatives on a faraway southern island so that their parents could be hospitalized—and suddenly my wife's body before me began to overlap in my mind with the image of those children. I smelled the sweet scent of milk of her body. I abandoned all resistance. I shoved my wife face down on the bed and hit her round buttocks three or four times in succession, until I began to have the hallucination that I was spanking one of the children. My wife squirmed and fought, but to me she seemed to be smiling cheerfully. OK, let's call it quits for now—I could almost hear her saying. All at once she became dear to me, and I thought how I would like to return to a casual, tranquil daily life with my wife and two children. When, breathing hard, I came to my senses, I was bathed in perspiration, so I took off my clothes and dried my body.

"You hit me, damn you. Some nerve you have to hit Miho with those dirty hands. I will never forgive you for this," my wife shouted, her face flushed. No matter how hard I tried to dry myself, the perspiration kept coming. In the meantime, I tried to put on a polo shirt.

"Listen and remember what I say. This time Miho is really going to die, I'm warning you." Finally, my wife was beginning to tidy herself up.

Oh no, I thought. This was a recurrent threat. Panicked, adopting an even more belligerent stance, I went up to my wife and gave her a cuff on the ear. "You are not to say such things," I ordered her; but then, spurred on by my own words, I said, "If you want to commit suicide, I'll show you how it's done." I grabbed the sash to my wife's nightgown (it was strong—once when my wife had tied herself to her bed and tried to strangle herself, I had been unable to untie the knot and finally had to cut it with a penknife), wound it around my neck, and pulled as hard as I could with both hands.

At first, my wife paid no attention, but when the sash dug into my skin, my face darkened, and I began to gasp, she grabbed hold of me. "Mr. F? Mr. F, come quickly. Toshio is getting violent," my wife shouted, and the attendant in the next room came.

"Toshio is trying to kill me. That's how he treats a patient, mind you. Who ever heard of such stupidity."

I could do nothing but entrust her to F's care and leave the room.

I went up to the large windows in the communal bath, and, clinging to the bars, I gazed at the relentlessly bright scene outside. My body would not stop shaking. I didn't care if my wife killed me for what I had done. But I could not stand being subjected to her repeated questioning, I thought in my excited state. Still, as the shock waves subsided, I felt my despair abate slightly—knowing full well that restoring my wife's normal state of mind would take a long time and require the self-control of walking on thin ice.

* * *

Indeed, my wife's lagging mood continued to affect her for a while, but that afternoon we were to leave the psychiatric ward and go to the outpatient clinic for treatment.

At this point, that was for us an absolute order. As the time of the appointment approached, my wife grudgingly began to tidy herself up. Then the nurse opened the door for us, and we left the psychiatric ward. To the two of us, the white billows of summer clouds, the grass, and the trees in the garden offered not the slightest comfort. The glaring midsummer sun shining down upon us was darkened, shaded by the thick folds of our brains, and, leaving the ward, we felt as though we had been exiled together from the world.

My wife's face was pale, and she looked as if she had suddenly aged as she strode on ahead of me.

Our back-to-back hearts were gently, softly warmed by the summer sun. This attack, too, would pass eventually, but the attacks that besieged us one after another began to seem like a vast sea. What was the problem? I raised my head and sighed, and the direct rays of the sun suddenly diffused over my retinae so that the inside of my head was strangely full of color. The seeds I had sown I myself would have to reap. But how far would I be able to swim, bound hand and foot, without being sucked into the deep maelstrom? Perhaps that was not an appropriate way of formulating the problem. I wanted to obliterate the nature I was born with! No, stamping out my sentimentality would accomplish nothing. Dangling in midair, I could find no support for my arms and legs.

At the convenience of the doctor, we were kept waiting for a while.

Seeing an opportunity, my wife came up to me, and, trying to drag me into her logic, she purposely rubbed my nerves the wrong way. I had to take this treatment in silence. But if I said nothing at all, I would stir up her attack even more: I had to go along with my wife's logic. But then she tripped me up and I stumbled. I tried to move away. When I did so, my wife moved with me.

"I'll follow you wherever you go. What do you mean by turning me into a lunatic. Make me the way I was before!" My wife and I had to walk around and around the hospital grounds. The sun was beating down on us. Someone was looking this way from the office in the outpatient clinic.

I heard recorded music. Mixed in was lively background noise, as though someone was stamping on the floor boards or something was being dragged.

When, without thinking, we went in that direction, I witnessed the peculiar circle dance of some mental patients.

How can I explain it? Brilliant color exploded before my eyes, as if someone had emptied a box of bright confetti near the edge of my field of vision, but a calmer look revealed, in fact, no gaudy colors. Possibly it was because there were female patients in the group—not that these women were wearing a lot of lipstick and rouge—that I was assailed by the impression of gaudiness, despite the fact that I was already living among these people and had grown rather accustomed to many things about them.

All ages, all manner of appearance and clothing were jumbled together. The male patients ranged from a boy of about high school age to an old man with white hair, some of them in soiled deshabille, wearing an assortment of white hospital gowns, polo shirts and slacks, army caps, knitted undershirts, and long underpants. Most of the women had on Western clothes. Only a few were wearing kimonos, one in a standard dark blue print with a red obi and another with a grey coat that looked like a raincoat or a smock over a kimono. Perhaps there were only those two. (No, there was one more, a woman who wouldn't join the circle but sat quietly in a chair in the corner of the room intently watching the dance; she was wearing a kimono.) That day while I was waiting for my wife when she was still an ambulatory patient, I had gone toward the psychiatric ward and had seen a woman, clutching the windowbars, watching me. I was sure she was the same woman. Now, however, I no longer felt that strangeness, or that sentimental attraction. The observer in me, who had made a wide circle around the outside of the building, ready to flee at any moment, was gone. I no longer watched as though I were viewing something rare and curious, and the fear had lessened. I had simply seen an inconspicuous woman suffering from a disordered brain. Once, later on, I caught a glimpse of her wearing a conservative blouse, tripping lightly down the corridor, singing cheerfully. The rest of them were wearing simple dresses, blouses that looked like underkimono, skirts tied at the waist with sashes, tights, and gathered skirts. Dressed like elegant married women, like farm girls, or like young ladies, like students or waitresses in low class restaurants, like office workers, or again like housewives and storekeepers' wives (strange how each looked terribly like her role), they were all dancing together in the circle, some well-scrubbed, some poorly groomed. I could pretty well imagine how they looked when they had their attacks. Now they suppressed their symptoms, affecting nonchalance. Yet every one of them had some obstinate vestigial signs of those attacks. They all (it was true of the male patients as well) had a morbid wound in a place on their body that hands could not reach, and whenever that part of their body flapped its wings and kicked up a fuss, they were driven to display an unsightly agony. When that had passed and they resumed their life with a certain bashfulness that set them off from normal society, there was something slightly odd about the way they presented themselves. In almost all of them an awkwardness of movement created a comic quality, like clay dolls that had come to life with a clatter. Trying with all their might to make up for their failures, they upset the disequilibrium even more. But that imbalance I found rather pleasing.

With expressions exaggerated by chronic illness, they lurched around in a circle like hand puppets representing various human types.

I was quite used to the faces and appearances of several of them. The past lives that each of them shouldered seemed not so very foreign to me: I could almost imagine I knew them very well.

The Western style circle dance pleased me especially. The men and women formed couples and held hands as the whole group moved around in a circle in time to the lively music. Then they stopped and stamped their feet in turn. Then they went around again, pointing to their partners, then skipping, then the men holding the women from behind; it was amusing how the dance showed up the individuality of the dancers.

As I gazed at the dancers going so energetically around and around in a circle, the bodies and faces of the couple at the front of my field of vision seemed to throb with life. With a vividness one might find symbolic, their now forgotten lives in society went around and around, cyclically entering, then leaving, my field of vision. Serious faces, droll faces, a secret smile, a tearful face, a grimace—in other words, the stock types of mental patients' faces—showed themselves fullface and profile. They left my sight, then the same faces reappeared and did it all again.

There was a simple purity about them that tugged at my heart and pulled me in.

Not that I had taken my eyes off my wife. When I went to watch the dance, my wife had tagged along at a distance, assuming a neutral attitude. No matter how much my wife might abuse me, she simply could not bear to leave my side. Knowing that she could not go away, she would draw me completely under her control, then have an attack, and pound me to shreds.

My wife, too, was watching the dance.

Keeping my distance, I pretended to take no serious notice of her, but out of the corner of my eye I was always watching. The full tide of my wife's attack began to echo painfully in my breast.

In a little while, a nurse from the outpatient clinic came looking for my wife and led her away. That meant it was her turn for treatment. As I looked after them to make sure that she had gone with the nurse, I realized that for approximately an hour during her session I would in a sense be free. Not that the dark clouds parted, but at least for that amount of time I would be able to give my nerves some respite.

As I continued watching, another group of dancers came babbling up. These were ward patients I had not seen before. Another veil was lifted from my eyes. These were the real, unmistakable mentally ill. Compared to them, the group until now had been absolutely normal. Had I been delirious? A chubby woman in short pants, her hair cut short like a man's and parted on one side, a young man walking around with his obi untied and his kimono open in front, a little boy with a surgical scar on his forehead, waving his arms meaninglessly in the air, an old disheveled hag, a woman with her stomach protruding as though she were pregnant. When these newly arrived patients let out a yell and joined the circle, everyone became confused: some people danced backwards, some broke away from the circle, and total pandemonium ensued.

It was strange how the patients I had been watching suddenly paled beside the new. I began to get a headache just watching this utterly haphazard attempt at a dance. I was assailed this time with a numbness, as if I had been anesthetized.

Suddenly, I began to worry about my wife. Wasn't it possible that today's session had ended earlier than usual and she had gone off by herself? I began to feel that she had; anxiety welled up, and I left the dancing. When I reached the breezeway to the outpatient clinic building, it seemed indeed that the therapy session had just ended, and there I saw my wife, heading in my direction. I was relieved. Why was it that at dangerous moments like these I always just managed to catch my wife?

I smiled automatically and waved to her, and, as though she had completely forgotten what had been going on until just a little while ago, her whole face broke into a happy smile; she stopped for a moment, stood on tiptoe, waved vigorously at me, then, her red skirt billowing in the breeze, she ran toward me.

For an instant, I forgot about my wife's attacks and the fact that we were in a mental hospital, and I had the illusion that it was a normal, tranquil day and I had just come home from work, greeted affectionately by my wife who had anxiously awaited my arrival—knowing only too well that those symptoms that resembled the dance of the black moth were right behind me, casting a shadow over me, their heels against my spine.

THE HEART THAT SLIPS AWAY

I was in a mental hospital, having been admitted along with my wife to tend to her personal needs.

I had managed to support the family until then on the proceeds from my fiction and essays and from my earnings teaching at a certain school. We had two children. Since it was not only my wife who was to be hospitalized but myself along with her, I resigned my teaching job, sold the house to raise money for the hospital fees, and left the children to be cared for in my wife's home town.

My wife was suffering from acute neurasthenia, and as long as we were in the clutches of her attacks, neither she nor I could live a single day in peace. Outsiders did not understand; they thought us ridiculous. My wife had fallen into a hell of suspicions and could not let me leave her side for a second. Even when I was in the lavatory, my absence made her anxious. Her anxieties piled up and up inexhaustibly, and, in order to possess me, she could not relax for an instant her relentless demands. But the more she persisted, the more her thirst increased and she was never satisfied. Consequently, her mind ran out of control, and her demands became frenzied and cruel; that made me all the more irritable, intensifying her anxiety and causing new suspicions to well up like clouds. I tried to turn myself into a machine that would unswervingly devote itself to my wife, but it seemed as though I would simply be overwhelmed by a futility not unlike trying to sprinkle water on a desert. I would never be able to quench my wife's thirst. I could not leave her side. The doctor had hinted that it was inadvisable to leave her alone, and it was also my diagnosis that this was the only way to control her symptoms, and that our life together had no purpose other than that. That one and only method, however, showed no results whatsoever, and often it seemed like a repeated exercise in futility, but I persisted. Not only spiritually, but physically as well, I literally did not leave my wife's side. I could no longer even consider going to work. When my wife's discontent mounted, she hit me and kicked me. I was not allowed out the front door by myself, yet my presence in the end invited despair (since it was I who incited her symptoms), and gradually my wife was beginning to notice that I—or one aspect of me—was the object of her hatred. Even so, she could not bear to lose me. I was driven further and further into a disadvantageous position. Embroiled in one of her attacks, I experienced a bottomless self-hatred. I felt like an ugly, deformed lump of flesh. I sensed the futility of my devotion like a bad odor. And as a snake raises its wide head, the phantom of my ego burst forth.

127

My wife feared any stimulus from the outside world. No matter how unsightly our life, I wanted to hold her close beside me and remain secluded in a deep, dark cellar.

*   *   *

The two of us were protected from the outside world first of all by the bolt on the door, then by the wire mesh, and the iron bars, and the wood fence topped by barbed wire, which obstructed casual traffic with society. The psychotic ward was the best possible environment, more than we could have hoped for. Not only did it approach my wife's fervent desire, it afforded me, as well, some respite from the nervous strain of remaining alert twenty-six hours a day: because of my wife's supersensitive state, the slightest stimulus from the outside world (a visitor, noise, the newspaper, or the radio, all the many sorts of lively commotion involved in daily living) was enough to incite her symptoms and send her into an attack. In any case, living in a ward shut off from the outside world allowed me some peace of mind since, even if I left my wife alone during one of her attacks, the physical danger was relatively slight.

And so for me, the bolts and barbed wire were symbols of a great relief. I would have welcomed more. In fact, it occurred to me that it might be better if the two of us were put in separate little rooms facing each other, a heavy bolt on the connecting door keeping us from opening it at will, and in the center of that door, thick like the door of a refrigerator, would be a small square peep hole so we could keep track of each other as we lived our daily lives.

*   *   *

One day, from around a bend in the corridor, I heard the following conversation.

"You know, it's because they lock us in and surround us with fences like a prison that we feel like escaping. We're not criminals, after all. Stuck in a place like this and left alone for weeks on end with no treatment, anybody'd feel like running away. If they'd just give me a shot or two I'd get well, but I can't stand it if they keep me in here forever."

"Well, it won't help to get so worked up about it. Once you're in here, there's no point in being impatient. Most everybody here's been in for five or ten years. I've been here two years already myself, and they don't give me any real treatment. But being set off from society like this and putting up with it, I guess that's the treatment. The doctors can't be trying to make us get *worse*, after all."

"I've put up with it for a long time. But there are limits to what a man can endure. If worst came to worst, I suppose it would be easy to break out of an old rundown building like this. You could escape from just about anywhere. Even S ran away."

"Yes, and you can hardly blame S. They really gave it to him the night before. After that, he didn't even eat; he just sat there dumbly, thinking. He must have gotten fed up and wanted desperately to go home. When he gets an attack, he really gets out of hand, though."

* * *

Both people who were talking were patients. I couldn't judge how far to believe what they were saying. In any case, they were patients who suffered from delusions and hallucinations. You never knew what they were liable to say. It was not an illusion, however, that a patient named S had escaped from the ward. There were several patients with the last name S, and at first I had not known which of them it was, but eventually I was able to establish that it was a young boy who looked like a beansprout, lank and pale, only his mouth red in contrast. That S I remembered clearly. Once I had gone along on an after-dinner walk planned for the patients' recreation. We were on a road atop a cliff on the old castle grounds, and S veered off onto a side road and gave the young nurse in charge a hard time. Seeing that the nurse could not reach S, who was trying to jump down from a high spot on the slope, I automatically held out my own hand to him. This gesture met with S's displeasure and rejection. Possibly my treating him like a cripple had made him angry. Or perhaps I had disturbed a secret fantasy. I tried to believe that it was not my fault, that he was in fact very ill, but still, at this brutal rebuff, I felt myself dragged into a lonely isolation.

Since then, I had retained some misgivings about S, so that hearing now that he had run away brought forth nothing but a wry smile. Serves him right. Even if a patient does manage to escape, do you really think there is any place where he will be able to find peace? Isn't it because you can't fit into society that you're all in here in the first place? I supposed he would go home; the trouble with that was that his family would just bring him back.

Even so, I could not conquer my feeling of bleakness. To shut a person up in one place, no matter how it was done, had overtones of tragedy. Someone who escaped from such a place aroused sympathy. I wondered where the little boy S had gotten out. Had he been carefully preparing ahead of time, giving the impression all the while of an extremely disturbed patient?

The person who discovered where he had gotten out was M, a patient who had been terribly zealous in the investigation. He went around looking everywhere in the ward. The way he acted suggested that he took a certain pleasure in S's escape, or that he was doing it because, on the contrary, he identified with the doctors, orderlies, and nurses and was outraged by the escape. Actually, from the point of view of the patients left behind, the incident might mean that yet one more of the areas to which they had been allowed free access would be taken away from them; there was precedent. Thanks to the old man K known as the veteran escape artist, for instance, the courtyard fence had been made higher and surrounded by barbed wire. They said that old man K had escaped as many as six or seven times. Usually, though, he walked around with his eyes downcast and rarely spoke to anyone. He held high in both hands a grimy teacup, and when no one was around, he would sip from it surreptitiously and smoke. He always appeared to be looking far off into the distance. Yet all there was to be seen were two hospital ward buildings (the windows covered with wire mesh and iron bars), the high wooden fence topped with barbed wire (which had been put there because of his own experience), the cramped little garden with its small concrete reservoir, and, other than a few shrubs and flowers, a limited piece of sky. From the old man's posture one might suppose that he was thinking up a new escape route. Hadn't old man K in fact now come back to the hospital? Having run away, the patients would simply realize anew that society was filled with gray anxiety and a difficult place to live, and they would come back.

That is what made incidents of escape by patients so disconcerting. Escape was just like deliberately sticking one's head into confinement. That was the inevitable problem. One could just dismiss such people as ill, but even healthy people, living their lives in such forced confinement, would eventually lose their sense of what was what.

Besides, patients who escaped made the nurses extremely angry. From the nurses' point of view, such an attitude was hardly unreasonable. They could not spend all their time watching one patient. Overwork and the disturbed nature of the patients were an oppressive burden. Even if there were one nurse for every patient, it would be difficult to stop a patient determined to escape. It was only natural that they should cease to feel good will toward patients who purposely did nasty things that redounded to the professional discredit of the nurses.

S had gotten out by squeezing through the windowbars in the dressing room of the employees' bath. When the assiduous M, in his search to ascertain the escape route, opened the door to the bath, there below the window bars were S's printed white cotton kimono, frayed black obi, and a pair of hospital slippers lying there forlornly, slightly dirty, discarded like an empty shell.

* * *

Instantly wondering what the nurses were doing, I checked the nurses' station. During the day there were usually three or four nurses on duty, but now I saw only one. Moreover, she did not seem especially worried, though she did look like someone in ill humor who was forcing herself to remain calm. Possibly she was rather optimistic of the result, figuring, after all, how far could he get in broad daylight in his shorts and an undershirt.

Why was it that I was disposed to imagine the Escape Incident (just thinking of it as such is an exaggeration, of course) in connection with a cacophony of buzzers echoing throughout the hospital, summoning ambulances (another out of the blue association), which come hurrying to the site. Were they conducting a search for S? Was it all right to dawdle so? Might he not commit suicide?

I wondered if the nurse in question, instead of worrying about the boy S, was considering punishment for the patients who were left so that nobody would ever try a stunt like that again. For some reason, my head tended toward unsettling thoughts—the idea, for instance, that the patients were being incarcerated in this prisonlike hospital in the name of mental health. And that there were frequent incidents of escape: the escapees were eventually caught and put into even higher security rooms, after which the hospital fortified and armed itself better and better. Perhaps the trouble was that, in hospital confinement, delusions arising from my debilitated state began to sustain germs of anxiety that I would not ordinarily have noticed. The only people with pass keys were the doctors, nurses, and janitors. In the event of fire or earthquake, or some other unforeseeable disaster, this ward would surely become a solitary floating island cut off from the outside world. Maybe one of the patients would suddenly be possessed by a frenzied attack. Or suppose some of the patients became violent. Every person in the ward, despite differences in the severity and nature of their symptoms (and among them were people who, like me, were not themselves patients), would be totally at the mercy of an unexpected catastrophe. (Awakened in the middle of the night by some strange noise, I was often terrified. We had entrusted our lives to a handful of people—at night to two young nurses who, despite their crisp night duty caps and pure white uniforms, were still inexperienced girls.)

I had overheard the patients' conversation earlier with vague pangs of apprehension. What one of them had said—deliver us from this hell—had planted an obsession in my mind. Was it that deep down I was crying out the same thing? But that was an awkward attitude for me at the moment. When my wife's attacks intensified, I walked blindfolded, head drooping, beckoned by the goddess of death. I thought I could not bear the burden of making up for what we had done to them: because of my wife and myself, the ward now had to be even more strictly isolated and confined. Something in the patient's tone of voice stirred my blood; would this mood not quickly diffuse throughout the ward, and the patients who had been daily without an outlet for their various dissatisfactions and glooms, would they not recklessly band together and evict the doctors and nurses? And would they not do something to those of us who were not patients but companions of patients and had simply gotten dragged into the struggle? In that case, what would become of my wife? Even she, whose nervous outbreaks I could not cope with alone, would wield no power before the violence of the masses, I supposed. That was my salvation. No, if I was dragged into the scuffle, it was hardly salvation—my head full of such contradictory thoughts, I felt as though I would lose all sense of what to do.

Presently, the usual number of nurses assembled, but they did not seem to be talking about S especially; I was imagining things, maybe it was nothing at all. The hospital rooms were there to heal sickness, perhaps there was no reason a patient should not leave by his own will. Still, I could not wipe away my loathing for S.

That S, as scrawny and thin as he was, had been able to squeeze through the bars on the window seemed miraculous, the result of his extraordinary determination. Since the dressing room was used only by employees, perhaps the bars were considerably farther apart than in other places, but even so, this was no mean feat. Had they during the day put a padlock on that door so that the patients could not get near the windows with the widely spaced bars?

* * *

As usual, my wife's symptoms showed no sign of abating. Would we never know when these nervous psychological tangles would end? Might not this condition go on and on forever?

I was gradually losing my staying power. Fragile and irritable, when my wife began to have an attack, I could not now repress my own unsightly symptoms, no less dramatic than hers.

Then my wife, despite her gratitude that ours was a locked ward, occasionally began to harass and perplex me even more by hinting that she was going to escape. That for me was a torment. I wished they would increase ward security, add iron doors, more locks.

Though in my distress I imagined a prison cell might bring us peace, the real problem was simply how long I could keep going, withstanding my wife's symptoms. Could I continue to sustain myself? If I managed, perhaps my wife's symptoms would disappear. I could then sustain my wife, and we could sustain the children. No, my brain was in a tangle. One of the patients had said that being in a closed cell caused their anxiety and made them want to escape, but in my case, exactly the opposite was true: it was because the restrictions weren't tighter that I could never relax.

*   *   *

It was natural that, having been hospitalized because we had become unable to deal with the world, we should have few visitors. One of our rare visitors was my wife's cousin, a university student who paid us a casual visit a little past the middle of August.

Certainly, my wife and I both had eagerly awaited his visit. This was because we knew that, having gone home for the summer vacation, he would come back with detailed news of our two children.

One way to avoid my wife's symptoms was to talk about the children. I often tried picturing various scenes from the children's daily life in my wife's native village on an island in the south and recounting them to my wife. We would recall the special little childish expressions they had used and write them all down in a notebook; then we would think of their unhappiness and their loneliness. All my own memories were of not having treated the children with loving kindness, and when I was demoralized by my wife's attacks, the mere mention of the children's names was enough to reduce me to tears. When, clutching the windowbars, I gazed at the outside world, the young voices of unknown children passing by made me envious. Weren't our own children perhaps quite ill, unused to the climate and the water? For all we knew something horrible had happened to them. At the thought I became so restless that I could not stand still. This torment would last forever; it seized me with such sheer, graphic power that it seemed to be accompanied by the physical pain of being in a wooden vise. When my wife said, "If anything happens to the children it will be your fault, and I will curse you for the rest of my life!" I began to think she was absolutely right. And I began to be sure that something untimely had already occurred to the two children, that, therefore, I had been condemned to have my chest and heart in an instrument of torture for all eternity.

In any case, our desire to find out at the first possible moment how the children were getting along was fulfilled by his visit. It did not seem, however, that we could rest completely assured. Both children had severe rashes all over the lower part of their bodies, and the younger one, perhaps for that reason, had been running a fever and lay in bed, her head on a cold water bottle. Even so, when she was feeling better, she amused them all by singing little songs off key, but she seemed rather listless, he said. It was just because of the rash, so there was nothing to worry about, he repeated, but I did not miss the slight shadow that passed over my wife's face. I had to anticipate that this cousin's visit would make matters worse and prepare myself: afterwards, without fail, it would induce a deep-rooted attack. My mind was preoccupied with that fear, plus the anxiety of being too far away to ascertain the children's condition, but all I could do was to check the expression on my wife's face with an air of indifference, yet carefully, as though I were making my way over thin ice.

Once the dark shadow had passed, my wife immediately regained her bright expression. After all, she seemed extremely pleased that her cousin had visited us. I thought I had better ask her cousin to spend the night and use him as an intermediary to prolong my wife's psychological tension.

That evening my wife was full of life. Had my worry been needless anxiety? Hearing, after so long, of the activities of close friends and relatives in her home town had calmed my wife's spirits. As far as the children were concerned too, at least she had been able to get a general idea of how they were doing directly from someone who had just seen them, and this was, for my wife, a great relief, I thought.

* * *

But my wife's usual attack visited her punctually that night. It was not long after we had crawled into bed that, thinking "Oh oh, here we go," I felt my body go numb, and in my impatience at having to do something (though there was nothing I could do), an oatmeal-like substance filled my whole head and I was forcibly dragged into a weary hatred. Taken quite by surprise, I had not been psychologically prepared for the attack; you could say that I began to show my own symptoms, in anticipation of my wife's.

I had completely relaxed at my wife's good mood just before bedtime. We gave one bed to her cousin, and my wife and I slept together in the other. Because of the cousin sleeping near us, I was breathing easily, thinking I had been relieved of the long and delicate nightly process of trying to get my wife to sleep without inciting her symptoms. Tonight I would be able to get a good night's sleep. Thanks to the reassurance of her native village air and the tension of her cousin's presence, my wife would sleep soundly. For me, it had become second nature to live in dread of my wife's symptoms, and I was somewhat worried now. But even so, I didn't expect them to start so quickly. I blamed myself for being off my guard. Yet even had I not been careless, I could have done nothing. At that realization my anger returned, at double its original intensity. After my miscalculation, the jolt was twice as dramatic as usual; I was dropped with a thud off my high cliff down to the earth that was reality.

My wife broke free of the arms I held around her. Ordinarily, that would not be an especially remarkable act. For the two of us now, however, it was a clear indication that my wife was on the verge of an attack. Even though I knew that from that point on any effort was futile, I continued to flounder in that pitiful futility. And I began to feel impatient with simply spinning my wheels. Somewhat stubbornly, aggressively, I tried to embrace my wife again after she had slipped out of my arms. Again my wife roughly brushed my arms away. I began to feel spiteful (I knew what my wife would say later: All I did was move your arms so I could go to sleep and you got rough and egged me on and *made* me have an attack!). Neither of us spoke because her cousin was sleeping in the bed right next to us. Her oppression intensified by the silence, my wife got up and sat on top of the covers. Here again, that in itself was nothing special. But for the two of us, it simply indicated that my wife was firmly attached to the rails of an inevitable attack. If I didn't attend to her in some way, my wife would pass the whole night in that position. Then the attack would be prolonged, lasting perhaps until the following day, even the day after that.

"Why, Miho? All right, then, what in the world do you want me to do?"

Losing control of myself, I hurled at her these ineffectual words. Already I sensed that I was being invaded and drawn into the mechanism of my wife's attack, but I was powerless to stop it.

"Sh, you'll wake up T. You go to sleep," said my wife quite calmly.

Even if her cousin did overhear, what she said must have sounded reasonable enough. He would be more likely to wonder about my attitude, I supposed. What would happen, however, if I took my wife literally and went to sleep (though of course I couldn't sleep), only I could know. Go to sleep! But the words did not mean what they seemed to mean. My wife had already assumed that other personality, the personality she assumed when she fell prey to an attack.

The only thing different that night was that the attack was not accompanied by my wife's persistent cross-examination, her seemingly unending spate of words. Possibly her cousin's visit had something to do with that.

Tense as I was, I had let myself doze off.

When I awoke with a start, I saw the effects of that blank in time. Perhaps I had snatched a brief instant of sleep, but my wife was in the throes of an attack, her nerves seething; I knew she had been gnawing away at the passing time. Realizing I had been caught off guard, I looked around for my wife and found her at my feet, curled up on the bed like a dog, her head facing away from me. This posture was menacing. At the same time, I felt my blood race with sudden rage. (How long are you going to keep tormenting me?)

"Miho, what in the world is wrong with you? Will you please sleep like everybody else? Is it that you don't like to be in the same bed with me, is that it? Why don't you just say so and I'll go sleep with T." In a tone of voice even I found disagreeable, I badgered my wife mercilessly.

Without saying a word, my wife rose and, throwing back the mosquito netting, opened the door and went out into the corridor.

You see what happens? You see? Stifling my inclination to wail, I was unable to check the tightening in my chest, the futile irritation at the fatigue of two hearts that now must pursue their separate parallel courses, back to back, until my wife's attack had finally subsided. Eyes gleaming in the darkness, I glared up at the ceiling.

In the moonlight filtering through gaps in the window curtains, I was able to ascertain the approximate position of the hands on my watch; I judged that it was about one-thirty. I was under the impression that I had just dozed off a bit, but what had seemed like a moment was actually quite awhile. Sure that during all that time my wife had been absorbed in her obsession, I shuddered and blamed myself—wasn't my wife so ill she was beyond being able to control herself? There was no excuse for my present state of mind. Once embroiled in my wife's attacks, however, despite myself I began to behave as though I were having my own attack.

I knew where my wife had gone. I did not doubt that she was either in the dressing room in the patients' bath or in the little storeroom. But since it was late at night and getting chilly, she certainly would not be able to stay where she was forever. She would come back. Then I would apologize abjectly and somehow or other get her to bed. My wife was ill. When her suspicious interrogation began, I would bear the tenacious constricting pain and go along with her. And in this contrite frame of mind, expecting her to return at any moment, I thought I heard her footsteps coming down the corridor, untimid, as though she had reached some decision, whereupon she came unceremoniously into the room. Suddenly, my good intentions drew in their horns and shrank back. I had been one instant late in responding and, as a result, just lay in bed where I was, holding my breath and observing her. My wife opened a suitcase, changed out of the simple dress she used as a nightgown (her wallet was under my pillow), and immediately left the room. Pretending to be asleep, I lay perfectly still. Now all I had to do was jump up and grab her. Doing so would not have eased her attack, but it would at least have avoided the extra anxiety that followed (anxiety accompanied by unforseeable danger). I let still another moment go by. I tried to make myself believe that she had come to put on more clothes because it was cold. At this rate, she might very well be intending to spend the whole night in the dressing room. In just a little while longer I'll go and get her. So thinking, I went back to sleep. That night the temperature fell much lower than usual, and the chill kept one from getting out of bed lightly.

Barely able to resist the sleep into which I was drawn, I had returned to my waking self. Thinking "Now I've done it," I went out into the corridor. According to my watch it was almost three o'clock.

I hurried to the dressing room. I went with the clear image in my mind, so clear I could almost touch it, of my wife with her back to me, pressing her body against the windowbars, forlornly watching the noiseless passage of time in the outside world that suggested the nearness of the sea. But emptiness reigned there; I saw no sign whatever of my wife. Immediately I went on to the storeroom and put my hand to the door. At that point I still expected to find my wife inside, crouching like a cat, her eyes flashing, determined not to let me open the door; but the door opened easily, offering no resistance, revealing only the stuffy, damp smell of mold. Had I finally let my wife slip away? The helpless feeling surged through me that this time it was not just anybody, but my own wife, who had escaped. Slowly and carefully, I opened the doors of every lavatory, and I checked the patients' kitchen. The door to the courtyard was locked from the inside. What had she managed to crawl under? Where was she hiding? Checking all those places one more time, I headed in the direction of the nurses' station. Maybe she was there, chatting with the nurses on duty.

But in the nurses' station time was passing in complete stillness. A nurse was repeatedly entering figures on a large sheet of white paper. Another lay face up on a sofa with her right fist raised to her forehead. I could hear the pen distinctly as it scratched over the paper.

"Nurse," I called in a low voice from the doorway. The nurse who had been writing figures looked up, and the one who was lying down hurriedly got up. Both of them had red eyes.

"You haven't seen my wife by any chance?"

"What? Oh your wife," said the nurse writing the figures. "She must be in the courtyard."

She said this in such a positive tone of voice that I found myself going along with her and even thinking I had flown into a panic for nothing.

"A few minutes ago I thought I heard the door open, so I went and looked around with a flashlight, but nobody was there, so I locked up again. I guess I must have locked her out."

My spirits lifted, I borrowed a flashlight and followed her out into the courtyard. Locked out by the nurse and unable to get back in, my wife was probably cowering, trembling in the bushes. The poor thing must be wet from the night dew and chilled to the bone. Dummy, see what you get for being so stubborn? It occurred to me that maybe her head had cooled by now and her attack subsided— but then again, having been ignored for nearly two hours might well have exacerbated it. In any case, it had gotten so cold outside I would have to warm her up. So thinking, I hurriedly shone the flashlight at the base of trees and around the shrubbery in the rather small garden, but, for whatever reason, there was no sign of her.

My sandals and my feet were drenched with the night dew. Without a word, the two nurses conducted their independent searches. I supposed it was their responsibility, since they were the nurses on duty. What did they care that I stood at the crossroads of fate? I searched painstakingly three times, but my wife was not to be found. I could not keep myself from feeling progressively sad and pathetic. What should I do? What to do? Not that there was really anything much I *could* do. If she wasn't in the courtyard, did that mean she had really escaped from the ward and run away? But where had she gotten out? Remembering my wife's expression when she was in the throes of an attack, I began to feel that she would go to any lengths to escape, but *where* would she escape from? Especially in the middle of the night?

"Where do you live? Maybe she went home," the nurse suggested.

"Home?" (Taken by surprise, I could not answer immediately.) "We have no home. She has no place to go but here," I said, feeling rather meager, and the small concrete reservoir in the center of the courtyard weighed on my mind.

"At any rate, I'll go report to the doctor in charge," said one of the nurses, and she walked back to the ward exit door (the doctor in charge was sleeping in another ward); the other nurse went back to our hospital room, so I followed her. If my wife had escaped, I would have to make the nurses understand the situation. The idea flitted continually through my brain. But I stubbornly persisted in thinking that even if I requested the nurses to begin a search, and even if the doctor in charge came, the situation would not change. The only reason for following the proper "procedure" in an orderly fashion was so that the hierarchy within the ward would be left intact. But the relationship between my wife and myself was not apt to be altered by something like that. Perhaps I had already unconsciously understood my wife's wordless action. It was true that, in a way completely unrelated to what the nurses were doing, in some unfathomable realm, my wife and I were in communication with each other. I did feel that the friendly sympathy, however awkwardly displayed by the remaining nurse, went beyond the fastidiousness engendered by a sense of responsibility to her job. If she noticed that her excess of sympathy was unappreciated, she would be hurt. Though I had no way of expressing it, I was overflowing with gratitude. She checked all the private and semiprivate rooms to see whether my wife might not be lurking in one of them. She was the nurse I had caught napping on the couch a little while earlier. As I walked on tiptoe with this nurse down the long corridor, my wife's disappearance sadly and clearly took on meaning. The image of her wandering crazed, disheveled, who knows where through overgrown weeds, her bold patterned skirt fluttering like pieces of paper, flashed before my eyes. Then all the many forms my wife's attacks had assumed since she began to show abnormal symptoms nearly a year ago assailed me, forming one solid, thick layer all around me. Despite the pain, the torture, a seductive murmur somehow lingered in my ear. Separated from my wife, I cannot live.

"Does a corpse float or sink in water?" I asked suddenly, and the nurse focused steadily on me, her pupils in the exact center of her eyes.

"It surfaces and floats for a while, then sinks again."

When had she acquired this bit of information, I wondered. But her manner inclined me to think that she must be right; I only half listened to her words, thinking maybe there is an etiquette for declarative statements. Realizing the knowledge was of no use to me now, I said, "I'll go look in the pond." I went back out into the courtyard, stood at the edge of the pond, and looked steadily at the surface of the water.

I thought I saw some weeds or something that the patients had thrown in during the daytime floating there—Or were they bubbles rising from the dark depths of the pond? Wasn't that a body washed up against the far end? I felt like jumping into the reservoir (in a courtyard where patients are allowed to come and go freely, it can't be so very deep), stirring up the whole thing, going around with just my head above water, checking every inch of the water and the bottom. And I had an intense desire to cry out at the top of my lungs. I could almost feel my wife's corpse, its spongy resistance to my hands as I tried to lift it. As if stuck to the bottom of the pond, for an instant it would not move at all, but it soon seemed to peel itself away and, without any support from me, float up with uncertain weightlessness, breaking through the water's surface. So my wife was dead; it had finally happened. Was it for this death, her long, long suffering? My sins will be judged inexpiable. For eternity I will never be able to crush the mountain of my guilt. I looked at the night sky and muttered to myself that that was the way it should be. I felt a lump in my throat, and one tear slid down my cheek. Suddenly, I seemed to see our younger child, matured to a girl of seventeen or eighteen, taking care of me, now old and feeble and tubercular.

There was a continuous ringing in my ear. It felt as though a highly polished brass wire hung abstractly in the empty space in my head, twanging out a high plaintive tone like a shriek. I began to sense in it my wife's raw, unalloyed will. Finding her attacks so hard to bear, had I not focused blindly on the phenomenon itself, so that I had become unable to see its naked form? My wife's voice, terribly pure, hung in my ear, inside my head, calling me on and on until I felt, along with that voice, her deep gaze pitying my stupidity.

Surely, my wife of all people would not have disappeared so cruelly. I felt a kind of certainty about it. There was no need to jump into the pond. Something whispered that. Taking a pole from the clothes drying rack, I plunged the end of it into the pond and began slowly moving it around.

The tip of the pole seemed to catch in the slippery, clinging water, and it was harder than I expected to move it around; after I stirred each area, I was impelled by the suspicion that I might have missed a spot, and I intently covered every inch of the small pond many times over.

While I was doing this, I began to feel as though I could talk with my wife through the tip of the pole. (Toshio, how unlike you to immerse yourself so completely in devotion to me. I'm impressed. Now at last I can believe in you.) I found myself feeling just like a little child running a race with his mother watching.

At some point the doctor in charge had joined us and was standing next to me. Arms folded, he watched without a word. The two nurses also looked on silently. Actually, I preferred their silence, because it allowed me to continue my invisible conversation with my wife.

Even so, from time to time I turned my eyes to glance at the doctor. His posture suggested strong will and rationality, precise judgment, ironclad rules. It was also the attitude of omnipotent science. Feeling tongue-tied, I was communicating with my wife through the tip of the pole. During the war, I had looked exactly as this doctor did now as, arms folded, I stood by and watched the soldiers under my command perform their night duties.

Then I spoke: "She doesn't seem to be here." The doctor still said nothing. When I considered the troublesome process the doctor and the nurses would have to go through now because of my wife's escape, my heart sank.

"Did she take her medicine with her?" the doctor asked curtly.

"There was some she was saving up instead of taking—I'll go look," I said and went back to the room.

Her cousin was still sleeping, unaware. Rummaging through the desk drawer, I found about ten packets of medicine. Grabbing them in one handful, I went back to the courtyard.

When I returned, lo and behold, there standing next to the nurse was my wife.

Without speaking, I walked up to them (the tower of tragedy topples with a crack). Still shuddering (the white film flutters and dances, and quickly unwinds), I hesitated as to how to greet my wife.

One of the nurses returned sullenly to the nurses' station. The doctor had already disappeared.

Seeing me, my wife smiled brightly. No, it wasn't because she saw me; she seemed to be smiling brightly for the benefit of the doctor and nurse.

"I suddenly felt like going home to Kitten (our nickname for our little daughter). I walked and walked, and then I got lost," my wife said to me.

I shuddered anew. My wife's home, where we had left the children, was a day and a night's trip by boat from Kagoshima. You couldn't walk there.

Laboring to keep my voice down (feeling as though the skin on my face were losing heat and might peel off), I asked, "Then where did you get in?"

"Over there." She turned all the way around and pointed at a six-foot board fence, on top of which there lurked in the darkness another six feet of barbed wire.

"I heard a thud and ran over to see, and there was your wife," said the nurse who always stayed behind, holding my wife's arm as if to support her.

"Did you hurt yourself?"

"Nope. I'm not hurt or anything."

Undaunted, my wife looked as if to say she couldn't imagine what I'd been so worried about. I stole a glance at her face and clothes. Were there no snags or scratches from the barbed wire? As I pictured her, fearless, slipping easily as a fox through a gap in the barbed wire, silhouetted against the night sky on the ridgeline on the board fence, I became somewhat agitated. I thought I would like to be alone with her in order to get a better look at her body.

It was not out of despair, in the extremity of an attack, that my wife had fled. Why had my gloomy thoughts dwelt so on that idea? She did not even think of herself as having "escaped" from the hospital. She had wanted to see her child on her home island because her cousin had said she wasn't well, so she had tried to go there—that was all. Ignoring the obstacles that stood in her path, my wife had scaled the fence and gone.

"But I came back because you cried."

"Did you hear me cry?" I asked, without contradicting her.

"Mm-hm. Miho, Miho, you howled, just like a dog."

The nurse had left my wife in my charge and disappeared.

Under the corridor lights, I examined my wife's face once more. Just on her large, white forehead, in one fine line just at the hairline, I could make out traces of blood. It was ever so slightly seductive. The observation was accompanied by the physical sensation of touching with my fingers the scar on her left buttock she said was from a childhood wound.

I was still worrying whether her attack was really over, and how to deal with the doctor and nurses after this incident, but my wife was strangely full of energy. It seemed as though she had drunk her fill of drops of dew and moonlight, and life had been blown back into her.

INTERPRETIVE COMMENTS ON THE STORIES

"The Farthest Edge of the Islands" and
"This Time That Summer"

These two stories, written some fifteen years apart, were both inspired by Shimao's experience as commanding officer of a suicide squadron on Kakeromajima in the Amami Archepelago of the Ryukyus. Read together, they show some obvious contrasts. They depict the days immediately before and after Japan's surrender; though separated by less than forty-eight hours, their worlds are at least superficially in stark contrast. Most of "The Farthest Edge of the Islands" takes place at night, from just after sunset to just before dawn, whereas most of the scenes in "This Time That Summer" occur in the daytime, between early morning and sunset. The village beyond the mountain pass is, for Lieutenant Saku, the quintessential "village of night," whose daytime aspect he is never to see, where flowering trees bloom "secretly, quietly, only at night." In the very middle of this village reigning over the darkness, giving it meaning, is Toë, who "lives only for the nights." The light from her silver candle–lamp, when all other lights in the village are hidden for fear of enemy air raids, draws him to her by "fate," as if to the center of his own being (he is after all the "daytime lamp," who also should come into his own at night, when he submits himself to darkness or to the symbols and passions of his unconscious), and compels him to visit her regularly thereafter. "This Time That Summer" is mainly an account of daily routine and the conscious daytime efforts of the commanding officer to give rational structure to his surroundings. Toë is relegated to a minor role, to the shadows beyond the reach of the lamp in the room where her father entertains the lieutenant. Now that the lieutenant can see her at will, he has lost his sense of urgency; he does not want to "burn up all at once" a passion that will now have to last him many years.

The style of narration in the two stories emphasizes the contrast. "The Farthest Edge of the Islands" is told as a fairy tale, in simple language and short sentences with desu-masu endings, occasionally addressing the reader directly in a rhetorical tone characteristic of children's books. The opening sentence, "This story takes place long ago, when the whole world was at war," sets the stage in an indefinite time in the distant past, very different from the present and no longer remembered by the reader; the place names are imaginary. Kagerōjima, presumably a verbal play on Kakeromajima, means, to use Waley's famous translation

143

of the word, "Gossamer" Island, suggesting a figment of the imagination. "This Time That Summer" is a much more matter of fact and specific first-person chronicle of events, in de aru endings. The sentences are long and full of technical, logical, and interpretive vocabulary. The title itself implies a temporal continuity with the present, and the use of initials, O, N, H, for names of characters and places suggests real details discreetly unidentified out of consideration for those involved.

"This Time That Summer" makes explicit comparisons between the tenor of life before and after the surrender. With the relaxation of the extraordinary tension created by the imminence of certain death for a transcendent cause, the activity of building revetments and training for the mission—in the atmosphere of anticipation that dominates "The Farthest Edge of the Islands"—is replaced in "This Time That Summer" by dismantling equipment (the torpedo-boat warheads), demobilization, and relinquishing what has been given them (the flat-bottomed boats, the carp, authority over the villagers). The intensity has faded. As he is going to the village to read the Imperial Proclamation, the lieutenant thinks to himself on the familiar mountain path that even the village has changed for him with the defeat:

> I remembered my own midnight visits there, constricted by my regulation death uniform: the red earth on the pass, the banyan tree and the growth along the roadside, the color of the sea viewed from above, the layout of the village, then the cluster of thatched roofs, the cries of frogs and owls, the smell of the trees and flowers, all vividly made their presence known. I, for whom ill fortune had closed off the road ahead, had felt the dubious intensity of being in a vacuum, a desire to burn myself out in a single instant. But now that things had gone back to the way they had been, the scene shifted to one of monotony, and I was apt to stagnate in weariness and repetition. I hoped to gaze again some day, after many years had passed, on the path over the mountain and the village below.

And with the loss of intensity come new complexities: reputations to restore, details to dispose of, the threat of court cases. Simple animosity directed uniformly at the enemy is dispersed, like the explosive powder in the process of defusing the warheads, into little feuds between men from different regions or of different rank. Directionlessness has become their overriding purpose.

So these two stories are in a sense "about" existential freedom, about what happens when the (disagreeable) limitations of space, time, duty, and ideology are removed. The reprieve from certain death represented by these two stories in combination raises, as it did for Dostoyevsky under similar circumstances, existential questions about the effects of freedom on human beings.[1] But the shift from night to daylight and the implied spiritual rebirth means accepting responsibility for life without direction from above, accepting responsibility specifically for what you have been doing in the past, worrying about the *atoshimatsu* (cleaning up afterwards), taking care of undone things that "resurrect themselves," and ultimately facing trial and atoning for wrongdoings.

Despite striking differences, however, there are remarkable elements of continuity in these works and the worlds they create. Consider the treatment of time, for example. In "The Farthest Edge of the Islands" are several scenes focusing on transition (the last rays of sunset), or on intimations of something to come (the Little Dipper heralding the appearance of the Morning Star). Yet fear and anticipation tend to stretch out the moment, to slow down time to the extent that change is imperceptible. On the brink of obliteration, when only a few may be left "to cry like crickets after a typhoon," time becomes meaningless except as the present moment. The past is irrelevant, and there is no future; there is only *now*. Each day seems "separate, discrete, as though there were no connection with the day before or the day after." Lieutenant Saku's vision of the future defies the flow of time: "All things . . . were to be cut off from him; on the other side of a deep rupture they would recede rapidly like the ebbing tide." "This Time That Summer" creates a similar sense of drawn-out time, a "vacuum" or "blank" (*kūhaku*) caused here, too, by anticipation of the unknowable. In the meantime, there is no way of calculating how long the "tensionless, monotonous life would last . . . and the hopeful swell of life just out of reach." This story focuses on the coming of darkness as the other does on the coming of daylight, and both stories end with sustained moments of anticipation just before a major change.

Both stories begin after one abrupt change and continue until just before another. The pattern is characteristic of other stories in this collection as well, but it is most obvious in "This Time That Summer," which begins, in fact, with the words, "The next morning," and presents a series of episodes, each paired explicitly or implicitly with a similar occurrence with which it is in dramatic contrast. Gradually, the emphasis shifts to prospects for beginning a new life in a new era that awaits them after the conclusion of peace agreements and demobilization arrangements. Elements of the same pattern are present in "The Farthest Edge of the Islands." The story begins not long after the suicide squadron has come to Shohaate, changing the face of the island and creating "something unsettled in the air" in Toë's village. When the lieutenant receives ominous dispatches suggesting that the time of their mission is at hand, on both occasions it is just after sunset (and the story ends, of course, just before sunrise). When the second dispatch arrives with the instructions to stand by for sailing orders, it is "one night past the full moon," and the lieutenant realizes that the inevitable attack will certainly come on a moonlit night. Even his name "Saku" is written with the character for astrological conjunction; its other (*kun*) reading is "tsuitachi," the first day of the month.

Toë, in contrast, seems in a way to transcend time, not to be bound by it—
at least until the lieutenant begins to take over her life and she becomes acutely
aware of the passage of *his* time. No one knows how old she is, but she looks very
young. No one knows, either, when or how she came to live in her house, in a
garden surrounded by roses that "bloomed the year round."

There is a strong sense of a lost past in this story, perhaps related to Toë's
lost timelessness. Toë is an orphan; the Bible with the gold embossed cross on the
cover is her only memento of her mother, who died when Toë was an infant. Only
the oldest people in the village know anything about Toë's mysterious birth, and,
one assumes, about other things as well. In "This Time That Summer," this past
has its counterpart in the lost intensity of an era of order, belief, and authority
that is suddenly invalidated by the end of the war.

One sees in these stories the alternation of two phases, a dark and a light,
and a main character who is somehow out of phase, "a lamp in broad daylight" who
misreads the tide chart, becomes zealous in executing his duties only after the
mission has been aborted, loses his intense desire for Toë when he is free to see
her, and realizes the necessity of looking over the text of the Imperial Proclamation only when it is too late.

Yet the two phases are essentially similar; each is a "vacuum" in which one
regrets the past and fears the future. The first episode in "This Time That
Summer" suggests such essential similarity.

> That same man, who one day before had affected a modest stoop and
> an ingratiating smile, the very next day had come all by himself,
> rowing his little wooden boat through the inlet right up to the base in
> order to get matters settled. On his face was no vestige of
> yesterday's smile; what it displayed instead was the confidence of
> self-sufficiency. There was even something that made one suspect
> that this self-reliance was no different today than it had been the day
> before.

Between the two stories is a rupture in time to which both stories refer.
Balancing a passage from "The Farthest Edge of the Islands" quoted earlier, is a
mirror image in "This Time That Summer": "The war had ended, with no exposure
to battle. The suicide squadron's mission stood poised for an instant, its back
turned, on the opposite edge of a chasm, then went away."

Barriers—chasms, walls, mountains, abrupt transitions between different
realms—are a prominent motif in both stories, analogous perhaps to the juxtapo-
sition of phases, or a vantage point from which two phases might be surveyed at
once. The mountain pass, marking the border between two worlds, contains elements of the dangers of both: the sentry and the eerie banyan tree with the
mythological threat of a *Kenmun* hiding beneath it. It is here that most of the
lieutenant's mystical experiences take place.

The progression of time is handled slightly differently in the two narra-
tives. "The Farthest Edge of the Islands" alternates between daily records with
explicit chronicling of the activities of night, and sections of indefinite time
introduced by sudden shifts to verb forms indicating repetitive action. There are
two such sections, both of which begin as the lieutenant is crossing the mountain
pass to return to the base before sunrise. The effect is to change the pace of
time: to create a bubble or a vacuum in which cycles are repeated indefinitely, on
the brink of a change of phase, after which the narrative continues on exactly as
before, so that the sequence of events would be totally intelligible without noticeable interruption if the "bubble" were removed. The shift in narrative time
creates the impression of attenuation, of walking in place.

> Each night when he had soothed Toë and was on his way home, he
> came to the foot of the banyan tree at the pass. A strange voice
> from the village below lingered in his ears and stopped him in his
> tracks. It put him in an unusual frame of mind, as if the entire village
> were submerged beneath blue waters and the sorrows of the people of
> the village crystallized into the cry of a curse. Presently, very
> faintly, like methane gas bubbling up from the depths of the pond, the
> voice assumed the tones of one young girl gone mad, insistently
> transfixing the youth who was crossing the pass and leaving the
> village behind. The voice echoed on and on in a melody like no music
> he had ever heard. The lieutenant put his fingers in his ears and
> hurried on, but the melody was still with him. It was Toë, who had
> run barefoot down onto the beach and was singing, singing "I shall
> never see my love again. . . ."

The crystallized voices, the water that slows down motion and communication, the
sound that rings on and on, all suggest suspended animation as the lieutenant is
"transfixed" by Toë's voice.

The passing of time in "This Time That Summer" is more regular. Like
"The Farthest Edge of the Islands," this story recounts the events of three days
and nights, but one passage suggesting repeated action of questionable duration
("But the dazzling summer days passed innocently on . . .") makes the total time
span of this story, too, indefinite, suggesting the plasticity and ultimate meaninglessness of time. Here again it is images associated with the mountain pass
(especially the frog with the human voice that becomes Toë's in the passage
above) that transport the lieutenant to another dimension, outside the rational
world of the base.

> Coming down that road, and when I left the village and went back to
> the base as well, the expanse of paddy fields redirected my inward-
> turned spirit, and at the chorus of frogs my body and mind were
> gently lifted and carried away in an unexpected direction.

This effect occurs on the mountain path, both going and coming; it marks transition. In another passage this dimension is more explicitly linked to a different progression of time. The scene this time is the lieutenant's own room, but the "mountain stream" and the frogs make the association with the pass:

> I could hear the deep mountain stream that ran beside my room and the hoarse croaking of frogs under the floor boards, but the stillness deepened until presently it invaded my ears, ringing on and on. Suddenly, I got up with the thought of slipping out to O, but the inclination soon withered. Ah, the dizziness: everything starting to return to the past, the sensation of reverting once more to those distant days. Then those days once again sidled up to the war, whirling around and around without cease; there was no possibility of survival—but the war had now ended. No matter how short the interval, for a while death had looked away and I could let myself do as I myself wished. . . . The cry of frogs, like the sound of hard, dry walnuts rubbed against each other—it was a soft, gentle, low sound, sinking off into the distance, marking off and protecting the area within its range as a comfortable hidden village. I listened, abandoning myself to those tremolos that made me desperately want to live, until I was no longer sure they were frogs. They might be insects hiding in the earth; it was like something I had heard before, yet somehow different, like something one heard only in the warm night air of the southern islands.

Unlike that quoted from "The Farthest Edge of the Islands," this passage deals at first with a dramatic transition, in this case a disturbance of time represented by the intrusion of "whirling" cycles from the past; the passage goes on, after a syntactical rupture, to prospects for the future. What it describes, therefore, is a transition between two transitions, a "brief interval in which death had looked away." And this brief interval is dominated by the time-transcendent image of the mysterious sound ringing on and on, the cries of the frogs that are both familiar and new, suggesting during the daytime the world of night.

When the lieutenant is on his way back to the base after dining at the deputy major's house, the cries of the frogs move him to reinterpret his immediate past:

> The life to which I had submitted in total earnest, obediently surrendering my body to preparations for a suicide mission, now seemed like a counterfeit, a phony. The croaking of the frogs overwhelmed my body and passed on, as if washing away the various toils and obligations of humanity.

They pass on by him, as if emphasizing his stillness. Their time and his time are different: their time works a purifying change in man's world, here, in a pattern of reversal common to these stories seen paradoxically as stationary against a backdrop of motion. In "The Farthest Edge of the Islands," the lieutenant's heart "races ahead" as he feels stalled in meaningless time just before the "inevitable crisis"; the cries of the frogs race on ahead offering some consolation, some promise of renewal—a negative and a positive version of the future that are characteristic of Shimao's fiction.

Particularly in "This Time That Summer," barriers and borderlines are a recurrent motif. As in "The Heart that Slips Away," walls and gates with restricted exit and entry confine the characters to an area markedly different from the world at large. Such restrictions, like the "walls of military regulations," make the characters want to escape but, at the same time, offer security and peace of mind. The secret naval base is, of course, a place of extreme danger and coercion; yet it is also the "hidden village" "marked off and protected" by the cries of the frogs.

The lieutenant is generally a solitary observer. When the lieutenant was in Officer's Candidate School, "a thin membrane that always stubbornly peeled itself off" had formed between him and the rest of the men. He is often pictured inside looking out, or outside looking in. He shines his flashlight into Toë's room and into the Fourth Flotilla barracks, where he oozes "an incompatibility irritating to the skin."

Inside-outside images are implicit in the contrast between interior and exterior views of characters in the story; one has the strong sense of being inside one mind and excluded from others, relying on judgment from external visual evidence. The words *kaotsuki*, "facial expression, countenance," and *ushirosugata*, "form seen from behind," appear frequently in this story (and the others in this volume) and are applied to events and abstract concepts as often as to people.

The alternation of light and dark phases, the recurrent pattern of crossing boundaries into the unknown, and many specific images (water, boats, the Morning Star) create a conspicuous motif in these stories of death and rebirth, both physical and psychological, as I have suggested above. But there are strong spiritual—in fact, religious—aspects to this motif. One, present in the "sick wife" stories also, is clearly Christian, associated with the death and the resurrection of Christ.[2] The cross is mentioned three times in "The Farthest Edge of the Islands." The lanterns that remind Ogusuku of "lights of the town that grew and shrank like crosses he had watched in painful ecstasy as a child," for example, draw the reader's attention because the reference is completely unexplained and we are allowed no other psychological insight into this minor character. Toë's Bible with the gold embossed cross that "steals the warmth from her cheek" is also associated with the distant past, with the death of her mother and her own birth. Toë spends the night on the beach expecting to die, clasping the lieutenant's dagger to her "like a cross," and in that position she greets the dawning of a new day. The food that Toë offers the lieutenant is fish:

In the village under the pale, pale moonlight, beyond the mountain
ridge, playing dead on a cutting board there lies a cool fish that has
swallowed a pearl.

another symbol of Christ, clearly associated here with a temporary death.[3] The
cape around which Toë makes her way to see the lieutenant late at night resembles at high tide "the stern image of a standing god." When she reaches the
"place where the banyan trees grew," presumably directly below the mountain
path, she kneels in the shelter of the rocks and prays. For Toë, there is a god
associated with the cape, the barrier between two worlds, a "stern" figure analogous to the night watchman on the mountain pass that the lieutenant must cross to
enter Toë's world—both protective and judgmental.

Shimao's main characters are often unseen observers, hidden by the light of
the flashlight they direct toward the human objects of their scrutiny. The lieutenant in "This Time That Summer," essentially a benevolent commanding officer,
makes the inspection rounds of the barracks, where he judges, reprimands, even
punishes the men ruthlessly. He has power and can be capricious. But at the same
time, Shimao's characters feel watched and judged—by the sentry on the pass, or
by unseen or abstract beings: the nighttime enemy planes, for instance, "with
eyes that could see in the dark," or the dead leaves in Toë's garden that "were wet
from the rain and gleamed like eyes." In "This Time That Summer" the lieutenant
envisions military regulations "turning a stern countenance toward those who had
ignored them." "Vengeance" is a recurrent word. Toë's midnight ordeal as she
makes her way past the stern god to the lieutenant's side of the cape seems to him
"bitter punishment intended for himself," and "This Time That Summer" is dominated by the apprehension that he will somehow be brought to trial, held "ultimately responsible" for the safety of his men, the maintenance of the torpedo
boats, and the legality of dealings with the villagers. Perhaps the final hour of
"This Time That Summer," when "everything would come to an end" is this last
judgment, for the lieutenant associated with the image of an old man "wearing his
ragged clothes, barefoot and empty handed, all alone."

Ryukyuan folk tradition provides another religious motif to these stories,
curiously reinforcing the Christian one in a number of ways. The Kenmun goblin
that lives under the banyan trees on the pass and the cape is feared, as I
mentioned earlier, for his dreadful interrogation and, depending on the outcome,
cruel punishment of passersby. When Toë pauses to pray on her way around the
cape, it is because she hears the sound of oars and thinks the spirits of the Dead
are passing by. According to Ryukyuan tradition, the spirits of the ancestors, the
guardian "father" gods, regularly visit the islands from across the ocean, beyond
the horizon, to communicate with the people, the "son" gods of the islands.
During an annual rite of praying and feasting in the family cemeteries, a
shamaness or priestess sings special songs to welcome the visiting spirits.

Yoshimoto Takaaki has pointed out that the lieutenant in Shimao's stories of the suicide squadron could be seen as a visiting god from across the seas, and Toë as the priestess who welcomed him and was ritually sacrificed to him, offering him her body and her life.[4]

It is easy to associate the Toë of "The Farthest Edge of the Islands" with the village shamaness. One hereditary group of Shamanistic priestesses (and, more rarely, priests) in the Amami Islands was called *yuta*. They traditionally lived alone, like Toë, in an isolated sacred dwelling, suggested by Toë's garden of roses, often located near a sacred grove, suggested in this story by the "ancient trees, from whose branches hung many roots, like beards," trees that "stood as if shoulder to shoulder, strangely encircling the village," giving off a mysterious scent, bearing "flowers whose buds opened secretly, quietly, only at night." The *yuta* priestesses were a hereditary nobility accorded special respect by the rest of the villagers. Toë's position suggests something of this sort:

> Among the people of the village, both children and adults, there were many who thought that Toë was fundamentally different from themselves. This was simply because for a long time Toë's family had been thought of in such a way. . . . Thanks to the entire village, Toë was able to spend her days playing with the children.

These priestesses were allowed to marry only other *yuta* or men from the mainland, called *Yamatonchū*.

In the Amami Islands there is a legend about the *Nirai Kanai* god, a sea god who dwells in a paradise to the East (the *Nirai Kinai*), where the dead reside and from which fire was originally obtained. (Notice Toë's association with fire, especially the flame of the silver candlestand in her room, with its overtones of sacredness, ritual, even self-immolation.) Death for the Amami people resulted in rebirth in the *Nirai Kanai* paradise. The shamaness propitiates the gods and acts as intermediary with the people. She is endowed with extraordinary auditory and visual powers (by putting her ear to the sand on the beach Toë can hear the lieutenant's footsteps all the way up the mountainside, and his conversation with the watchman at the pass; and somehow or other she knows about the torpedo boats hidden in the caves and of the squadron's secret mission). The priestesses are also susceptible to possession by spirits and serve as mediums (Toë can feel "in her own breast the lieutenant's taut, frayed nerves"). They are the villagers' sacrifical offerings to the gods, whose mistress they may become (as Toë gives herself to the lieutenant, and intends to kill herself in a scene with ritualistic overtones at his death). But mostly, the priestess waits, as Toë waits, for the return of the guardian deity.

The lieutenant's similarities to the *Nirai Kanai* god are clear. He, too, comes from across the seas, from the East, to protect the island. His nickname associates him with fire. The indoctrination of the special attack forces during the war, telling them that they will die for the sake of their sacred ancestors and that they themselves will then become gods (*kamisama*), intensifies the association. By ritually sacrificing herself and dying clutching his sword, Toë may hope to be reborn in the *Nirai Kanai* paradise, where she will live forever with the lieutenant, her guardian spirit. In order to gain that realm she must brave death, as she does when she makes her precarious way around the cape that separates her world from his.[5]

The syntax and imagery of the two stories echo thematic patterns and motifs. Let me cite one example, in both Japanese and English:

Sore wa watakushi hitori de seou koto de wa nai ga, tashikame mo sezu, tōzen no koto no yō ni nariyuki ni makase, tegiwayoku omoeta buntaishi no shochi ni makasete kita koto ni hozo o kamu omoi da. Uka to ochita mōten datta to shite mo, sore ni kizukanakatta jibun ga utomashii. Ima oshiyosete kuru seikatsu no, atsui kabe ni nita okite. Sakujitsu made kageusuku shisanshite shimatta to omoeta sore wa, sentōjōtai ga torihazusarete miru to, katakuna ni ne o hatte ite, mushishita mono e kibishii sabaki no kaotsuki o mukete ita.

Though the responsibility would ultimately not rest on my shoulders alone, I bitterly regretted having thought it so perfectly natural to entrust matters to the discretion of the assistant squadron leader who seemed so able and decisive. It was only an accidental blind spot on my part, but I hated myself for not having noticed it. I felt surrounded by regulations, like a thick wall, in the new life that bore firmly down on us. Regulations, which until yesterday might just as well not have existed, the minute wartime conditions were lifted, spread their roots firmly, turning a stern countenance toward those who had ignored them.

One characteristic of Shimao's prose is the length and unpredictability of his sentences; one must be content to read them without knowing in what direction they are ultimately headed, as another sort of perpetual state of transition to the unknown. One could easily find more and better examples of difficult passages than the above, but it does exhibit, in some measure, several aspects of Shimao's tortuous style. Here there is a preponderance of thinking and perceiving verbs, four of them in negative forms reversing the reader's perspective on the preceding clause; in fact, what is being described is a series of changes in perspective, reflected by pairs of thinking verbs, often in the negative and positive. The difficulty is increased because there may be more than one pair of negative and positive verbs not in parallel construction, as in the first sentence quoted, so that it is occasionally (although not here, really) difficult to judge instantly which are the major breaks in the sentence and which the minor, which independent clauses and which dependent.

There are also frequent time shifts, here corresponding of course to the changes in perspective. In this short passage there are eight time shifts, not counting shifts between what translate as simple perfect and progressive forms in English, which would increase the number by at least two. The passage could have been organized to present previous impressions first, followed by the change, then by the new outlooks. Or, past and present could have been arranged in strict alternation in parallel clauses. As it is, however, one has the sense that the time sequence has been deliberately disrupted. Consider, for example, the last two sentences. The first of these is not, in fact, strictly a sentence at all, since it ends in a noun, so that there is a grammatical break between the two sentences (appropriately after *atsui kabe ni nita okite*, "regulations, like a thick wall"). This break makes it possible to sandwich a phrase referring to the past between two phrases referring to the same present, reversing the natural order of the first two parts. There is also the intrusion of *mushi shita mono* ("those who had ignored them"), which takes the reader very briefly into the past once more before the final verb. The final verb itself, *mukete ita*, "was turning," though it refers to what I have been calling the present, is in fact a perfective, telling the reader that the whole passage, narrated in present tense, is to be thought of as having occurred in the past. This technique, not uncommon in modern Japanese fiction, is particularly striking in all the stories presented here, with the general effect of slowing down and speeding up time and creating subtle shifts in perspective.

Another characteristic of Shimao's style that occasionally creates difficulties for the translator is his apparent predilection for mixed metaphors, of which there is a splendid example in the passage above; the *shisanshita* "scattered" *atsui kabe* "thick wall" that *oshiyosete kuru* "comes rushing and crowding," *katakuna ni ne o hatte* "strongly puts out roots," *kibishii sabaki no kaotsuki o mukete* "turning a stern judgmental face." The effect is one of confusion, certainly, and also one of unforeseeable development, as a stationary inanimate object begins to move, then comes to life, then becomes human. Like the frogs that cry like human beings, that protect and seem to offer absolution for all mankind, it resonates with animistic elements of Ryukuan folk religion implicit in other aspects of the text as well.

A final special difficulty of Shimao's prose, particularly in "This Time That Summer," is the frequent vagueness of his grammatical antecedents. The effect is not so noticeable in this passage. Sometimes one such term, ostensibly with the same referent throughout, changes in specific content or connotation with repeated occurrence, creating a gradual shift of perspective as the reader follows helplessly where Shimao's mind may lead him. This effect is generally obscured in translation. Deleted subjects intensify this effect and create additional confusion, to the extent that it is occasionally unclear, at least initially, just who is doing what. In the dialogue between the narrator and the commander of the Fourth Flotilla, Lieutenant F, partly because subjects are deleted and partly because being of equal rank, the two men use the same term of address for each other. It is at first impossible to tell which is which; the more natural reading is in fact the wrong one, as one discovers incontrovertibly midway through the conversation. There are two places in the text of this story where the narrator finds himself face to face with a hostile group, and convolutions in the sentences describing the emotions involved make it difficult to determine to which side they are to be ascribed. When the lieutenant goes into the Fourth Flotilla barracks, for instance, and finds the newcomers to the squadron playing the guitar, *somebody* seems "to ooze an incompatibility irritating to the skin with respect to him/those who had newly arrived" (*atarashiku haitta mono ni taisuru hada ni najimanu iwa mo nijimideta fū da*). Since the lieutenant has just come into the barracks and the men he is talking to have recently come from another squadron, "him/those who had newly arrived" is not enough information to distinguish between them; *ni taisuru* "with respect to" is ambiguous, so that we do not know whose skin it is, and *ni* does not tell us for certain whether the disharmony oozes *from* the skin or is disagreeable *to* it. Such situations create still another shift in perspective, a logical break or gap analogous to the many discontinuities in time. They also reinforce a pattern suggested earlier, of observer and observed identified, the inspector and judge himself inspected and judged, the *Nirai Kanai* god watched over by a god whom he resembles and yet who mysteriously resides in the natural surroundings under the gaze of that superior *Nirai Kanai* god.

"Everyday Life in a Dream"

This story, whose title *Yume no naka de no nichijō* might mean either a dream of daily life or daily life as though lived in a dream (*muchū*), has often been called surrealistic by the critics because it is not a realistic, coherent account of theoretically possible events.[1] More recent critics now generally read this and other Shimao Toshio stories written in the same vein—*Matenrō* [Skyscraper], 1948; *Asufōto to kumo no kora* [Asphalt and baby spiders], 1949—specifically as accounts of coherent "reality" as experienced in a dream or by the unconscious, according to its special logic and symbols.[2] It has also been pointed out that the logic and symbols of these stories are more subtly at work in Shimao's "realistic" fiction, especially as one might expect in the "sick wife" series.[3] His characteristic associative logic is apparent even on the sentence level in his syntax and word choice. "Everyday Life in a Dream," therefore, brings to light aspects of the rest of the stories in this volume that might otherwise go unnoticed.

The obvious importance of this story, of course, is that it presents an interpretation of the formation of a writer and the process of creating a literary work. It may be read as a statement on the relationship between life and art, such an important issue in Japanese literary history and central to the body of his works as a whole.

The young narrator of "Everyday Life in a Dream" has "defined his existence" as a "novelist" (his term is not *shōsetsuka* but, rather pretentiously,
noberisuto), partly because he feels it is a respectable label for someone without
useful "skills," who observes but does not participate in life. Now, having labeled
himself a novelist, he must become one. Like the two Amami Islands stories, this
story presents a transition, in a sense a metamorphosis, a process that involves
unknown danger. Believing that art is based on life experience, the narrator, who
has "sold off cheap" everything he has to say on the basis of his uneventful life so
far, now has to "embark on a new lifestyle" in order to keep writing. He first
intends to remain an onlooker, taking out a sort of guest membership in a juvenile
gang so that he can learn how to pick pockets without risk of arrest, having been
promised that he may incorporate any of their activities into his fiction without
fear of recrimination. But, of course, just as he is on the threshold of this safe,
vicarious existence on the roof of a bombed-out building, he is called back down
by the woman at the reception desk and exposed to leprosy. Extraordinary experience is necessary to a writer, and there can be no such experience without serious
risk. The narrator then subjects himself to a series of experiences in which he
gradually participates more and more: first through an imaginary conversation
with the woman on the train, then playing a role, taking his mother's place and
receiving punishment intended for her, then becoming the observed instead of the
observer, finally dealing as himself, in his own right, with a woman whom he
knows. Gradually, too, his experience is not of others but of himself; he learns
who he is and was, and he, not the gang of juvenile delinquents, will henceforth be
the material for his stories. At least that is the case in the story at hand (the
next product of the narrator). In the process, he has become a "novelist"; his first
work of fiction has appeared, and he has, after all, created another—but at great
personal sacrifice. He has broken out with a strange skin disease, metaphorically,
the leprosy to which he was exposed at the beginning,[4] and he has turned himself
inside out, exposing his private pain to the world. His life, his physical existence,
has been subordinated to his art, and ultimately used up by it.

The obvious interpretation of the strange, itching excrescences all over the
young man's head is as a manifestation of leprosy, but careful reading suggests
other possibilities. When the narrator goes "home" and confronts his unclean
house and the dubious morality of his mother, he comments,

> A normal family, safe and sound, had been my reality until the war.
> But what about now? Think how adversity comes, one misfortune
> after another in such thick profusion. I no longer know what I am.
> How wonderful! All this is my reality. As the feeling spread over me
> like pox, I was stung by that simple comment from my father. To me,
> father seemed like the immovable iron wall of society.

These pox are the "novelist's" reality, different from that of ordinary people, more dramatic and experienced with greater intensity. But this "reality" in fact concerns his parents more than himself; he gets just a taste of a "novelist's" reality before his premature exhilaration at indirect suffering is stopped by a more sober, prosaic reality.

The pox also suggest venereal disease, an association natural from the mother's promiscuity. Perhaps it has something to do with the unrecorded terrible comment by his father.

> I would do anything to restore my mood of sentimental generosity, so ruthlessly taken to task as if for an inexpiable sin. "Father, the truth is I have leprosy": I wanted to satisfy my vanity, to state that no reality could startle me. But the only result was the realization that, faced with the all too human disharmony between my father and my mother, I was utterly powerless.

> My father said something. These were terrible words. When I heard them, I wondered if my mother's skin were not also my own. Those words gave that skin a glimpse of the brothel.

One assumes that the narrator's father refers to real pox as opposed to the imaginary pox associated with the narrator's "mood of sentimental generosity." (The word I have somewhat recklessly translated as "brothel" is *jigoku* "hell," which is an old slang term for unlicensed prostitutes, or an abbreviation for *jigoku no yado*, pleasure houses.) Through experience he has exposed himself to leprosy, but he has inherited a venereal disease from his mother. Most likely, the excrescences at the end of the story are the realization of both potentialities.

The origins of a "novelist" are an important factor in his development. Seeing the child of mixed blood on his mother's back, the narrator feels self-important: "the thought that I possessed this truly 'novelistic' background mysteriously encouraged me. I felt I held my own will in my bare hands. Don't forget, I had defined my identity as a novelist." What makes a novelist, this story seems to be saying, is experience and identity. "Everyday Life in a Dream" represents the "novelist's" supersensitive, excruciating, dangerous exploration of both inner and outer worlds, in prose strangely coordinated to both outward (conscious) and inward (unconscious) experience.

The narration of "Everyday Life in a Dream" seems to move both forward and backward in time. When the story begins, the narrator has sold his first piece of fiction, but it has not yet appeared; just before the end, the issue of the magazine carrying it has appeared, so some unspecified period of forward time has elapsed. The period corresponds, presumably, to the incubation period of his leprosy. During this time, he has subjected himself to various adventures and he has traveled, but, in a sense, his travels carry him backwards in time, toward his origins—his first journey, of course, is to his mother's home town, which one assumes to be Nagasaki although it is never named. His father turns up on the scene as well. That time has gone backward is clear from the fact that the town that "the newspapers had reported as totally destroyed" in the war is still there, that the house "where the hills and the buildings had turned to ashes and crumbled, virtually melted, to the ground" "by some whim of fate . . . was still standing." His mother too, is not so old as he had expected, retaining "a surprising bloom of youthfulness." The little albinolike Eurasian boy he remembers having seen playing in the streets long ago is still a child, young enough to be carried on the narrator's mother's back. The decision to go looking for his parents was made in reaction to fear that the end of the world was coming, a fear prompted by planes flying overhead and dropping things on the land below, an image certainly related to the war. So, his attempt at present life experience falters because of a threat from an acquaintance from the past. He instinctively abandons all connections with that present, but he immediately feels a similar threat from airplanes associated with the recent past (moving from the bombed-out building to the planes that bombed it), which remind him that his mother's home was bombed. He decides to go home, and by the time he gets there, it has not in fact been bombed.

After this point the time and direction of the narrative become more complex. While he is home, of course, the narrator learns about his origins, his birth heritage. The realization that his skin is his "mother's skin" comes immediately after the strange *fumie* scene:

> My mother took what looked like a tray and set it down on the tatami. Apparently, whenever my mother wanted to say something to my father, it was agreed that in order to prove there was no falsehood in her words, she would perform a sort of *fumie* ritual, trampling on a sacred image. I suppose there was a portrait painted on the tray. It happened to be upside down so I could not see it; I wondered whose portrait it was. I felt an unnatural curiosity to see. Lifting high her skirts, my mother stepped on the tray. The sight was so bewitching that I could hardly believe she was my own mother. Intuition told me that this extremely critical, taut moment was the best possible chance for reconciliation. I felt almost like praying. But what in the world. The words my mother finally blurted out were an expression of her true devotion to her Caucasian lover.

This confusing scene is pivotal to the narrative and the development of the narrator, through experience that he shares with his mother. The association with Christianity of course suggests death and spiritual rebirth, but the *fumie* ritual, specifically, is a renunciation of the possibility of rebirth. The mother's actions are similarly ambiguous. Because we do not know whose portrait was on the tray —that of Christ or her Caucasian lover—we do not know whether she apostatizes or not. The association of Christian devotion with devotion to a lover is a motif evident in "The Farthest Edge of the Islands" as well as in the three "sick wife"

pieces that end this volume. The mother does step on the tray, but if the image
on it is that of her Caucasian lover, she then immediately renegs on her apostasy
when she invokes his name. Whether because of apostasy, deceit, or simply
adultery, the mother's action may be read as a sin, for which she is to be punished
by the narrator's father. Or perhaps she is being condemned as a martyr for
refusing to apostatize. Metaphorically, the narrator participates in the ritual and
the sin: he feels like praying, but he is physically attracted to his mother, and it is
in fact he who receives the punishment, whether for spiritual or carnal devotion.
His beating (as that intended for his mother) might be interpreted as either the
punishment of a sinner or the martyrdom of a saint. The possibility of rebirth is
therefore ambiguous, as is the narrative that ensues. This episode seems to be a
central point in the narrative, from which time again branches out in two directions, forward and backward. On one level, the character, having investigated
his birth, seems to begin to grow up again, passing a building that makes him think
of a school house, with children looking out at him (reminding us of the leprous
elementary school friend early in the story), then coming to a woman who must be
an acquaintance from the more recent past, with whom he has a sexual relationship—though sex is merely anticipated in this episode—echoing his adolescent
sexual fantasies in the first half of the story. At this point, he sees his first story
in print and develops his skin disease, so we are back to the present. In another
way, however, the narrative may be read as extending further into the past after
the *fumie* scene.

After being beaten by his father, the narrator loses his teeth, suggesting
physical degeneration (or return to infancy). Then he passes through a scene filled
with ambiguity and with images of psychological transformation or liminality: the
flowing water he can hear but not see, for example, and, most conspicuously, the
chemical smell of sulphur.   The road slopes downhill and the houses are off
balance. He next encounters the building full of school children, then the still
younger child, terminally ill, who dies looking at the ocean. The narrator then
goes into the woman's room, from where he is mysteriously transported to a
stream where he bathes himself as if in a womb beyond death.   By a similar
process, gradually from the seemingly rational, if bizarre, opening scene, the
narrative has come farther and farther from the logic of consciousness.

External time—history—as well seems by implication to have gone backward. We have already seen how in the first half of the story postwar images lead
to images of war, which lead to those before the war. The Eurasian child has been
a natural association with Nagasaki since the Dutch settled there during the
Tokugawa period beginning in 1641; the next image, the *fumie*, is associated with
the same area in slightly earlier times (the Amakusa Rebellion of 1637-1638, most
notably). In the liminal scene, when the cherries have not yet bloomed, people
pass by who are not quite human; they seem "insubstantial," have "pale shadows"
(*kage ga usui*). By the time of the last scene in "Everyday Life in a Dream,"

human beings have disappeared completely, giving way to animals from prehuman evolution—first birds, then insects. Surveying the outside scene, the narrator seems to have reverted to an earlier stage of evolution, a squid with no marks of individuality, "smooth and blank and transparent," wishing in fact to do away with the crows and the insects. This reversion to a prehuman stage of evolution is a motif that reappears in the "sick wife" stories, as we shall see.

Since "Everyday Life in a Dream" is about the development of a novelist through life experience and exploration of his own past—and the novelist in the story writes about his personal experience—one might expect to find in a story created by this process of development elements from the author's own life. It is not difficult. Shimao Toshio has written volumes of autobiographical essays in addition to his fiction (in language and detail occasionally almost indistinguishable from the fiction), and probably, because of the close relationship between Shimao's life and art, Japanese critics have paid even more attention than usual to the particulars of Shimao's life from childhood on. The analytical essays (*kaisetsu*) included in paperback editions of his works typically come in pairs, one on the work itself, the other elucidating relevant events of Shimao's life.[5] In interviews published in literary journals, Shimao is questioned again and again about his life. Recounting experiences, he answers sometimes as though he were quoting his own essays verbatim. Interviewed in *Kokubungaku* by his friend Okuno Takeo, talking about how he resumed his writing career in Kobe immediately after the war ended, he mentions having taught English at Democracy Hall (*Demokurashii Kaikan*). Okuno immediately interrupts him with the comment that Democracy Hall was the building described at the beginning of "Everyday Life in a Dream." Shimao says no, that was another building in Kobe.[6] The story was written at a time (1948) in Shimao's own life that corresponds to the starting point of his narrator. Elements of the exploration that ensues echo themes in the same *Kokubungaku* interview and also in Shimao's essays—the spiritual, intellectual mother, for example, married against her will to a man too prosaic for her tastes, who continued to be attracted to other men who approached her ideal;[7] the Eurasian children who both reassured him and made him aware of death during his early years in port towns, especially Kobe;[8] or his fascination for solitary travels. In one essay, he mentions the Eurasians (and movies) as a factor in his decision to become a writer.[9]

In "Everyday Life in a Dream," one looks for elements that are common to other fiction and related in some way to the author's implied past. And here again, there are many.[10] The narrator's conversation with his "mood" near the end of "Everyday Life in a Dream" has a resonance with other fiction that is not so obvious in the English translation.

(You're cheating. You're a fake [*inchiki, inchiki, inchiki*]) my mood whispered.

(You know, the trouble with you is . . .) my mood whispered again.

(This isn't "Nothing ventured, nothing gained." It's venturing something after losing everything.) *Atatte kudakero de wa nakute, kudakete kara atatte irunda.*

(And just what do you mean by that?) I challenged. (Suppose you tell me exactly what it is you are trying to say?)

Whereupon my mood answered me in an intimidating singsong, (These days you've been making such a big deal about NO-thing VEN-tured, NO-thing GAined.) *Omae was kono aida, iya ni shitsukoku shuchōshite ita zo. A-ta-t-te ku-da-ke-ro.*

(What would I make a big deal about a dumb thing like that for?) I shook my head.

Inchiki inchiki inchiki echoes the leper's comments at the beginning of the story, but it also calls to mind a novel (*Nisegakusei* [The phony student], 1950), written some two years later, set in Nagasaki in the commercial high school Shimao attended, which deals with what he calls *nisemono ishiki*, the sense of being a phony, of not participating in life, of always being spared consequences. The most dramatic consequences that Shimao and his characters were spared is, of course, the final suicide mission of the torpedo-boat squadron, suggested, in fact, in the next comment by the narrator's "mood," *atatte kudakero* (literally, "set to and crack open").[11] In the collision both the torpedo boat and its target are blown apart. In context here, *atatte kudakero* is an injunction to become a genuine novelist rather than a phony, to create a real work of art and, in the process, obliterate both himself and his object. Creation is destruction; like the ditch that Lieutenant Saku digs all alone at night in "The Farthest Edge of the Islands," it is "a job of rapidly progressing destruction (*gungun hakaishiteyuku shigoto*)."

It is possible to read "Everyday Life in a Dream" as a series of confrontations resulting in penetrating, symbolically dismantling, the object, then fleeing to another similar confrontation. When the narrator fixes his gaze on an object, he begins to see inside it, to know things about it that cannot be apparent from the surface: the gasoline drums inside the planes flying overhead, or the narrator's imaginary conversation with the young woman he encounters on the train.

But, of course, like the torpedo-boat pilot, the narrator of "Everyday Life in a Dream" is also cracking himself open, splitting himself apart. The dialogue quoted above is a conversation between "himself" and his "mood"; a third internal voice is added a few lines later: "(Don't trust your mood.) I wonder who could have whispered this?" Just as the imaginary conversation with the woman on the train was really a conversation with himself, in this dialogue, at the turning point of the story, all voices are the narrator's. He has been split into subject and object. On the train it was clear which voice was subject and which object, but by now no such distinction is possible. In the scene that follows this dialogue the narrator is stared at by children at the windows of the large wooden building. This scene has counterparts in much of Shimao's early fiction, (Kōshi no Me [The eyes at holes in the lattice], for example), in which a character is both the observed and the observer. Again, one character is split into two, subject and object. This is the plight of the novelist, especially one who writes autobiographical fiction. It is also a pattern discernible in the other stories in this volume. We have seen it clearly in the two military stories, in which the lieutenant's story is in fact recounted once in third-person and once in first-person narration.

"Everyday Life in a Dream" begins with an abortive attempt to go "upward," to the roof of a building open to the sky, then precedes on an inward journey, but a "downhill" road. Another story, Matenrō [Skyscraper], written immediately before this one, assumes a similar pattern. Having gone up the skyscraper and wandered through various empty rooms, the narrator finds himself going down into some kind of basement, then through successive iron doors into a secret chamber in which he is to learn something essential (about himself). He tries to flee from this ultimate confrontation, penetrating one by one the metal doors through which he came, but he is held back at the last door, on the verge of escape.

Atatte kudakero de wa nakute, kudakete kara atatteirunda (literally, "you're not setting to and cracking open, you're first cracking open and then setting to") suggests the possibility of rearranging the sequence of life and death, so that life begins only after death, resurrection from total destruction. This, too, is a pattern easily discernible in "The Farthest Edge of the Islands" and "This Time That Summer." Here it is art that rises from destruction. Perhaps the division of the writer into subject and object, or observer and experiencer, is related to the rebirth motif. The little boy who dies in the narrator's arms after the meta-phorical observer-observed split that occurs at the big wooden building gives us a clue. The scene recalls Shimao's own mysterious childhood illness, from which the doctors did not expect him to recover, a crisis in his life that is treated in Kōshi no me and other fiction of the same period as "Everyday Life in a Dream." Here the "author" is again split into observer and observed, and while one part dies, the other lives on. Another possibility, of course, is that the inward psychological journey will cause a crisis that will end in the death of the "observer-observed" dichotomy and precipitate the reintegration of a fragmented psyche that will no longer be a nisemono.

Just as the individual episodes show essential similarities, the cast of characters assume similar roles. There is a series of four young male characters—the self-deprecating, aloof youth gang leader, the leper school friend, the illegiti-mate Eurasian child, and the little boy on whom the doctors have given up hope. All are loners, different and somehow "inappropriate" to their surroundings, like the narrator himself. There are also four encounters with women—the receptionist, the woman on the train, the narrator's mother, and the "woman" he finally goes to visit. All have some strong claim on him, to which he gradually submits in the course of the story—that is, in fact, the sense in which he becomes more involved with his environment. Intending at first on joining the juvenile gang to become intimate with a "blatantly bad" "twenty-year-old girl" and "snatch from her willy-nilly the acrid flower of her adolescence," the narrator is unwilling to surrender anything of his own in return. Sex is associated with leprosy. The first woman he encounters, the "receptionist" who calls him back down from the roof of the building, he does not describe as being physically attractive to him, and in the end he allows her to be touched by the leper, "leaving (her) to die."

The woman on the train he describes in considerable physical detail. He is irresistibly attracted to her until she actually speaks to him and takes the encounter out of the realm of pure fantasy. Her act makes him lose interest and flee again. The next encounter is with his mother, described again in sensual detail—lover and mother and religious symbol combined; sex is associated with syphilis and contamination, with punishment, perhaps with original sin, with death and rebirth. She seems to incorporate the basic aspects of Jung's elementary feminine archetype: mother, anima, and Sophia, characterized by the unity of antithetical qualities: life-giving and death-dealing, old and young, mother and virgin, good and evil. The narrator identifies with her, as the Uroboric mother contains a masculine principle, the womb surrounding a male fetus or the unconscious surrounding the infantile ego. The narrator shares in her identity but does not actually interact with her.

The final encounter is with an unidentified, completely undescribed woman, who appears first as a disembodied voice "behind him." She is associated with his past, and, despite himself, he is drawn to her in some level of his psyche more basic than the voices that speak to him. He does, finally, interact with this woman. Ostensibly, his purpose in visiting her is sexual, and though no such scene occurs in "Everyday Life in a Dream," it is here that he suffers the leprosy or syphilis associated earlier with sex. She also shares the other aspects of the undifferentiated Great Mother. He enters her "room" and is reborn—physically as a smooth, unindividuated squid in a pure stream, spiritually, as a "novelist."

What Erich Neumann calls the great uroboros is the original state of man's unconscious, the seed of consciousness or ego contained within it. As the ego begins to develop by differentiating itself from the unconscious, it conceives of itself in masculine symbolism, and it perceives the unconscious in more clearly feminine terms, as the feminine archetype. As the ego develops, the archetype shifts from the elementary or eternal character suggested by the images discussed so far to the "transformative character." A common early image of the transformative female archetype is the "lady of the plants" or the "tree of life." They are associated with growth, nourishment, and decay and stretch from the earth to the sun, the unconscious to consciousness. Again, according to Neumann, birds are common symbols of spiritual transformation through feminine powers. The image we are left with in "Everyday Life in a Dream," then, may be that of the rebirth of ego consciousness after regression, but it is an ambiguous image: the tree is withered, the nourishment offered is to parasitic insects, and the birds are crows, ominous birds associated with the coming of night, and with death.

The course of events and progression of images in "Everyday Life in a Dream" seems determined by the logic of dream, but the narration itself is not.[12] The story is told consistently in the past-tense, with perfective verbs— more consistently, in fact, than any of the other stories in this volume. The reader does not know for whom the narrator is relating the story or under what circumstances; the tone and word choice are informal, even blunt, at first suggesting the style of an earnest, fashionably intellectual ("I had defined my identity as a 'novelist'") young writer hoping in part to shock his less progressive readers by his frank, vivid portrayal of the unpleasant and the unmentionable. So we assume it is a story written by the "novelist" narrator. The occasional appearance of the copula *de atta* (but *da*, not *de aru*) tells us that it is not a spoken account. The effect is of a summary organized by waking consciousness after the fact, of a dream—not daily life experiences by the unconscious, as I suggested earlier, so much as dream interpreted by consciousness. Time is not at first a straightforward sequence of experience, as one might expect of a dream, but a summary, occasionally even flashback, especially in the first few pages. There is an abundance of words like "because," "since," "but," "although," "therefore" putting a logical construction on the experience recounted. One layer of this logical apparatus is clearly set in the time of narration rather than the time of action: *naze darō* ("I wonder why"), *jitsu wa* ("to tell the truth"). But as the story progresses, such logical rhetoric becomes gradually less intrusive, especially after the *fumie* scene. By the final paragraph it has become considerably less frequent, and time reversals have disappeared altogether. The dream experience has become more immediate. Negative verbs, so common in the first few pages, gradually become rarer. Negation or absence becomes possibility, as the little boy who "didn't look sick at all" suddenly goes into convulsions and dies. Negative experience, it has often been claimed, is impossible without the logic of consciousness.[13] In the long last paragraph there are still many negative verb forms, but they apply to the time of narration ("I saw an old tree, what kind I do not know") and to the thinking or reasoning verbs, which have by no means disappeared, rather than to the verbs of action or experience.

Despite the logical, explanatory nature of the language, the images themselves develop, overlap, and succeed each other as in a dream. There is no possibility of escape or diversion, as there is in waking life; flight from one situation merely brings him face to face with another similar or more serious one. Every implication is eventually manifested, every fear is realized (except death or absence): at his attempt to keep the leper from touching him, the leper touches him; the thought "that something might fall out of the planes" flying overhead makes gasoline drums fall from the sky. When the narrator thinks of the planes themselves as a threat, they become more numerous and fly lower and lower. The thought of his father produces the realization that he has been there for some time. Everything is off balance, changing relentlessly.

The development and sequence of images is not always what the surface, verbal logic of the narrative would seem to suggest. At the train station on the edge of his mother's home town, for example, the narrator buys a ticket "from an old woman on the roadside by the terminal" in a "boxlike stall," which she folds up and "shuts down." The narrator says that since he was apparently her last customer, he hurried onto the train, so the ticket he bought from her must have been a train ticket. But such a woman in a collapsible stall near a large train terminal might ordinarily be selling lottery tickets, or reading palms and telling fortunes. What follows in "Everyday Life in a Dream" is, in a sense, an investigation of the narrator's identity in order to predict the possibilities for the future, much as a physiognomist or a palmist would do.   Word association is an unobtrusive sequencing mechanism. Just before the *fumie* scene quoted above, for example, the dirtiness of his mother's house (*kitanai*) suggests to the narrator that his mother, too, is "unclean" (*fuketsu*).   Immediately he asserts as fact her "loose living" (*fushidara na seikatsu*) till now in that house, whereupon she suddenly becomes a sensual being to the narrator. There is an illegitimate Eurasian child on her back, the issue of her loose living. Then he recognizies the child and realizes that he has known the truth all along. A few paragraphs later, the narrator expresses that the feeling that his background was properly sordid for that of a novelist "began to spread like pox" (*kasa no yō ni habikoridashita*).   Then the narrator mentions leprosy, which produces an association with his mother's skin, syphillis, and the brothel.   Such sequences of word association are characteristic of Shimao's more "realistic" fiction as well, particularly in the "sick wife" stories in which there is strong undercurrent of irrationality. The pattern of repeated confrontations with constantly developing inescapable "reality," in which every fear is realized and nothing is ever settled—the same problems occurring over and over in slightly different configurations—is essential to the "sick wife" stories.

Time is meaningless in "Everyday Life in a Dream," as elsewhere in Shimao's works, because it is not an organizing or constraining factor in the action.   The narrator and the reader are locked into the present moment; like Toshio in "The Sting of Death," we are "not allowed the leisure of climbing to a high place and surveying the path just traveled, or looking to check out the road ahead."   We have no temporal context to help us evaluate events, because what happens so often contradicts what we know from the waking past—the survival of the narrator's mother's house after the bomb, for instance, or the mother's unexpected youthful sensuality. Often the present moment in fact determines the past instead of the other way around. The narrator supplies a past to accommodate immediate conditions, so that the past develops by association from the present moment just as the future does, as the narrator, seeing the Eurasian child, suddenly "remembers" that his mother was a loose woman all along. This principle governs both the sequence of images and events and the structure of the story as a whole. And the perpetual present moment, again, is the moment of transition to the unknown, the brink of personal transformation.

"The Sting of Death," "Out of the Depths," and "The Heart that Slips Away"

These stories, and the group of "sick wife" stories from which they have been chosen, are the most narrowly focused of his works because they are closely bound to the particulars of the lives of Shimao and his wife, who give their names to the characters once called the lieutenant and Toë—the stories themselves have played an important therapeutic role in the events that inspired them.[1] Yet, they have had the broadest appeal of all of Shimao's works and are mainly responsible for his recent popularity.

Of course, these stories are easier to read and to interpret than his avant garde works (some critics, like Okuno Takeo consider them regrettable concessions to the mentality of the masses),[2] and the events, rooted in the everyday life of the family, are more immediate and familiar than those of the exotic military stories set in the Ryukyu Islands. But there is a basic universality to the terms and images of these stories not so easily explainable. Despite the specificity of the context, they describe human experience reduced to an elemental state, a common essence.

It is perhaps to be expected, therefore, that recurrent basic patterns discernible in the structure and imagery of Shimao's other works should be evident in these stories as well. The alternation of opposite phases is a striking example.

"The Sting of Death" opens with a passage that reminds us of "This Time that Summer":

> On the following day, I noticed that the alarm clock on my desk, which had stopped long ago, was running again. Since I had not fiddled with it, or given it a shock of any kind, I have no idea why it decided to work again. In the past it had not responded even to vigorous shaking. But there it was now, ticking away diligently. My first thought was that my wife's will had lodged itself within.

Like "This Time that Summer," "The Sting of Death" begins after a mysterious transformation, with the start of a new phase in which the laws of the old no longer hold and the characters must learn by trial and error the rules that have replaced them. The laws of time, for example, have changed. Toshio's personal clock has started running again, but it shows a different time from clocks in the outside world; perhaps even its pace is eccentric, controlled as it is by his "wife's will."

In the new era "Toshio," like the lieutenant in "This Time That Summer," is responsible suddenly for the "aftermath" of the past, suddenly judged, held accountable, and made to suffer retribution for his sins. A change of heart is not enough; he cannot escape his own *ushirosugata* ("receding figure") but must expose, acknowledge, and expiate every detail of his past existence.

The story begins "at the change of seasons from summer to fall" and ends with "preparation for winter." Several times the characters are depicted as going to bed at night and awakening in the morning. Each time the narrator awakens, he has to start over again learning the rules, which, like the time, are dictated by his wife. Following a pattern evident in the military stories, there is a close relationship between today and yesterday, if not with the intervening night:

> What had led me to awaken I did not know, but the reality from which I had been cut off until just a moment before now formed a continuum from the instant of my awakening to the reality that existed before I went to sleep. Remembering what I had been doing when I entrusted that section of reality to sleep was painful. But to one who has awakened, reality comes back to life completely unabridged.

Another kind of alternation of brief phases associated with light and dark is, of course, Miho's vacillation between rational and irrational moods. Her "attacks" are signalled by the "dark cloud" that appears on her countenance and the "dark stain" she sees on her husband's face. When they begin, "the gloriously shining sun" is "abruptly hidden behind a giant black curtain" and the surroundings "turned into a vast ice field." These dark miniphases, if you like, have elements in common with the larger phase that begins with the first sentence of the story and extends beyond the last. Darkness and cold are associated with the larger phase in general.

> As the days went by, I was quietly invaded by the hopelessness of waiting, shut up at home. . . . I began to feel as though the two of us were huddled close together under the heatless rays of an eclipsed sun.

Miho used to drape the bedding outside to air in the sunlight, but rain dominates the time span of the story. The bedding is in the closet, chewed and soiled by the mice.

In an earlier phase, the ardent housewife Miho had left all the doors and windows open to let fresh air and sunlight into the house; now the shutters (*amado*) are closed, and husband and wife, "unsightly" as "shrimp that shed its shell," must withdraw into darkness because of threats from the outside world and restrictions imposed from within, by each other and, ultimately, by themselves. In turn, husband and wife repeatedly try to escape, but like the cat they always come home of their own accord. The only ostensible progress in the course of the story is that they have rebuilt the fence around their house, so that it is stronger and looms "conspicuously . . . apart from the rest of the neighborhood," containing the family, making them different. In this dark phase, the fence becomes even more prominent as it soaks up the rain and swells with the moisture.

Withdrawal to closed quarters is characteristic of the miniphases, too, of course. At the climax of "The Sting of Death," husband and wife remain closeted in their room for a night and a day, unable to deal even with the needs of their children, "the curtain to the hallway unopened" at noon. Inside the room, Miho reverts to her darker self and burrows into her husband's deepest secrets and into the past.

Withdrawal into darkness leads inevitably to confrontation with death, a drive to self-obliteration: extreme passivity (at least in the husband), stripping away of the conscious persona, and finally attempts at suicide. In the miniphase "Toshio" bangs his head against the dresser, and he and "Miho" vie to strangle themselves with her obi. On the first page of "The Sting of Death" the closed rain shutters lead to a vision—the more startling because it is at first incomprehensible—of a family suicide, the bodies lying still, submitting to insensitive examination by strangers. In the following passage cited above, one finds hopeful signs as Miho begins to leave the darkness, however briefly, to attend to the activities of daily life.

> Maya came in as if to check on us and said, "Birdie died," and my wife rose immediately and went out back. I couldn't bring myself to go look; sighing, I couldn't even muster the energy to open the curtain to the hall. As I was sitting there dully among the bedding strewn about the six-mat room, my wife came back and explained that one of the chickens had stuck its head in the water trough and almost drowned, but when she grabbed it and pressed its neck, it had revived. Then Tama came back from somewhere and meowed to be fed, so my wife stopped her interrogation temporarily and went to fix the cat something to eat. I thought the interruption might change my wife's mood, but as soon as she had finished, she sat down and took up where she had left off.

The "birdie" Maya reports as dead (having stuck its own head inexplicably under water) in fact survives. The description of how Miho revived the chicken has a negative counterpart in the same story: the scene remembered from an unspecified past in which Miho, "with a faraway look in her eye," kills a chicken by pressing her fingers on its neck. Miho takes life and gives it; again, like Jung's eternal feminine archetype, she is the agent of psychological or spiritual death and rebirth. The cat mentioned immediately after the bird is described earlier as "a reincarnation of something" and is given the name of their old cat "Tama" (a homophone for "soul"), whom it so resembles. This cat has mysteriously arrived to take care of the mice that now "run rampant in the house."

Like all the other stories in this volume, "The Sting of Death" presents the reader with transition, though from what to what is never clear. The train is the quintessential image of transition. Typically, train scenes occur in pairs, carrying the same impatient characters in opposite directions with equal urgency and in almost identical vocabulary. Each time "Toshio" sets out on the train, he does so with "unshakable conviction," expecting dramatic resolution when he reaches his destination: his wife will be at Ujikka's house; she has gone to the other woman's apartment and murdered her; she has returned home. Each time he goes to the station, he imagines that his wife will be on the next train. But *before* he reaches his intended destination, he realizes that the resolution is an illusion and heads off in another direction. The repeated cycles seem to offer hope that the larger dark phase, too, will give way to light, if only after the ultimate physical, psychological, and spiritual sacrifice. But as in "This Time That Summer," there is nothing in the story to suggest in concrete terms what the new phase might be.

Moreover, entire scenes in "The Sting of Death" (and the two stories that follow) tend to occur in pairs in which Toshio and Miho exchange roles. They take turns threatening suicide, dissuading each other, forgiving each other, being contrite, rushing to the door to escape. As Shin'ichi says, "When Daddy tries to run away, Mommy and I are too strong for him, and when Mommy tries to run away, Daddy and I are too strong." In all three stories, whenever Miho has an "attack," Toshio eventually becomes hysterical along with her, so that when her attack subsides, he is still in the throes of his and Miho must use his tactics to subdue him. When the ordeal is over, they react in exactly the same way, like two entities moving clockwise and counterclockwise around the same radius that reach a common point twice each revolution. When Miho tells her husband that she had hired a private detective to investigate her husband's activities and she herself questioned his friends about him, even following him on occasion to the other woman's apartment, the narrator remarks:

> From bits and pieces of what she had told me time and time again, I
> had basically guessed as much, but hearing the details in so many
> words directly from my wife's lips, I shuddered anew. Looking back
> on my past and my friends, they now seemed so strangely different
> from what I had taken them to be; I no longer understood what I had
> seen in the world, or how I had interpreted it.

He reminds us of Miho, who is incited to an attack every time she hears in her husband's own words details with which she is already quite familiar, and who is disillusioned with her perceptions of the world because of her husband's dishonesty. As Toshio tells himself, each has his "ego," each has played the role of the deceiver and of the deceived. Perhaps their reaching common ground represents the goal that is itself a transition to a new divergence.

"Out of the Depths" focuses on the (deceptive) distinction between inside and outside and the existential illusion of both freedom and confinement. Inside—identified with the abyss, with darkness, mental illness, the locked ward, the hospital grounds—seems different from the outside mainly when viewed from the outside. The people with the keys, doctors and nurses, simply do not notice that the occupations of the world at large are "all, every one, taking place on the brink of a dark chasm from which one could never climb out again." Before Toshio and his wife are hospitalized, he has a view of the women's psychotic ward:

> All the doors were securely closed, and the windows were covered with wooden lattice or wire netting and iron bars. The inside was dark, and, as if I were looking at strange tropical fish in an aquarium, I could make out dimly, on the other side of the bars, patients' faces gathering and separating.
>
> Occasionally, there erupted from this ward a loud laugh like that of a monstrous bird, and I envisioned a disheveled mad woman laughing raucously, running and running through the ward corridors.

Later on, this woman, viewed from inside the hospital, loses her grotesque associations and is described simply as "wearing a conservative blouse, tripping lightly down the corridor, singing cheerfully."

This particular woman is from the first identified with Miho in the narrator's mind and described in terms that suggest Toë from the earlier stories.

> Her hair swept straight back, her brightly figured kimono, and her youth almost gave me the illusion that she was my young wife just after our marriage, when I had brought her to our old house in the countryside, so far from the city. Her tired, defenseless eyes made me think of my wife's. . . . those feverish, thin-skinned eyelids, those abnormally keen, observant eyes, slightly childish, filled with perplexity at having lost control of her own actions.

Typically, though, she is the object of the narrator's curious stares; it is she who is at the window, and it is her eyes and keen powers of observation that are emphasized. This pattern of the observer observed is familiar from the military stories where, too, it is associated with two realms or phases that are actually positive and negative images of what is essentially the same scene. It is remarkable that in the passage above the woman reminds Toshio of his wife not as she is now, suffering from mental delusions, but as she was when she was "healthy," in the days preceding the ostensible causes of her illness.

If the two phases are associated with the hospital and the outside world, hospitalization itself represents an unstable transition period. Toshio prays "to the stones by the roadside" that Miho will recover, but her condition could instead get worse. When he watches the circle dance of the first group of patients, they call to mind subhuman images: "puppets representing various human types," awkward "clay dolls that had come to life with a clatter," huge bugs with "wounds in a place on their bodies that hands could not reach." He thinks he is seeing the essence of mental illness and congratulates himself on having become used to it. The woman associated with his wife is one of this group. Then another group appears, and "a veil" is "lifted" from his eyes. "These were the real, unmistakably mentally ill. Compared to them, the group until now had been absolutely normal. Had I been delirious?" From some standpoints, Miho might be seen as in a light phase rather than a dark, and she could as easily get worse as better. The sight of the new group of patients makes him "suddenly . . . worry about his wife."

Here again is the eternal moment of transition, seen as endlessly repeating cycles severed from the past and from an unknowable future. Time becomes meaningless. Inside the hospital the narrator has a dream that jumbles familiar images from childhood, the Amani Islands, his family life in Tokyo, and the institution itself, exemplifying the reordering of time by the domination of an irrational mind. Indeed, narrative time in all three stories seems to speed up and slow down at random, as Shimao broadens or narrows his focus, attenuates his prose with almost incantatory repetition and a shifting to present tense, then quickens his pace with longer and longer sentences made up of breathless short clauses that, unlike the labyrinths quoted earlier, occur in a logical sequence that does not require re-reading. Such slowing down at first, then a gradual quickening of the pace until the narrative reaches a frenzied pitch is characteristic of the passages describing—one might almost say simulating—Miho's hysteria.

The patients in the mental hospital have dropped most social defenses; even the narrator learns to scream in front of other people and to behave in socially unacceptable ways to his wife, often assuming the weaker or feminine role. The dark retreat of the mental hospital, like the house in "The Sting of Death" and Toë's village in "The Farthest Edge of the Islands," is associated with the realm of the unconscious, with the verbal "free association" of Miho's treatment, self-knowledge, original sin, the elemental drives and symbols of the human personality, the "shrimp that had shed its shell," unprotected by the conscious persona. Reduced to this state, the patients are not individuals but stereotypes. Watching the first group dance, the narrator muses:

As I gazed at the dancers going so energetically around and around in a circle, the bodies and faces of the couple at the front of my field of vision seemed to throb with life. With a vividness one might find symbolic, their now forgotten lives in society went around and around, cyclically entering, then leaving, my field of vision. Serious faces, droll faces, a secret smile, a tearful face, a grimace—in other words, the stock types of mental patients' faces—showed themselves fullface and profile. They left my sight, then the same faces reappeared and did it all again.

They all behave the same way, go through the same cycles, over and over, partly of their own accord and partly not. The beginning of the cycle is arbitrary, determined simply by the vantage point of the observer. None of the characters in these three stories is portrayed in particularizing detail. We know nothing about the "other woman" who so mesmerized Toshio for ten years, not about her appearance or even her name. The frequent dialogue is stereotyped, almost ritualized, indicating the roles adopted by various characters without giving them individual personalities. Characters, moreover, may adopt various roles at different times, and the changes are evident in their speech. Miho is the best example. When she is angry, she speaks roughly, uses men's vocabulary (*aitsu* for "her"), and calls her husband by his first name. When she feels helpless and clinging, she adopts the speech of a child, calling herself Miho and her husband "Daddy." At other times her speech is that of an average housewife.

Twice (once going toward home, once away from home) Toshio has a vision of an original landscape that he knows he has never seen yet seems to remember.

Across the intersection the road went uphill. As I gazed at the Jidō temple halfway up the hill, smoke from the incense stick offerings rising unceasingly, there flashed before my eyes a vision of the same neighborhood as I had never seen it, back in the days when it was heavily wooded and there were few passersby—a dark, deserted, uphill road.

The vision is of a dark woods, associated with the past and with death, perhaps a symbol of the unconscious. It appears in connection with the images of transformation (hill, smoke) we noted in "Everyday Life in a Dream."

Toshio is undergoing a transformation that leads him into unconscious realms of his psyche, so that he becomes like the mental patients he is observing. This process resembles the young writer's "Everyday Life in a Dream." When at the end of "The Heart that Slips Away" Toshio stirs through the water in the courtyard reservoir searching for his wife's body, a metaphorical union, and certain resolution, is achieved:

> While I was doing this, I began to feel as though I could talk with my wife through the tip of the pole. (Toshio, how unlike you to immerse yourself so completely in devotion to me. I'm impressed. Now at last I can believe in you.) I found myself feeling just like a little child running a race with his mother watching.

The communication immediately precedes Miho's return from outside the courtyard wall; it seems to *cause* her return, since she has heard him, howling like a dog (an image mysteriously appearing earlier, in "The Sting of Death"). The pond, the "immersion" (*bottō*) in devotion, the child, and the mother all suggest the unconscious. And that Toshio can communicate silently with her places her in his mind. The reader begins to see Miho and Toshio, fundamentally similar yet assuming alternating opposite phases, as two essential components of the same psyche, symbols in which the mind conceives of itself, like the great uroboros continually chasing its own tail.[3]

Shi no toge, the title of the first of the "sick wife" stories here, is actually a reference to the familiar lines from First Corinthians 15:55-58,[4]

> O death, where is thy sting? O grave, where is thy victory? The sting of death is sin, and the strength of sin is the Law. But thanks be to God, which giveth us the victory through our Lord Jesus Christ. Therefore, my beloved brethren, be ye steadfast, unmovable, always abounding in the work of the Lord, for as much as ye know that your labor is not in vain in the Lord.

The word *toge* (literally, "thorn") for "sting" occurs in the Japanese translation of the Catholic Bible. The thorn image, lost in my translation, is related to other concrete images associated with pain as punishment for wrongdoings. The barbed wire that tops the walls around the hospital garden in an attempt to prevent escape and to punish those who try is one example. Another is the butcher knife Toshio imagines in the hands of his wife, the judge and executioner. After he has broken his promise and secretly visited the other woman, he fears the knife himself. "On the road back to the station, I still had the feeling that I was being watched; several times I conjured up the pain of the butcher knife plunged into my side." This makes him remember the woman standing at the station (watching him leave as his wife had done earlier): he sees the glowing red tip of her cigarette as her "will" (like his wife's will that had lodged itself inside his alarm clock) trying "to think of a fitting punishment for the man who had beaten such a hasty retreat when the going got rough." Later, he hears a voice saying "Vengeance, vengeance." There are "eyes everywhere" in his environment, judging him and threatening retribution for secrecy or evasion.

The complete quotation from First Corinthians offers hope of salvation through death. Salvation for both the narrator and his wife may come as a result of his total devotion, the expiation of his sins through a symbolic death and a rebirth, at which the stories hint; as the title indicates, however, these stories are about sin and the pain of death, a possible transition to something unspecified.

In "Postscript to a Prayer to My Wife" (translated in the appendix), Shimao explains that, for him, the process of writing is itself a way of expiating his sins and demonstrating his total, religious, devotion to his wife. He adds,

> "A prayer to my wife"—perhaps these words make no literal sense. I suppose the prayer must be addressed not to my wife, but to God. What I meant was "A prayer to God for the sake of my wife." But to me, my wife was God's way of testing me. I could not *see* God; what I saw was my wife. In that sense, the title was an accurate expression of my mental state.

It is by now clear that, to a certain extent, the character "Miho" plays this role in the stories themselves. She has absolute knowledge ("My wife's tenacity and her abnormal sensitivity meant that I had to assume that she had positive knowledge of every single fact surrounding her husband"); she has total power over him; she requires ritual confession of sins and affirmation of faith and devotion ("From now on I will never fail to come home at night. I will not go out alone. If I leave the house I will take my wife and children with me. I will have nothing to do with women other than my wife"[3]; "vengeance" is hers, she is the agent of death and life, of his damnation or his salvation. In a different way from Toë in "The Farthest Edge of the Islands," she is associated with fish, the symbol of Christ. When her husband leaves her at the station early in the story, on the excursion that eventually leads him to the other woman's apartment, he is "like a fish freed from the small hatchery into the open sea." Later, when she questions him and finally forces him to confess that he has in fact hidden away some pictures taken with the other woman, he describes her as "a veteran fisherman" who "reassured me as she drove me into the area of danger." In a narrow sense at least, she is a fisher of men.

Notes to the Interpretive Comments

The Farthest Edge of the Islands and *This Time That Summer*

[1]Shimao had been an avid reader of Russian novels from his Nagasaki days, partly because of his acquaintance with White Russian emigrants in Kobe and Nagasaki. The July 1938 issue of *LUNA* carried his essay, "Karamaazofu no kyōdai o tōshite mitaru Dosutoefusukii ni kansuru dampen" [Comments on Dostoyevski as seen in *The Brothers Karamazov*]. The following year he published a similar article. See *Shimao Toshio hishōsetsu shūsei* 4, pp. 15-18, 21-24.

[2]Christian missionaries came to the Amami Islands in the early 1890s. Catholicism, in particular, flourished, espoused and encouraged by local leaders as a respectable alternative to Buddhism, associated with the long domination by Satsuma. During the war the military stationed on the islands gathered and reprimanded native, practicing Catholics.

[3]The wife who is actually a fish that has assumed human form in order to marry a human male is a recurrent motif in Ryukyuan legend. She tends to be a sacrificial victim. See Tanigawa Ken'ichi, "Shimao Toshio ni okeru nantō" [The southern islands and Shimao Toshio], *Kokubungaku* (October 1973): 150-52.

[4]Yoshimoto Takaaki, "Shimao Toshio no sekai" [The world of Shimao Toshio], *Gunzō* 38 (December 1983); also "Sei to zoku" [The sacred and the profane], in *Yoshimoto Takaaki zenchosakushū* 9, pp. 194-201.

[5]See Shimao Miho, *Umibe no sei to shi*, for a portrait of such customs. It is apparently true that Miho's own family was *yukaritchu*, a kind of hereditary nobility. See "Shimao Toshio no genpūkei" [Shimao Toshio's original landscape], an interview with Okuno Takeo in *Kokubungaku* (October 1973): 41. Miho suggests, half in fun, much later in an interview with Kaikō Takeshi (*Bungei* [March 1968]: 142) that she is herself a shamaness (*miko*) with fearsome powers.

Everyday Life in a Dream

[1]See "Shōsetsu no sozai" [Material for my fiction], in *Shimao Toshio hishōsetsu shūsei* 5, pp. 84-87; and "Hichōgenjitsushugiteki na chōgenjitsushugi no oboegaki" [Recollections of an unsurrealistic surrealism], Ibid., pp. 62-65.

[2]See, for example, Kuritsu Norio, "Kaitai to sanran" [Dissolution and dispersion] in *Yume no naka de no nichijō* (Tokyo: Kōdansha, 1971), pp. 264-71.

[3]Shigematsu Yasuo, "Shi no toge," *Kokubungaku* (October 1973): 167-72.

[4]Leprosy was apparently seen in the Amami Islands (as elsewhere) as a sign of divine retribution for sins. See Yoshimoto Takaaki, "Sei to zoku," p. 197.

[5]See, for example, the paperback collection of stories, *Shuppatsu wa tsui ni otozurezu* (Tokyo: Ōbunsha, 1973).

[6]"Shimao Toshio no genpūkei," p. 33.

[7]Ibid., pp. 21-22.

[8]"Shi o osorete—Bungaku o kokorozasu hitobito ni" [In fear of death: To aspiring writers], in *Shimao Toshio hishōsetsu shūsei* 5, pp. 211-17.

[9]Ibid., pp. 214-15.

[10]There are far too many examples to cite, from tenuous associations with leprosy in the military stories (perhaps Lieutenant Saku's name associates him with the lepers, gradually accorded the status of gods, who come to beg and to entertain the villagers traditionally on the *first* and fifteenth of the month; see Yoshimoto Takaaki, "Sei to zoku," pp. 197-201) to echoes of "Yado sadame" ("Finding a Place to Sleep," first published in *Kindai bungaku*, January 1950; reprinted in *Shimao Toshio sakuhin-shū* 2, pp. 37-54) in the last traveling sequence.

[11]See Kuritsu Norio, "Kaitai to sanran."

[12]See Karatani Kōjin, *Imi to iu byō* (Tokyo: Kawade Shobō shinsha, 1975), pp. 78-89.

[13]See, for example, Gregory Bateson, "Style, Grace, and Information in Primitive Art," (1967), reprinted in Bateson, *Steps to an Ecology of Mind* (New York: Ballentine Books, 1972), pp. 138-42.

The Sting of Death, Out of the Depths, and *The Heart that Slips Away*

[1]See "Tanba Masamitsu e no henji" [An answer to Tanba Masamitsu], *Shimao Toshio hishōsetsu shūsei* 5, pp. 113-20.

[2]See his essay included in *Shimao Toshio sakuhin-shū* 4, pp. 295-96.

[3]Yoshimoto Takaaki comments that, unlike many other writers (he cites Sōseki), Shimao never creates triangular situations of conflict in his fiction but always deal with tension between two poles. "Shimao Toshio no kagi" [The key to Shimao Toshio], *Zenchosakushū*, pp. 256-60.

[4]"Ware fukaki fuchi yori" is a reference to Psalm 130, beginning, "Out of the depths have I cried unto thee, O Lord" (Van C. Gessel, "Voices in the Wilderness: Japanese Christian Authors," *Monumenta Nipponica* 37.4 [Winter 1982]: 450) and suggests special meaning to the abyss image that permeates the "sick wife" series. There are many biblical references in Shimao's works. Another title, *Shutsu kotō-ki*, must be patterned after *Shutsu Ejiputo-ki*, the Japanese translation of "Exodus."

APPENDIX

The three brief selections included in this appendix are, at least in theory, nonfictional accounts by the people on whose experiences the stories in this volume are based, Shimao and his wife Miho.

Shimao's "fiction" is generally so similar in language, detail, and tone to his "nonfictional" essays (even to transcripts of his responses to interviewers' questions about his personal life) that one begins to see "Shimao Toshio" as an imaginary construct, a fictional character who extends beyond the bounds of his works into the realm of public personality. That transcendent character and his "personal history" are to a certain extent the products of a collaborative effort, since his wife participated in the writing of many of his autobiographical stories, editing them to correspond with "reality" as she saw it. These pieces, then, might be read simply as telling more about "Toshio" and "Miho," the characters that transcend the occasional and temporary roles they assume in individual stories. Like the six stories, the three accounts appear here in chronological order according to the content, rather than date of publication.

One might look to the last selection to find out what happened next.

"Letters from the Bottom of My Writing Box"[1]

Shimao Miho

During the time when our family of four was living in Koiwa in the old merchant section of Tokyo, I often thought of the blue sea and the blue sky of the southern islands where I was born, and each time, I wept.

How often I long for them,
Now so far away:
The color of that sky,

[1]Shimao Miho, "Kyōtei no tegami," in *Umibe no sei to shi* (Tokyo: Sōjusha, 1974), pp. 148-51.

The special color
Of the southern seas.

Understanding the depth of my homesickness, my husband moved our household back to Amami Ōshima. What with one thing and another, seventeen years have flowed by since then, but it is hard for me to believe that so much time has passed. Our two children have grown up and gone off to school, one in Tokyo, the other in Kagoshima; life for the two of us who stayed behind is now a monotonous repetition of routine. My husband gets up in the morning, goes to work at the Amami branch of the prefectural library, and comes home in the evening to sit at his desk. What is more, in the subtropical climate of the southern islands, one season is not clearly distinguishable from the next. There are two wet-rice crops a year, and violets and morning glories bloom even at the New Year. Only the relentless rays of midsummer clearly announce once each year the cycle of the seasons. And yet, summer is also the season when in the evening the sea breezes blow without cease from the ocean, and the air is fresh and clear; at night, moonbeams wrap the whole island in a deep blue, and even the stars twinkle more brightly; people often stroll along the moonlit beaches and gaze up at the starry sky, man and nature blending into one.

Late at night, from the dark lushness of the tall tropical trees in the garden, sometimes an owl begins to hoot in a soft voice that pierces the heart. Whether the sky is clear or clouded over, I go out into the garden, and as I gaze upward, I call to my husband sitting at his desk inside, "Let's look at the stars." On nights when the owl cries, for some reason I find myself in a gentle mood, and my heart goes out to the stars, the birds, and the insects.

When low rain clouds hang heavy in the night sky, my husband says, "I don't see any stars," but the stars are always in the sky. No matter how thick the clouds, I can see quite clearly the starlight that fills the heavens. Doesn't he know that those stars so familiar to me since childhood (the boat-shaped star; that cluster of little twinkling stars, the Little Dipper; the placid star, Nebuggwa) are there, scattered over the sky, shining among the constellations?

Enveloped in the sweet, pungent scent of hamayū blossoms drifting on the chilly night air, and the loud, compelling, cries of a profusion of insects in the dew-laden grasses that wet our toes, the two of us stand side by side and gaze up at the misty river of the Milky Way; we remember, sadly yet fondly, the summer night sky we watched together twenty-eight years ago, toward the end of the war, when he belonged to a Special Attack Unit facing certain death. By a fortunate turn of fate, this summer I have been given an opportunity to recall with renewed immediacy those days of the distant past. I was asked to compile the letters my husband and I wrote to each other at the height of the war for a book scheduled to appear sometime this fall. In those extraordinary times, there was of course no good paper to be had, and the letters are written in blunt pencil on pages ripped from notebooks, unfolded medicine packets, and scraps of Japanese paper—whatever we could find to write on. Some are covered from edge to edge with writing so small I now need glasses to read it; many words have become so blurred with time that they are almost illegible.

As I began copying out these letters onto my manuscript, their recurrent salutation, "To the Commanding Officer," sent my heart back to those days. I began to feel as though even now, across the mountain pass at the farthest end of the inlet, Lieutenant Shimao waited in his death uniform—and I longed desperately to see him again. But this is no more than an empty wish, for that person disappeared with the end of the war.

If I close my eyes, I can see him vividly, so young and vigorous. Can it be true that I will never, as long as I live, see him again in reality? Searching for some vestige of that Lieutenant Shimao, I stare at my husband's face and form, but to no avail. When I tell my husband so, he is put out and says impatiently, "I wish you'd hurry up and finish with those letters." I have already sent nearly a hundred letters to Yudachisha, the publishers, but there is no end in sight. For some reason this occupation seems to annoy my husband, but many summer days still stretch before me, days full of the intensity and heightened experience I knew when I was young.

"Lieutenant Shimao in the Days of the Special Attack Force"[2]

Shimao Miho

It was with the intention of writing about Commanding Officer Lieutenant Shimao that I sat down to this blank sheet of paper. Recalling how, being close by, I was caught up in the very midst of the battle along with him, I am seized anew by violent waves of emotion; mentally, I return to those dizzying days, and as if possessed, the fingers that hold my pen race over the page in the impossible effort to depict him as he was then, in wartime.

* * *

When the Shimao squadron of the torpedo-boat special attack forces first came to the narrow inlet called Nominoura on Kakeroma Island of the Amami Archepelago, the local people, having always thought of the military as something

[2]Shimao Miho, "Tokkōtaichō no koro," in *Umibe no sei to shi*, pp. 143-47.

to be feared, were quite amazed. Since the whole of the Amami Archepelago had been designated an appropriate site for military bases, the people were used to being subjected to restrictions in all aspects of their lives. Base commanders had rounded up native Catholics and threatened them with drawn swords, proclaiming that anyone who dared to believe in the heretical religion of the enemy would be shot or nailed to the cross, and they had been persecuted in other ways as well. So the people of the island were well aware of the cruelty of military men, and hearing that the special attack unit had arrived, they trembled in anticipation of the outrageous verbal abuse to which they would surely be subjected. But Lieutenant Shimao, the commanding officer of the special attack unit, was exceedlingly courteous to his men, addressing the other officers respectfully, calling them "Mr. Wakino" or "Mr. Tabata" as if they were civilians.

He usually went out unaccompanied by his orderly; seeing an old woman shouldering a heavy load on the mountain path, he would casually take it and carry it for her up to the pass; encountering a group of children on the ridge, he would go down the road with them, singing and holding hands. The people of the village gazed at this strange commanding officer in surprise. All the men under his command were well-mannered and kind; when a villager had been bitten by a poisonous snake, they were on the spot immediately to perform an operation and save his life. The commanding officer himself had personally supervised camouflage in the village as a precaution against air raids. And when people were alarmed by groundless rumors, he would gather us together in the village square and talk to us. Because of his generosity and solicitude, the people of the island began calling this twenty-seven-year-old commanding officer "our benevolent father" (*waakyajuu*), and they gave him their affection.

From about the time news began to reach us of the severe attacks on Okinawa, raids by enemy planes became daily more terrible; elsewhere in the Amami Islands, two or three houses built on the beaches were bombed and burned, and there had been some human casualties. But the inhabitants of Nominoura and Oshikaku, near the Shimao squadron, held a conviction so firm it approached religious faith, that "Lieutenant Shimao will protect us, so everything will be all right." They were convinced that the enemy planes that crashed at sea or in the mountains had all been shot down by the antiaircraft guns of the Shimao squadron, interpreting those successes as certain proof that Lieutenant Shimao was their guardian deity. And strangely enough, the villages of Nominoura and Oshikaku continued to survive unscathed. This fact intensified their devotion to the commanding officer. People were inspired by the soldierly way Lieutenant Shimao carefully collected the bodies of enemy pilots whose planes had crashed, burying them with proper grave markers in the village. "That man must represent the ultimate in human existence" (*Anchuukusa, ningin tushi, umarekahannu chuu daroyaa*), they proclaimed, and there was even a popular song that went, "See, what did I tell you? Lieutenant Shimao is both compassionate and heroic . . . for you would we gladly lay down our lives"; one heard it in the mouths of toddlers barely old enough to talk. When little children saw a man in uniform, they would call out to him, "Lieutenant Shimao," apparently thinking this a general term for all military men.

When Okinawa fell and the mission of the special attack squadron was at hand, our hearts were bound together by the knowledge that all of us—Lieutenant Shimao, his men, and the people of the island—would share a common fate in life or death. The crisis was now an imminent reality. It had been arranged that after the suicide pilots had departed on their mission, the men of the island, in cooperation with those left on the base, would take up their bamboo swords; the young women had been instructed to serve on the battlefield as nurses; and the elderly, the women, and the children were to gather in one place and commit mass suicide. This was to be done in a U-shaped tunnel in the valley near the barracks, which the unit and the villagers had joined forces to dig. The order to assemble in that tunnel was given late on the night of 13 August, and the people came, resolved to die. But the Shimao squadron remained on standby alert all that night, and they were still there to greet the dawn. One more night passed, and the war was over. On 1 September, Lieutenant Shimao, having escaped inevitable death, took his leave of the people of the island and, leading the chain of little motor boats that carried his men, left Nominoura inlet and went away.

More than twenty years have passed, but even today at Nominoura inlet you can see the decaying remains of the base, and the people of the island still have a group that meets to talk of Lieutenant Shimao; they sing the "Lieutenant Shimao Song" and reminisce about those days. And every once in a while, Lieutenant Shimao appears in my dreams—to the evident chagrin of my husband.

"Postscript to a Prayer to My Wife"[3]

Shimao Toshio

Just about two years ago I wrote, also for *Fujin Kōron*, a personal account called "A Prayer to My Wife." It was basically a record of the particulars of our stay in a mental hospital. The title it appeared under at the time was "A Prayer to My Wife Who is Sick of Spirit," but not only were the words "Sick of Spirit" and the subheading and accompanying footnote gratuitous, in fact I felt slightly uncomfortable about the whole account. Thinking back now, however, I wonder if I

[3]Shimao Toshio, "Tsuma e no inori: hoi," in *Shimao Toshio hishōsetsu shūsei* 5 (Tokyo: Tōjusha, 1973), pp. 68-78; originally published *Fujin Kōron* (September 1958) as "Yomigaetta tsuma no tamashii" [The revived soul of my wife].

was not being overly self-conscious. If there is a suggestion of defensiveness in my account, that will erode away eventually of its own accord; I could write nothing better at the time, and in the end I will reap what I have sown. But let me venture to say that in fact I wrote the account with an entirely different goal in mind. "A prayer to my wife"—perhaps these words make no literal sense. I suppose the prayer must be addressed not to my wife, but to God. What I meant was "A prayer to God for the sake of my wife." But to me, my wife was God's way of testing me. I could not *see* God; what I saw was my wife. In that sense, the title was an accurate expression of my mental state. In short, it seemed to me that I would be willing to write absolutely anything if it would give my wife some comfort. I wrote and rewrote that piece until it pleased my wife. Sometimes the effort put me in an extremely bad humor. My becoming irritable was for us an exceedingly bad sign. Knowingly going against my wife's mood meant that a dreadful past would once again rear its ugly head. Irritability in me was something my wife could not forgive. It was tantamount to a breach of faith in our new life. Whenever I began to succumb to bad humor, I found myself on the threshold of the desperate dizziness of having to pull us through the crisis that would surely ensue. I was afraid that provided with a suitable target, those symptoms that had at last begun to abate would now recur. In such times, I derived psychological support from a particular expression. I'm not sure whose words they were, but I suspect they come from some German children's story: "Everything grandmother does is right." This was for me both a sacred precept and a comfort. In our case, it was "Everything Miho does is right." Miho—that is my wife's name—had loved her husband to the point of madness. After a long and circuitous course, that fact had now stung to the quick even my dull and insensitive heart—or so it seems to me. Not just in a manner of speaking, but in the broad daylight of reality as well, our family (my wife, our two children, and myself) had walked slowly step by step along that circuitous course. Aside from minor details—in fact, *including* the most minute detail—"Everything Miho does is right" became the standard by which our family lived.

Soon it will be three years since we came to the city of Naze on Amami Ōshima. To make a long story short, we have managed to return to a normal life. Before long the days of sickness will have disappeared without a trace. Why should we leave our healthy existence ever again to return to the din and clamor and the verbosity? My wife and I are now accustomed to our rule of rest and repose. We no longer have defenses.

The crucial change occurred within me, most dramatically during our stay in the mental hospital. My faults had driven my wife to illness. For all intents and purposes, she was treated as a schizophrenic (on her chart, the doctor had written *"symptoms of nervous disorder"*). Our normal way of life was obliterated. I completely lost my balance until I myself was almost hallucinating, and our young children sustained deep psychological wounds. Losing my own sense of perspective, I prostrated myself before the pathological reasoning of my wife.

In retrospect, it seems there was no other way for my wife and me to go on living, and that was probably in fact the case. It is strange how I remember those days almost with nostalgia: that cramped, tense, day-to-day existence within the barred windows of the mental hospital, two people picking at each other's entrails. I had to recognize then that I was no more than an undignified, badly made puppet. I could discover in myself no source of spiritual support whatever. At the slightest indication of confrontation, my wife was like a surgeon poking around in the open wound. My wife was never wrong. And it was my wife, plagued by auditory and visual hallucinations, hardly distinguishable from the mental patients, who guided her theoretically sane husband. Strange how that happened.

When the doctor reluctantly allowed my wife the faint hope that she might be able to return to a normal life, she and the children and I pulled up stakes in Tokyo and moved to Amami Ōshima. While my wife and I were in the mental hospital (I was there simply to attend to her personal needs), the children had been sent ahead to the island without us. The account I wrote for this journal two years ago traces the path of our lives that far. What convinced me to publish it was the prospect of the pleasure it would give my wife—at least I think it is fair to say that that was a large part of my motive. For strangely enough, my wife was absolutely delighted by it. Time and time again she read that reprint from *Fujin Kōron*, her cheeks flushing with excitement. Seeing her emotion, I too was moved, and yet each time I felt an inexpressible shame.

The kind of illness to which my wife had succumbed did not respond immediately to treatment. Where my previous account ended, the children and I were still trembling in fear of the recurrent darkening of their mother's mood. For us, this shadow was quite simply a reflection of hell. We noticed the slightest clouding over of Miho's mood, which, even on days when the cool north wind blew, bathed us immediately in a cold sweat. At such times we were thrown together not so much as father and child, but as fellow prisoners. Of course the pain was not ours alone; Miho herself was the victim of far greater torture. Wracked in the violent clutches of her darkest attacks, she experienced even now the hell of knowing that she might very well revert to the pathological symptoms that had plagued her in the hospital.

"If someone told you right now that you would be granted just one wish, what would you wish for?"

My wife was fond of tossing out questions about "just one wish." By now I was able to give her an immediate answer.

"Never again to see the dark shadow on your face," I would say, and the children always took up the refrain, "The best wish is for Mommy not to get angry anymore."

When my wife's heart clouded over, we would shut all the rain shutters and spend the whole day without stirring from our sunless room; when, on the other hand, her expression was bright, a lively day of gentle tropical breezes came our way. The children and I had tacitly joined forces in a common strategy, to avoid anything that might irritate or annoy Mommy. It was a sort of unwritten law—at least we saw it as the countenance of the reality of "law." And we knew how happy we would all be if only we obeyed that law. That there were no restrictions on what Miho did, that she was always in the right, became the rule of the house. Miho was never wrong. Of course, this was an attitude we had adopted only gradually, in reaction to a pattern that had evolved from the time of her extremely unusual (according to the diagnosis of the doctor who had examined her in the hospital) childhood on Amami Ōshima, developed during the days of her illness, when she was removed from her normal way of life, and continued now in her dealings with the children and me.

I think of ten years as a kind of landmark. To a considerable extent our family life has remained closed to the outside world. Unquestionably, there is something unhealthy about that. But it is my goal to remain steadfast in our present style of life for ten years. My job is to extirpate the ill feelings I have planted in the hearts of my wife and our two children. I cannot believe that there is any other job for me than that. I shall, of course, have to continue fighting a battle both externally and within my own heart, a battle that is beyond the limits of my strength. Then, after ten years, counting the four years that have now gone by, we will reach a vantage point full of hope. One might say that the measure of peace and security that we now enjoy is more than I deserve.

* * *

Let me write about an experience that proved fortunate for us. About a year ago, for the first time since moving to Naze, my wife and I took a trip together, just the two of us. Half a day's bumpy ride on a bus took us to Koniya on Minami Ōshima. From there we went by motorboat to a deserted little village called Kuji, where they were excavating buried explosives. A Naval special attack unit had once been stationed on this site, and the thirty-meter U-shaped tunnel that contained their torpedo boats had caved in. Near it stood a stone marker, still new, reading, "Here lie the accident victims from the suicide squadron." At the height of the Battle of Okinawa, one torpedo boat had malfunctioned and exploded in front of the tunnel, killing more than ten men. Among the casualties was Commanding Officer Miki. The tunnel entrance had collapsed at that time, and the boats had remained buried until now. If the 250 kilograms of unexploded warheads were still there, the situation was extremely dangerous. They must be exhumed and disposed of at any cost. There was also the hope of recovering the bones of the men who had died in the secondary explosion inside the tunnel. There was a chilling "certainty" about the tunnel, which we were finally able to enter after the dangerous excavation was completed, that made one feel as though all was exactly as it had been twenty years before—so much so that I half expected to see all those torpedoes, lying there before my eyes. But we saw instead the wooden posts that had supported the tunnel, now fallen and entwined like tangled skeletons, and beneath them the plywood torpedo boats, rotted through and turning to earth. We could discern the engines, the fuel tanks, and the steel frames of the trailers that carried the boats, buried in the caved-in tunnel. And sure enough, here and there, the dreadful crescent-shaped warheads displayed their rusting casements.

After that, my wife and I boarded the motorboat once again and went to the village of Senku on Kakeroma Island. It was of course difficult to discover any trace of the defense forces that had once been stationed there. Only the embankment along the pier, disproportionately long, too carefully constructed for this small, out-of-the-way island town, still suggested soldierly activities. But I could not rid my mind of a shrill phantom whistle emanating from the direction of the desolate, grass-covered village square, where the barracks once had stood. We went still farther, over the mountain path to the village of Nominoura. There I heard with my own ears villagers address me even now as "Lieutenant." Like Lieutenant Miki, who had died in that explosion, I had been stationed on the base at Nominoura. Along both banks of the quiet narrow inlet, the entrances to twelve underground boathouses faced each other, their concrete-filled mouths wide open; as I gazed at them, I realized that in this journey there lurked a subtle danger. An indefinable shudder ran down my spine. Hadn't we come here a little too soon? Shouldn't we have waited until the waves of Miho's symptoms had more nearly subsided? As I stood on the site where headquarters once had been, gazing absently at the gradually fading afterglow of sunset reflected dully on the water, I began to lose myself, to feel helpless as though my heart would break into tiny pieces and scatter in all directions.

Presently my wife and I crossed the pass to the village of Oshikaku. How many times, I wonder, had I crossed that pass in the still of night? When we had climbed all the way up and started down again on the other side, we saw the lights of the village. The sun had now set, and the bright moonlight gave the inlet an uncanny luster, like a casting net over the water's surface. What deep inspiration, what anticipation, this sight had instilled in me in the past. Now, however, as we ran down the path to the village, we could not help realizing that there was no place here for us to go. After the defeat my wife had left her aged father all by himself in his large house and come to be with me in Kobe. Later, the Amami Archipelago had been removed from the jurisdiction of the Japanese and governed by foreign military rule. Her father had died old and alone. Though he had a legal heir, he had taken sole comfort in thoughts of his only daughter. Moreover, he had taken the initiative in offering me her hand. Until her mother died, the three of them had lived in a warmth of affection and mutual understanding almost beyond belief. As the doctor at the mental hospital pointed out in the course of her analysis, my wife showed a filial devotion of an intensity ordinarily unimaginable. How can one conceive of never ever having been scolded by one's parents? Miho was just such a rare case. She had no inkling of the difficult parental complexes that plague our relationships these days. True, the traditions of her environment were gradually crumbling, but as long as her parents were alive, she continued to enjoy special treatment by the other people of the village. She alone in the village was addressed affectionately as "Kana." Her childhood was like a tale now lost, of a small southern island where the old Ryukyuan ways of life persisted until relatively recently.

In her early childhood memories, Norwegians hired to catch whales and women divers brought from Tottori on the Sea of Japan for the artificial cultivation of pearls still shift beyond a curtain of blue. By now all concrete corroboration of such memories must surely have disappeared. We had heard rumors that many of the houses had been sold off to Okinoerabu Island. What had happened to the cedar forests, or the palm tree nurseries, we did not know. I bitterly regretted my rashness. Having come all this way, as cautiously as if carrying a plate of thin ice, wasn't I now suddenly being tempted by some demon into committing an error that would lead to ultimate defeat? Supporting my wife as I walked, I could not stop the trembling that came from deep within me.

Presently we entered the village, which was little more than an empty shell. And there we mourned. I watched my sobbing wife rub her cheek against the gravestones of her father and mother; her grief was so intense that I despaired of ever being able to drag her away. Finally we left the cemetery and visited the site of her family home. Of the house itself, there remained not a trace, and the garden her aged father had named The Garden of a Hundred Flowers and allowed to bloom at random was now completely overgrown with weeds. Was there nowhere for us to go? The only homes we felt comfortable approaching were those of the old people in the village. And indeed, except for Kei-samma, Uncle Sai, Cousin Kei, and Miho's childhood friend Zumi, all of whom welcomed me as they had during the war and treated my wife once more as "Kana," weeping over her changed fate, we could not help realizing that we no longer meant anything at all to this village—in spite of the moonlight that even now, just as long ago, poured that soft light peculiar to the southern islands into every corner.

The next morning I awakened before daybreak from a shallow sleep in the hard bed of our shabby inn; my wife was muttering in her sleep: "Where am I? I have to hurry back to Juu." "Juu" was her father. As she spoke, I could picture the expression of helplessness in her unfocused eyes. I shook her. And I thought that we must get away from this village as soon as we possibly could. Many villagers were gathered at the pier to see us off. We were by now people in a legend. I could not hold back the tears as the motorboat left the pier. Zumi came with us as far as Koniya. Strangely enough, after the long, tiring bus trip from Koniya to Naze, my wife began to regain her equilibrium, almost as if a fever had left her. What was going on inside her then, I do not know, but after that Miho began to recover by leaps and bounds. Having been baptised into the Catholic Church as an infant, in the four years since we returned to this island she has regained her faith, adding to her baptismal name Maria the confirmation name Agnes.

I am writing this account at an inn in Kumamoto; my wife's health is now sound enough for her to endure my being away from home for a little while on business. While I am traveling, we talk to each other every day by letter. One might even say that the Straits of Kagoshima make a pleasant intermediary between us. When I have fulfilled my business obligations, I will undoubtedly head straight back to the island. And after this experimental business trip, I expect to find that my wife has become even stronger emotionally. We do not want to move away from this island for a long time to come. Our children have grown up. Even Maya, the younger one, is now capable of composing a poem like the following to send to me on the road:

Maya's Song

The *hamayū* blossoms are white,
And they smell good.
I think they are pretty.
A cool breeze comes;
The stars are pretty too.
In a clear voice
The insects are singing;
Many people walk in the streets.
Inside the house, older brother and Maya
Hold a pretend mass.
Father is far away in Kumamoto;
Maya is sad.
I pray to Mother Mary
That he will come home soon.
The *hamayū* blossoms are white.

SELECTED BIBLIOGRAPHY[*]

Shimao Toshio. *Shimao Toshio sakuhin-shū*, 5 vols. Shōbunsha, 1962-1967.

_____. *Watakushi no bungaku henreki*. Miraisha, 1966.

_____. *Yume no naka de no nichijō*, Kōdansha, 1971.

_____. *Garasushōji no shiruetto: yōhen shōsetsu-shū*. Sōjusha, 1972.

_____. *Shimao Toshio hishōsetsu shūsei*, 6 vols. Tōjusha, 1973.

_____. *Shuppatsu wa tsui ni otozurezu*, Shinchō Bunko, 1973.

_____. *Yōnenki*. Yudachisha, 1973.

_____. *Nikki-shō*, Shio Shuppansha, 1981.

_____. *Shi no toge*, Shinchō Bunko, 1981.

Secondary Sources

Single Volumes

Aeba Takao. *Shimao Toshio-ron*. Shimbisha, 1967.

_____, ed. *Shimao Toshio kenkyū*. Tōjusha, 1976.

Matsuoka Shunkichi. *Shimao Toshio no genshitsu*. Sambunsha, 1973.

Morikawa Tatsuya. *Shimao Toshio-ron*. Shimbisha, 1965.

Okada Kei. *Shimao Toshio*. Kokubunsha, 1973.

Shimao Miho. *Umibe no sei to shi*. Sōjusha, 1974.

Tokushū: Shimao Toshio: Shukumei toshite no bungaku, Kokubungaku: Kaishaku to kyōzai no kenkyū 13.10 (October 1973).

Yoshimoto Takaaki. *Sakka-ron 3: Shimao Toshio.* Keisōshobō, 1975.

Articles

Aeba Takao. "Shimao Toshio-ron." *Shimbi* 6 (May 1967).

Akatsuka Yukio. "Shimao Toshio oboegaki." *Bungakusha* 127 (June 1963).

Gessel, van C.   "Voices in the Wilderness: Japanese Christian Authors." *Monumenta Nipponica* 37.4 (Winter 1982).

Karatani Kōjin, "Yume no sekai: Shimao Toshio to Shōno Junzō." In Karatani, *Imi to iu byō.* Kawade Shobō Shinsha, 1977.

Kuritsu Norio. "Kaisetsu: Kaitai to sanran." In *Yume no naka de no nichijō,* by Shimao Toshio. Kōdansha, 1971.

Okuno Takeo. "Shimao Toshio-ron." *Kindai bungaku* 10.5 (January 1954).

_____. "Shimao Toshio no bungaku to yume." *Bungakkai* 17.3 (March 1963).

_____. "'Katei' no hōkai to bungakuteki imi." *Bungakkai* 17.4 (April 1963).

Terada Tōru. "Shimao Toshio no sekai." *Shin nihon bungaku* (April 1963).

Yamamoto Kenkichi. "Kaisetsu." In *Shi no toge,* by Shimao Toshio. Shinchōsha, 1981.

Yoshimoto Takaaki. "Sengo bungaku no tenkan." *Bungei* 1.2 (April 1962).

_____. "Shimao Toshio no sekai: Sensō shōsetsu-ron." *Gunzō* 23.2 (February 1968).

*All places of publication (if not indicated) are Tokyo.